Shades of Gray
The Hochenwalt Files

ADDIE J. KING

DEDICATION

For the real Nadia, who never had a chance to realize her own potential, and to my friendship with her mother

ACKNOWLEDGMENTS

Special Thanks are due to...

Ray Westcott, my husband, my best friend, and my biggest supporter.

The Dayton Area Novelists Group, for endless hours of critique and enthusiasm.

The world's best parents, Karen and Alvin King, because they are mine

The world's best in-laws, Sandra and Eugene Westcott, for the same reason

One of my biggest fans, my grandmother, Mary Jane Woodruff

All of the law enforcement officers I've worked with over the years, from the Dayton Police Department, Montgomery County Sheriff's Office, Sinclair Community College Police Department, University of Dayton Police Department, Five Rivers MetroParks Police Department, Ohio Highway Patrol, Ohio Department of Natural Resources, Ohio Liquor Control, Urbana Police Department, Champaign County Sheriff's Office, St. Paris Police Department and Mechanicsburg Police Department; even if they didn't know that they were helping with research at the time, it was invaluable insight.

All the writers who encouraged me with this project for the last many many years; including but not limited to, Jenna Bennett, Kit Ehrman, Elizabeth Bevarly, Julianne Lee, Clay Stafford, Jaden Terrell, Steven Saus, Eldon Hughes, C.H. Valentino, Diana Woodward, Tim Dawe, Linda Johnson, Diana Rankin, Amy Zook, and many more.

My friends, Steve, Melissa, Audra, Chris, Sarah, Sara, Rebecca, Rebekah, Anissa, Andrea, Amy, Tara, Erin, Erin, Jane, Tracy, and Ted

My loyal booth minion, Savannah

The former staff, faculty, and attendees of the Novels In Progress Workshop, Killer Nashville, and the Writer's Symposium at GenCon, for teaching me more than I could ever have begun to ask about the business andthe art of writing and editing.

Also to Todd Hostetler, my cousin, my friend, and cover artist extraordinaire. You couldn't have captured the book better.

CONTENTS

CHAPTER ONE

The wet dog smell should have tipped me off that something was up, but I don't think I'd have ever made the mentalleap from sweaty canine to werewolf because of it.

"Damn you. Get back here," I yelled, as I sped down Wayne Avenue, one hand on the grip of my gun in its holster, and the other hand clapping my patrol cap to my head as I ran. "You're under arrest, asshole!" The heat of the day sat like a soupy, fetid fog, carrying the scent of unwashed bodies and barbecues in backyards. I smelled wet dog, but I didn't see one nearby as I ran. How far away would those kinds of odors carry when the air wasn't moving?

On that day, I was just plain old Officer Samantha Jane Hochenwalt, rookie cop for the Dayton Police Department, in good, old Dayton, Ohio. Just like every other day, I was riding with my training officer, Justin Noble. And yet again, we were after a bad guy, but he wasn't your typical bad guy. He was more like a sort-of bad guy. But he'd still committed a crime, even if it was a little crime, so it was our job to catch him.

My partner, Justin Noble, was right behind me. Justin normally outruns me, since he's got longer legs. This time, I'd seen our suspect spin away before he did, so I was a couple of steps ahead. I heard him yell into his shoulder mike for the backup that wasn't quite here yet.

The jerk we were chasing ran with an exaggerated stride, holding tight to the waistband of his pants, his knees bending sideways as he scooted away from me. I was surprised at how fast he moved, for such a short, overweight man. He looked like an addle-pated leprechaun, with his short legs bowing out sideways and his bald head screaming red from exertion. I'd have laughed, but I was annoyed. I hate running. In my mind, only crazy people and maniacs run for fun. Oh, that, and people who have to stay in shape for work, like me.

He didn't get much farther before a cruiser pulled in ahead of him as he tried to cross a side street. He hesitated and that gave me my advantage. Before he could spin away, I grabbed his elbow and slammed him down on the hood of the cruiser that had been our backup. Justin came up behind me on foot and grabbed his other elbow as the cop driving the cruiser got out of the driver's seat.

"Damn, Hock, you sure got him good," our backup said, grinning at me.

I didn't let go. I didn't know if our perp had a gun or a knife hidden in his pants as he ran down the rundown, historic residential streets of Dayton's South Park neighborhood, but there was something hidden in the front of his pants.

"Sam, lighten up. He's not fighting you," Justin said, taking our prize away from me to pat him down. Thank

God he'd started using my nickname. I'd never thought of myself as a Samantha, and my last name, Hochenwalt, is a mouthful in everyday conversation. A lot of the other cops call me Hock, but Sam sounded much better coming out of Justin's mouth.

"There's something in the front of his pants," I gasped, still a bit out of breath from running in the heat and humidity. I was drowning in the soupy air. I gagged from the stench of dirty wet dog in the not-breeze, and shook my head to concentrate. "Is it a weapon?" I stood slightly off to his right, one hand on my gun, ready to back him up if the moron moved.

"Would you look at that?" Justin asked, as he patted him down and pulled a large, square, foam backed package of T-bone steaks out of the front of the man's pants.

The other officer laughed. "Hey, you think he has to register this as a deadly weapon?"

I glared at them as the stitch in my side started to ease. "Is that it?"

Justin held the steaks in his left hand, and the cuffed wrists of our suspect in his right, as the other cop held his sides from laughing.

Damn them, it was funny. I mean, no man has a bulge in the front of his pants the size and shape of a T-bone steak, especially one attached to a perfectly square sheet of foam board. I grimaced, knowing I'd never live it down. "I wasn't staring at his crotch. It's hard not to notice that something's wrong when he's running like that."

They kept laughing. I'd probably end up with butcher paper and coupons for hamburgers hanging inside my locker before it was all over. I just hoped they stopped there. Cops don't practice restraint when they play practical jokes on the rookie, and I was still a newbie less than six months out of the academy.

After we dropped our thief off at the jail, we headed back out to the cruiser. The heat closed in on us once again, but the dog smell hadn't made its way downtown, thank goodness. I felt sweat run down my neck into the fabric of the t-shirt I wore beneath my Kevlar bulletproof vest. If I thought I could stand the vest chafing my skin, I'd have gone without the t-shirt, but hot, sweaty, and chafed wasn't my idea of fun. I figured all the sweating would earn me some Ben and Jerry's therapy at the end of the night.

I grumbled, under my breath. "Why are we so busy? I mean, why aren't criminals sitting inside in the air conditioning like rational people? This is crazy."

Justin laughed. God, I enjoyed his laugh. It came from his toes, a sudden shout of laughter that welled up inside him. He'd been assigned as my field training officer even though he was only a couple years older than me, and they'd kept us together even after the initial two week training period. The rareness of that laugh brought out the smartass in me, in hopes of hearing it more often. I'd been wisecracking like a maniac for six months. Of course, it wasn't just the laugh, or the good looks, or the dependable personality. He had a cute butt, too.

Once we were underway, I took my hat off and ran my hand through my hair.

He smiled. I probably looked like an angry troll, with my dishwater brown hair in sweaty spikes and horns sticking up in different directions and my cheeks flushed from the heat. Justin was as hot and sweaty as I was, but guys look good even when they drip sweat. It made me want to punch him on principle. I settled for a nasty glare, and jammed the cap back on my head.

When was I going to catch a break? Police work wasn't glamorous, but maybe someday I'd get to work on something more exciting than chasing a meat thief or arresting a druggie for passing a note to his daughter despite the restraining order. That was last night. I mean, come on. Those are crimes, but I wanted to be where the action was, and it definitely wasn't here. I'd always thought when I became a cop that I'd get to solve murders and lock up violent rapists and drug dealers, not deal with all this piddly crap.

Justin offered to stop for a bathroom break and a chocolate banana malted milkshake before we took our next call. There wasn't much else I could say but to accept his peace offering for laughing at me and cool off. I was frustrated with the mundane police career I had, but I had no way of knowing that my life was about to get one hundred and eighty degrees off mundane, and in a way I could never have expected.

If I'd have known, I think I'd have refused the milkshake that night.

CHAPTER TWO

We headed for the United Dairy Farmers store on Woodman Drive. I settled into the front seat of the cruiser, clipboard in hand, knowing that Justin would go first and be back faster than I ever could. Why didn't he let me go first? Well, it doesn't take nearly as long for a guy cop to go to the bathroom.

I had never really thought about it before I became a cop, but I was always worried about pulling down my pants in bathrooms with multiple stalls. Going to the bathroom is a big deal when in uniform. It's especially difficult for women. The guys have it so much easier. Not only is the concern about the time to get through the layers, but I didn't want to report keys or cuffs or a gun yanked off my belt under a stall door. Because of all my precautions, it took me way longer to do what I needed to do, so we'd fallen into a routine of him going first.

Justin parked the cruiser toward the back away from the gas pumps. He ran inside and I stayed to finish the paperwork and report forms from our last stop. I'd get my milkshake after I was done. I was planning to get the biggest size they carried; the ice cream would help cool off my frustrations from the crazy night.

I heard a growling noise outside of the cruiser and turned my head. There was nothing there; at least nothing I saw. A moment later, I heard a scuffling noise from behind the store. I stepped out of the cruiser, and didn't see anything. I chalked it up to the normal sounds of a residential neighborhood settling down for the night. As I turned to get back in, I caught the smell of wet dog again. I shook my head. My imagination must be on overdrive. Either that or every dog in the neighborhood had found a mud puddle to cool off in, not out of the question with the heat today. Heck, if I thought it would work, I might be tempted to try it myself, even though I really didn't want to wash mud out of my uniform later.

Before I could do much of anything else, something grabbed my left arm. I started to turn and face whoever was dumb enough to grab a cop from behind, but my hat was knocked off and a hand snaked into my hair, pinning my head and pulling hard. I felt a pop in my shoulder when I tried to wriggle away. I'm ashamed to admit that I didn't even think of reaching for my gun.

I tried to move, but my arm was caught in a vise-grip. Struggling only made it worse. I let out a shriek, and reached for my radio. Whoever had grabbed me swung me sideways like a discus thrower at the Olympics. My head was pinned by the hand fisted in my hair and I couldn't see who it was. I heard a voice whisper, "Now you'll understand."

Tears ran down my face as I hit the call button on my radio. Any words died on a scream when I was thrown into the drugs still in his system, fogging his hearing? Strong hands dragged him into the van, where he faced the man who'd made him.

"What the hell did you do? Why do I have to clean up your mess? I should kill you."

The wolf whined, tucking his tail further between his legs, his body huddled in a ball.

His maker was angry, and he couldn't blame him, not one bit. The wolf had taken the biggest risk of his life. Officer Hochenwalt had to help him. He couldn't even stand up to this guy, not without worrying for his family's safety. Where he regretted what he'd done to the pretty young cop, he still thought it was the right thing to do. She'd help him, he was sure. He'd just gambled his own life on it.

CHAPTER FOUR

I opened my eyes as someone jarred my shoulder. I was on a stretcher. An ambulance stood nearby, with other cruisers parked around it. The red and blue flashing lights made the night sky look like the inside of a pinball machine.

I saw Justin's face, pale and worried above mine. I tried to speak, but couldn't get enough oxygen to do more than whimper. A weight was sitting on my chest. My left arm felt useless and I wondered for a second whether it was still attached.

I was distracted from my mental inventory when I realized that the inside of my right elbow was bleeding. It felt like something had been injected; hot, liquid lead scored straight into my veins. I felt it sear through my body, burning me alive from the veins out.

I cried out and tried to move, but they had me tied to a stretcher. "Burns, it burns, it fucking burns," I moaned, writhing against the restraints. "Make it stop, someone make it stop." I was caught in a loop of pain, between my head, my shoulder, my ribs, my elbow, and the liquid fire as it spread blazing heat to my fingers and toes. Every time the heat rose, I convulsed, and pain exploded in the other injured parts of my body.

Justin's face came into view, and I saw my district sergeant behind him. "Hock, hold still. They're trying to help you," the sergeant ordered. I wanted to hold still, but I couldn't do it, writhing against the furnace blast of agony that swirled through every inch of my body. The stretcher tipped precariously and the paramedics rushed to right it.

"Sam, please hold still. They can't help if you don't hold still." It registered that he'd used my first name in front of the sergeant, something he'd never done before. Justin sounded worried, and I could feel his hand on my wrist as he held me down. My response died on a scream, and I don't remember much beyond that. It's all a big blur of pain, fuzzed voices and bright lights until I realized I was in the emergency room.

I vaguely remember when the doctors manipulated my shoulder. I woke up periodically as they poked and prodded and ran their tests. I opened my eyes at one point and noticed that there was a large machine in the room that they wanted to use on me. I had the irrelevant thought that it looked like something out of a science fiction movie, and found it funny. That thought didn't last long. Once I was inside the machine itself, the combination of the tight space and the secure wrapping on my ribs made me panic, hyperventilate, and pass out yet again.

The next coherent moment I remember was when I woke up in a strange hospital bed. Mom held my hand, and Dad stood right behind her with a relieved grin on his face.

"Hi sweetheart, you gave us quite a scare," Mom said, as she leaned over to kiss my forehead.

I noticed Dad setting aside a tattered paperback book when she spoke to me. He always had a book with him. That's par for the course for a bookstore owner. Dad owned and ran a small second hand bookstore, and I can remember smelling the peculiar smell of old, musty pages and his favorite butterscotch candies on him when he came home from work at night when I was a kid. Sure enough, I caught that same smell when he leaned over to check on me. That alone reassured me. It was a smell of home.

"You think you were scared? That's the scariest thing that's happened to me since I broke my ankle trying to sneak out of the house when I was fifteen." I smiled weakly, trying to ease the worry on their faces.

Dad laughed. I could hear the stress bleed out of him. He rubbed his hands over his face, and then quickly through his hair, a nervous tic he'd had for as long as I could remember. I noticed he hadn't shaved since the day before and was struck by how much older he looked. Dad was always clean shaven. It surprised me to see gray hair on his chin and cheeks.

"She'll be fine, Kathy," he said to my mom, who was already moving to tell the nurses I was awake. As she walked away, he turned to me and kissed my forehead, right on the spot Mom kissed a moment ago. "It takes more than that to knock the spirit out of my girl."

Mom missed the last comment as she left the room, but it made me smile. She came back with a nurse. I wasn't surprised that they knew each other. Mom's been a trauma nurse for almost thirty years. She used to work here at Miami Valley Hospital, but moved to a different hospital five years ago. She still knew a lot of people here. I caught snatches of their conversation as Dad tried to distract me. I heard "don't know what caused the bite" before Dad realized I wasn't paying attention to him, and shrugged as he strained to hear the conversation outside as well.

"Hey, someone tell the patient what's wrong with her." I called out to Mom and the nurse. Mom had a guilty look on her face. Her being a trauma nurse meant she was organized and efficient, but she sometimes got wrapped up in treating something and forgot to be a mom. I guess it evened out; she would overcompensate for it in the end, and I'd get spoiled while I was sick because she felt bad about it. I hoped that the injuries this time rated more than lollipops. I was thinking pie. Homemade Dutch apple pie. A la mode. Extra ice cream. With caramel sauce on top. Yeah, that'd work for me.

The tender look on Dad's face as he watched the emotion fly across Mom's was priceless. They'd met when Dad got hurt in a car accident, and realized that their parents knew each other. She'd taken care of him after he left the hospital, and the rest, as they say, was history. They were a good match; best friends, partners, confidantes. I hoped one day to find a match like that for myself.

Mom sat down and brushed my hair back from my face. I felt Dad's hand on mine. It felt good to have my daddy hold my hand and my mom comfort me. Sometimes the simplest things feel good, no matter how bad of a day it's been.

CHAPTER FIVE

I didn't get a chance to savor my parents' comforting gestures for too long; I had a visitor.

My best friend, Nadia Jeffries, stuck her head around Dad's shoulder. "Hey, look who's awake. Good grief, girl, you scared the life out of me. Thought I'd have to go find a new best friend, and I'm not ready to trade in for a new model yet."

I smiled at her. Nothing made me feel better than talking to Nadia when I had a bad day. I'd known her since grade school and we'd taken care of each other through junior high dances, braces, girl talk, bad breakups,exams, graduation, and college. We've got a million blackmail stories on each other, but we'd never use them.

I was the person who'd pushed her to go to school when she'd worried about leaving her father alone to leave town for veterinary school after her mother died. She'd been a big supporter of my plans to join the police department, and helped me talk to Mom and Dad when I became a police officer. She also knew all about my feelings for Justin, which went way deeper than I tried to let on to him.

Nadia leaned in and stage-whispered in my ear as she cupped her hand to her mouth. "Officer Yummy's out in the hallway, losing his mind." Her face split into a grin, a punctuation of white teeth in the smooth and perfect mocha color of her skin, her curls held back from her forehead by a multicolored scarf.

"Nadia," I warned, in a hoarse voice. She'd coined the nickname for Justin after I'd confessed my crush to her. I didn't share that kind of information with Mom and Dad, and if Justin was somewhere within earshot, I'd have to kill her slowly. God, she made it sound like we were still in junior high. I certainly didn't want him to overhear that. Good grief, what had she told him while I was unconscious? Luckily, Dad was busy talking to Mom about finding the doctor and getting more information.

I wasn't sure I wanted him to see me like this. I reached up and found a bandage wrapped around my head. I wasn't imagining a head injury, then. It felt like pixies were playing conga drums with ball peen hammers inside my skull.

The doctor came in with a smile on his face. "Mr. and Mrs. Hochenwalt, Ms. Jeffries, if you could step out so I can examine my patient, I'd appreciate it."

Nadia's face fell. "But we just got in here," she pouted. "She just woke up."

When the doctor held his ground, they shuffled out. Dad was dragging Mom behind him. Nadia chattered a mile a minute, distracting them. I had a funny feeling she'd been doing something similar since she'd arrived. How long had they all been here? How long had I been there? I wondered if the doctor would tell me.

As they left, I heard Justin's voice in the hallway as he argued that someone should be in the room to hear what the doctor said. I heard Mom calm him down with the promise to listen at the door and I smiled. Some things are just too predictable. I was her daughter. She'd insist on knowing my condition, and the care I'd get, no matter what she had to do to find out.

The doctor snagged my attention from the hall. "I'm Dr. Wilson. You've got quite a crowd out there." He bent to check my head. As he probed my skull I grimaced and he umhm'ed, without explanation. Eventually he shone a light in my eyes and asked about my sight. Nothing was wrong with my eyes: I could very clearly see Mom sneak back into the room.

He continued with the torture as he manipulated my shoulder. I gasped.

He asked if he'd hurt me.

"No. It's sore, but not bad." I was surprised more than hurt.

"That's not unusual. Your shoulder was dislocated, but it popped out clean. We were able to reset it easily. Nothing was broken there. It'll be stiff for a while and we'll have you in a sling until the swelling goes down, probably a week or two."

I saw Mom nod out of the corner of my eye. She'd snuck back in and she had her nursing face on, like she was taking mental notes. I love my mother, really I do. Mom, in Super-Nurse Mode, could be really annoying. I tried to sigh, and it hurt.

There's only so much a person can sigh when ribs are strapped up, and deep breathing is impossible. I had a mental image of Scarlet O'Hara laced into her corset and silently gave thanks for living in the twenty-first century. I understood now why women used to carry smelling salts all the time. There'd be a real danger of passing out if I had to exert myself. The edges of my vision went a little gray as I breathed out slowly and winced.

Dr. Wilson saw it, and shook his head in disapproval. "Here's the deal. You've got a couple of broken ribs, but the vest kept the damage from being worse. The bad news is there's not much I can do for them, other than strap them to prevent you from moving around and hurting yourself worse. They'll have to heal on their own. You also have a concussion. Your initial tests showed extensive swelling and bruising to your brain. There was a strong possibility you wouldn't wake up. You made me very happy regaining consciousness long before anyone thought you would. We repeated our tests about an hour ago, and the improvement was astounding."

"Well, I guess confusing doctors by getting better faster than expected can't be a bad thing, can it?" I asked.

"That's very true. I'll take a surprise like that any day." He probed the bandage on the inside of my elbow. "It sure beats surprising us in the other direction. Either you've achieved a miraculous recovery or our CT equipment is on the fritz. The truth, however, is that there was probably some error in the equipment that produced the earlier result."

I moved my right arm to shift in the bed and felt the pull of stitches inside my elbow. "So what's the damage on stitches?"

"You've got forty-six stitches inside your elbow. You weren't on a dog-fighting case, were you?" He picked up my file and scribbled some notes.

"No." I was puzzled.

"I'm not sure even a pit bull would tear you up like this. The bite mark looks too big. Any idea what it was?" He unwound the gauze from my arm to check on the stitches.

"Um, no, I don't have a clue. I never got a look at his face."

"If we weren't in a city, I'd think you were attacked by a wild animal."

"Why?" I didn't get it.

"Human teeth bruise flesh before they break skin. Carnivores in the wild have teeth better adapted to piercing or ripping flesh without bruising because their teeth are sharper. Whatever bit you had some mighty sharp teeth."

"I'm confused." I shut off the memory of the teeth digging into my arm and concentrated on what the doctor was trying to tell me.

"So was I when you came in. We couldn't tell what bit you, and no one seems to have seen what happened, so we treated it as if you were bitten by a wild animal. That means we've given you an immunity booster to fight against rabies as well as the first round of rabies shots, and you'll have an additional four shots in the next month. We'll also be keeping you on antibiotics for awhile."

Yuck. I hate taking medication. Of any kind. "Doctor, whoever did this to me spoke perfect English. I'm pretty sure it wasn't a wild animal, unless you count the human wildlife here in Dayton."

"I wish I'd known that. It would've saved you a few injections." He smiled. "Oh, well. It'll at least save you the second round. Get some sleep. I'm going to talk to your fan club outside, and then we'll run more tests. After that we'll know more about how long you need to stay here. Something tells me you're going to want out of here as fast as we can make it happen. I hope you won't be a difficult patient." That sounded more like an order than an observation. He patted my hand and stepped into the hallway. Mom followed him out to get the official update in medical-ese. That wasn't surprising.

I grimaced. Dr. Wilson had my number. I could be difficult when I was sick. Hospitals were the worst. But who likes to be disturbed every hour to be poked with needles, woken up at the crack of dawn for crappy food, and having to worry about exposing yourself in drafty sleepwear?

Not me.

CHAPTER SIX

Justin sat in the hallway with his eyes shut; his world disintegrating around him. Sam was hurt, and hurt badly. And it was all his fault.

He glanced down to see just how bad he looked. He still wore his uniform pants, but had removed the Kevlar vest, and unbuttoned the uniform shirt, showing the t-shirt underneath. It had been two days since the attack, and he hadn't left the hospital. He was wrinkled and tired, and just wanted to be alone, but he couldn't leave. It didn't matter if the doctors said she'd recover. He wouldn't blame her if she never wanted to speak to him again. He had been the one to suggest stopping for ice cream and a bathroom break. That made it his fault.

"Hey, good-lookin', why the long face?" Sam's friend Nadia had deviled him all night. He couldn't seem to shake her. Sam's parents and Nadia had been nothing but nice to him, thanking him for his help, and asking how he felt. Medieval torture would've been kinder.

In his mind, her father should've been beating the tar out of him for letting it happen. He'd let him. Justin had hoped for that. It would've hurt a lot less than the misery in his head and his gut. After all, he'd been the senior officer on the scene. Sam's safety was his responsibility. Instead, Nathan Hochenwalt just smiled, put an arm around his shoulders, and called Justin's foster dad, John, to come talk to him.

John and Nathan had become friends since Sam had joined the police department, going golfing together on weekends. John was a retired detective, and Justin had asked him to speak with Sam's parents when she complained about how much they worried about her on the street.

When he'd arrived, John herded him away from Sam's folks. His dad knew better than to jolly Justin out of the mood he was in. John tried to talk to him, but it didn't work. He didn't deserve that kind of help, anyway. After a while, John finally gave up, and went off to look after Sam's parents instead. He wished Nadia would do the same.

"Leave me alone." He tried to ignore her. Nothing doing; she was worse than Sam with the constant chatter. At the moment, he wondered if Sam would ever chatter at him like that again. He promised himself he'd never complain about it as long as she'd do it just once more.

"No. I'm annoying that way. How're you feeling?" She sat down on the bench next to him and crossed her legs, slouching down beside him with her foot bouncing in the air.

"I'm fine." A lie, but one calculated to get her to go away.

"I know you like her, and more than just as a friend and co-worker."

Justin's jaw dropped. He'd been careful to avoid Sam finding out how he felt. He was her training officer. The guys at the station would be brutal. She didn't deserve that, but Nadia was right. "What's your point?"

"Didn't even try to deny it? Even if I hadn't guessed, you just clinched it."

Damn. She had him there. "Stop gloating and tell me what you want."

"I want you to decide what you want. And then I want you to do something about it."

He launched himself off the hard plastic bench outside of Sam's room, too confused and upset to sit still. The others had wandered off for coffee and food after the doctor came out and said she'd be fine. He'd refused to leave, terrified that someone would come back to finish the job on Sam. He still had no idea who had hurt her. He wouldn't be able to forgive himself if he left and her attacker returned. "What the hell are you talking about?" Justin blurted, loud enough to attract attention. Would he have been able to keep his voice down if he'd slept more than twenty minutes or so since she came in?

"Shhhh," the nurses at the station hissed at him.

He repeated himself in an angry whisper.

Nadia took a deep breath. "If you like her so much, why don't you tell her?"

"That's none of your business." Though he'd started to wonder the same thing, now just wasn't the time to complicate things. Maybe after she'd recovered, after she'd passed her training evaluation, after...well, damn.

"She's my best friend. She's been hurt. I want to know if you're gonna hurt her more."

"Damn it, Nadia. Haven't I already hurt her enough?"

"You have no idea."

His head jerked up. "What the hell are you talking about?" What else could he have done? Maybe ritual disemboweling was too good for him.

"You've had her wondering about your feelings for months. Why don't you tell her? It'd do her good to hear something positive, something life-affirming. Can't you see that now isn't a bad time to tell her how you feel? It'd be something to take the pain off her mind, giving a silver lining to this awful thing. Why not make up your mind and go get the girl?"

"You've got no idea what you're talking about," Justin started, raising his voice.

Nathan Hochenwalt came around the corner just then, coming back from dinner and loaded down with coffee and doughnuts to settle into the waiting area for the evening. "You two kids want to keep the noise down? She's supposed to be sleeping." He took one look at Justin, and lifted his one free hand in surrender. "You guys want to take a swipe at each other, that's fine now that she's out of the woods, but don't wake her up." He handed them each a cup of coffee, and walked down to the waiting area where his wife sat with John.

Justin turned back to Nadia, who winked at him. He turned away and crossed his arms.

"Look, I'm going out on a limb to tell you this is a risk worth taking. I'm her best friend. I've known her since we were kids. A woman's best friend is someone who knows things."

He got it; he wasn't completely oblivious. Sam would return his feelings. He'd figured she would, but it was nice to have it confirmed. The question was whether he deserved it. "You don't know what you're talking about. I'm not fit to be with anyone. I don't know how. I'm damaged goods, Nadia." He heard the whine in his voice and winced. "She deserves better." No way would he go any further. No one got to hear the ugliness of his childhood in an abusive home. It was bad enough to know himself what he'd come from. He was terrified he'd turn into his biological father, even though he hadn't seen the bastard in twenty years. No way would he mess up a woman the way his mother had been messed up. He'd spend his entire life alone before he let that happen.

She leaned back and crossed her arms. "Bullshit. You have feelings for her. It's plain as the nose on your face. Right now she's gonna need as many friends and family and as much love and support as she can get to work through this and go back on duty in one piece. I'm telling you plain, make up your mind and go for it. It's a risk worth taking. You'll be glad that you did."

He stood in front of the door to her room, glancing inside at the shadows around the bed. "It's my fault, Nadia. She'd never have been hurt if I hadn't suggested stopping."

Nadia crossed her arms over her chest and shrugged. "I don't agree, but it's obvious you believe that, and I'm betting there isn't anything I can say to change your mind. So make it up to her by making a choice. Be there for her or make a clean break. You'd be happier if you were there for her, and so would she. But be all the way there for her or leave her the hell alone."

He stood in the doorway with hope dawning on his face while he made his choice and took a step toward it.

CHAPTER SEVEN

I fell asleep soon after the doctor left. I don't know how long I was out, but the sky, bright and sunny when the doctor talked to me earlier, was darker now. I could hear angry whispers in the hallway. I tried to listen, but could only catch bits and pieces of the conversation. Justin and Nadia were arguing. I heard "all my fault" and "leave her alone if you can't decide." Every time their voices got loud enough for me to make out more than a few words, Dad told them to shut the hell up because I was asleep and shouldn't be disturbed. I smiled. I'd coerce Nadia into explaining later. After all, that's what friends are for.

Justin stepped into the room. I heard Nadia in the hallway mutter "stupid boneheaded man" and heard Dad call out to her, keeping her from following him in. I didn't see what Nadia did, because Justin made a beeline for the chair beside my bed, blocking my view of the hallway.

Though the lights were off, a soft glow from the streetlights filtered around the edge of the blinds. Even in the dim light, I could see that his hair was a mess, sticking up in the back and on the left side, as if he'd run his hands through it over and over, or as if he'd fallen asleep on one side. His face hadn't seen a razor, and when he got closer, I realized he still wore his uniform pants and the blue uniform shirt, open over a wrinkled white t-shirt with a University of Dayton football logo on the front. He looked like he'd slept in his clothes, and I wondered how long I'd been unconscious.

"Hey," I managed through a mouth that felt like it was packed with cotton. I spied a water pitcher on the table beside me and asked for some water. He looked in the pitcher and went to the bathroom to refill it, coming back to pour me a glass.

"Jesus Christ, Sam, you scared the living crap out of me. How do you feel?" He leaned forward, as if to look me in the eye. When the light from the streetlights outside hit his face, I was astonished. Holy moly; he had dried tear tracks on his cheeks. Did that mean he cared? No, it couldn't be. I'm not that lucky. Or was I?

"I've been better, but I'll be okay. I promise."

"You don't look okay."

"Gee, thanks, Justin, exactly what every woman wants to hear when she feels like crap. Your bedside manner sucks eggs." Yikes. I didn't know how to handle this. Laugh. I could make him laugh. Yeah, that might make it better.

Instead of the laugh or smile I was going for, a look of sheer panic crossed his face.

I hurried on to another topic, confused by his reaction. I mean, I was on painkillers, so maybe I was just a bit slow at reading his reactions, but that's the same kind of comment

I made to him all the time. What was wrong with him? "Who's here?"

"Your dad just got back from getting something to eat. I don't think your mom's had a solid meal besides doughnuts and coffee since you came in. John and Nadia have been with them. Nothing would convince them to go home."

"How long have I been here?" I hadn't gotten the answer out of the doctor earlier.

"Two days, Sam. Tonight'll be your second full night here."

I didn't know how to respond to that. "I saw Nadia."

"God, she's as much a smartass as you." He laid his hand on the back of mine.

I grinned. "Great minds think alike. Please thank John for watching out for my folks." I was glad that my plan to ease Mom and Dad into accepting my career choice had included meeting my partner and his family, small as it was. John was the only family Justin ever talked about. Soon after we were assigned together, I arranged for John to talk to my folks and ask their questions about life as a police officer. I hoped he'd help smooth things over with them now that I'd been hurt, because I had no plans to give up my career.

"He and Nathan are good friends now; it made sense to call him. Dad would want to be here." It was strange to hear someone refer to my dad by his first name, but he was right. The two went golfing together on a regular basis these days.

I noticed how tired Justin sounded. Even though it hurt, I turned my hand over to hold his, but I wasn't prepared for what he did next. He laid his head down on top of my hand, and I felt the stubble of his cheek on my fingertips.

He was strung tight in every fiber of his body, and I moved my hand to bring his chin up to face me. "It's gonna be okay, Justin. I promise." I looked into his eyes. They looked scared, but he had an intense look on his face, like he was determined to do something.

"I came out of the bathroom just in time to see you fly past the window. I couldn't see what did it, but by the time I got to the door and then outside and around the corner, you were lying still and bleeding. If I hadn't gone to the restroom first, this wouldn't have happened."

"And you might be in the bed beside me if you'd been outside. Nice try, Justin, but we can play the 'what if' game all night and I still might be hurt at the end of it. This might've happened with you standing right beside me. There's no way to know."

He held up the water glass for me to take a sip through a plastic straw. I could see he wasn't convinced. Even I didn't believe everything I'd said, but it was true. There was a part of me that screamed for an explanation. I had to remind myself that time for answers would come later, after I'd healed enough to look for them. Of course, I wasn't able to convince myself of that either, but he didn't need to hear that right now.

Justin had something else on his mind. "Sam, this is bad timing, but I can't wait for something else to happen. I care about you. I need you to know that."

My heart cracked when I saw a single tear slide down his cheek. "I feel the same way," I whispered, hoping that this wasn't a dream.

His whole face lit up, like a little kid opening presents on Christmas day. I realized he hadn't been in the loop on how I felt, and Nadia hadn't opened her big mouth. Or, if she had, she'd made sure he felt the way he did before spilling the beans. Now that's a true friend. I owed her huge amounts of chocolate for doubting her.

He pressed the palm of my hand to his mouth and kissed it with relief, as if he'd taken a huge chance when he confessed his feelings to me. Okay, so maybe there is such a thing as karma, the good balancing out the bad and all that crap.

He gathered me carefully in his arms. I winced when the bed dipped, but enjoyed the feeling of him holding me. I heard a noise from the doorway and turned my head. Mom was doing a happy dance in the hallway as Nadia giggled. Apparently, my best friend was giving Mom and Dad a play-by-play commentary, and they approved. I heard laughter that sounded like Dad and John as I drifted off to sleep, exhausted, but in Justin's arms with a grin splitting my face from ear to ear.

CHAPTER EIGHT

The next time I opened my eyes, it was morning and I was alone. Well, almost alone.

I looked at the clock. It was seven in the morning. I don't ever get up at seven in the morning. I work the night shift, and I'm just not human and coherent yet at seven in the morning unless I'm still awake. As in, haven'tgone-home-yet awake. The light screamed in my eyes with an insistent glow I couldn't hide from. If I'd been a little kid, I'd have rolled over and yanked the covers over my head, but with the bandage on my head, the sling on my arm, and the sore ribs, I couldn't quite manage it.

Grumpy and wanting coffee, I heard the whisper of a nurse's footsteps in the hall and low voices, but I didn't recognize them from the night before. I panicked. Who was going to stop the jerk who did this to me if he decided to come to the hospital to finish the job? It wasn't like me to panic at the thought of being alone. I just needed a plan. Or a gun. Or something.

I hit the button to adjust the bed to a sitting position, and took slow deep breaths to overcome the pain in my ribs and force myself to relax. It was better to daydream about Justin and last night than to worry about deadly assassins coming in to kill me, but that didn't mean I shouldn't be alert.

As I sat up, I noticed that I wasn't alone after all. A good looking man with shoulder length blond hair sat in the chair beside my bed and smiled at me. I wondered what kind of cologne he wore, because he smelled of musk, forest air, and the loamy smell of earth after a summer rain. I was a little surprised to have noticed the smell. It was a comforting smell, and that confused me. I'm not the outdoors-y type. Normally I'd have wrinkled my nose and wondered when he'd bathed last.

I noticed he wore a hospital identification card clipped to his belt, and breathed a sigh of relief. He at least belonged here. He wasn't wearing a white coat or nursing scrubs, so I assumed he didn't have any needles hiding behind his back. I hadn't had any shots since I'd woken up, but after the doctor's statement about rabies, I was on the lookout.

"Hi, you must be Samantha," he started, as he leaned forward in his chair.

"It's Sam. I'd shake your hand, but I'm a little wrapped up," I said, as I indicated the sling on my left arm and the IV and bandage on my right. "And you are?"

"My name's Logan Boyd. I'm a social worker. I specialize in helping trauma victims."

Oh, goody. Relive the worst night of my life with a stranger, no matter how good-looking he is? No thank you. "And you're here to talk to me about what happened, right?"

"Yeah, I am. And you should talk to someone about it."

"And I'd have to talk about it over and over again, right?" I cocked one eyebrow at him.

"That's how it works." His nose was oddly shaped, as if he'd broken it and it never healed correctly. Even so, it fit him.

"Do you work here in the hospital?" I was eager to change the subject.

"I consult with the hospital. I don't get called in unless someone's hurt really bad."

"Only take the big cases?"

He grinned. "That's one way of putting it. I specialize in counseling for post traumatic stress disorder, and provide ongoing treatment for those who develop symptoms. I also work with the veterans' hospitals."

"I'm fine." I smiled. "Nothing wrong here, Mr. Boyd. In fact, I'll do even better once I'm allowed to go home."

"A sentiment shared by many in your shoes, I'd say. In fact, you look like you're in a good mood, your injuries notwithstanding."

I smiled. "I got some good news last night when I woke up and realized I'd be okay."

He gave me a skeptical look and his card. There was an odd, loopy symbol on it I didn't recognize. Circles upon circles of different sizes in a triangle embossed on a white card meant nothing to me. The symbol was followed by his name and three numbers. I assumed they were home, office, and cell numbers. "Be sure to call if you change your mind," he said, as he got up.

"I'll be fine."

"That may be, but if things change, don't hesitate to call. Day or night," he said again as he stood and I was struck by how he moved, with a smooth athletic prowl to his walk as he left.

I'm so not calling him, I thought. *He's cute and all, but I've got Justin, and my family, and Nadia. I'm fine.* Besides, I had bigger things to worry about, like what'll happen between us at work if the guys at the station figure out Justin and I have become sort-of a couple.

It's not unheard of for officers to date. In fact, it happens more often than people think. Police officers work a dangerous job with long hours, especially on night shift with court during the day. Once a relationship got serious, the higher ups would separate the couple, so they aren't assigned together or in the same district, to avoid any conflict on the job.

The bigger issue would be the teasing I'd take. Female police officers don't have it easy. The guys joke around a lot, and a woman who doesn't guard her privacy ends up being the topic of the week. Police officers are worse about gossip than junior high girls. I had no desire to parade my personal life in front of the rest of the department.

Right on cue with my inner monologue, Justin walked in. In his hands was a single large white flower in a heavy glass vase, and I smiled. I noticed a strange look on his face. He didn't look very happy.

I didn't get a chance to ask what was up because Mom was right behind him. "Hi, baby, who was the guy that just left?" She dropped a kiss on my forehead.

"That was Logan Boyd. He says he's a trauma counselor, supposedly one of the best." I didn't care. Justin was here to see me, and he'd brought flowers. That was a better topic. "Nice flowers, Noble. Someone might think you like me." I smiled at him.

He went red from his collar to his hairline. "They're not from me. I picked them up for you at the nurse's station, so you'd get them before you go home. They were sitting at the front desk waiting. I asked who brought them and no one seemed to know. I was hoping you'd know who they're from. There's no name on the card."

I glanced around the room. There were a few baskets of flowers. Mom went around and read off the cards, so we could figure out who'd sent what. The guys at the police district sent a basket of daisies (though they'd probably been picked out by the district secretaries). Mom and Dad sent some carnations, and Nadia left a teddy bear holding a spray of wildflowers. Everyone that I'd thought would send me flowers was accounted for, except for Justin. Made sense that I'd assumed they were his, and I said so.

He handed me the card, silently. It was a symbol very similar, though not exactly, to the one on Logan Boyd's business card. No question about it. Justin wasn't being coy. They weren't from him. "I don't know who they're from, Justin. I don't even know what kind of flower this is." I didn't want him getting jealous just when we'd figured each other out.

Mom spoke up. "Honey, that's an orchid. It looks expensive."

I rolled my eyes. Thanks Mom. Just make it a little worse. Justin's shoulders slumped. I didn't know quite what to say. Mom continued to prattle on, changing topics at light speed. "You know, after you get home, it might not be a bad idea to talk to a counselor."

If steam could come out of a person's ears, Justin was whistling like a teapot. Time to distract her, before he completely lost it. Obviously the flowers bothered him. I'm sure finding that another guy visited me in the hospital, even if it was a counselor, wasn't helping. "We'll see, Mom. Have you heard any more about when I might be going home?"

"Last night before we left, the doctor said he wanted to run more tests. If they came back with good results, then you'd go home today."

"Is someone taking care of Doyle?" I didn't want to think about my poor cat going without food or someone to scoop the litter box. That would be a very stinky welcome home.

"Nadia's been taking care of him. She picked up more cat food for you last night."

Even though it was hard to bend at the waist with my ribs taped up, it wasn't nearly as hard as it was the night before. I wasn't dizzy as I was sitting up and talking with them, and the headache was less. I hoped that meant good things for the tests the doctors wanted to run.

Mom helped me to the bathroom while Justin waited in the hallway. The doctor came in a few minutes later, and a nurse wheeled me off for the next round of tests. I crossed my fingers, toes, and everything else, hoping the tests would show enough improvement for me to go home.

CHAPTER NINE

We didn't have to wait long. The tests came back in less than an hour, and the doctor said I could go home. He seemed puzzled and wanted to order more tests, but I declined. If I was well enough to go home, I didn't see any benefit to more tests. That was kind of the point of a hospital, anyway, to get better, so why stick around if the job was done?

The doctor explained I'd be off work a couple more weeks before he'd sign the paperwork the department required for me to return to work. I figured I'd be on light duty for a while when I did go back. It's standard to ease back into the job if someone's off on serious medical leave. Light duty sucks, and entails an endless paper chase around the department. Hey, anything's preferable to lying in a hospital. There's a limit to the poking and prodding I can take, and I was well over it. I'd happily file old speeding tickets for weeks just to be out of here.

After the paperwork was complete and the doctor gave me his office number to set up a follow up appointment, an orderly wheeled me to the curb. Justin lifted me out of the wheelchair over my objections, and placed me in the back seat of Mom's SUV. Next to me on the seat was a huge bouquet of lavender roses, and several large shopping bags. Mom settled into the driver's seat with a big, knowing, grin on her face.

I didn't want him to think of me as a mooning kind of girl, but I couldn't help myself. Justin turned around to check on me as I lifted the roses to my nose. The look on his face was worth it. As I sighed over them, I noticed a smug grin on his face. "Those are from me," he said.

I kept a blissful smile on my face for the entire drive home. Well, almost the entire drive home. I swear Mom hit each and every bump in the road, jarring my shoulder and ribs every single time.

She waited until Justin carried me inside to the couch and then went to get the flowers and shopping bags. They must have bought out the supermarket. "You know," she said, "all the stuff he's bringing in was his idea. I had nothing to do with it." She raised her hands in front of her, as if holding back an accusation from me.

"What're you talking about, Mom?" I sat up on the couch gingerly, curious enough to take one of the bags from her and look inside.

"He insisted on going shopping before we went to the hospital, since the doctor said you might come home today. He wanted to make sure everything was right, so he wanted me to go along, but he's got you pegged." She helped me sift through the bags as she laughed.

Grand slam in the attentive boyfriend department. He'd gotten my favorite roses, a teddy bear, Gummy Bears, women's magazines, action movies, and most of my favorite kinds of junk food. The kicker was a very cold box of Esther Price candy at the bottom of the last bag, with a blue cooler pack keeping them cold.

"He got me chocolate covered potato chips? They don't even sell them this time of year. I wonder where he found them." I exclaimed, hugging the box with my good arm. My favorite pick-me-up when I felt down, they're a perfect blend of chocolate and grease. Some people go to bars to get drunk. When I've had a bad day, I head straight for the local Esther Price store. It's a good thing I work out, or it'd be a problem. I'd have to watch it on the junk food while I recovered.

Justin walked in just as I tore off the plastic wrapping. "Be careful not to break a tooth, Sam. They were still frozen this morning."

"You've had them in your freezer?"

His cheeks went red with embarrassment. "Yeah, I heard you talking about them and bought them a long time ago." Wow. He must have bought them four or five months ago. How long had he held them for me? How long had he been considering this?

Mom made some excuse about checking Doyle's food and water as she left the room. I crooked my finger to bring Justin closer. When he got within reach, I put one hand on his cheek to bring him closer and kissed him firmly on the lips. "Justin, if you don't watch out, you're gonna have me spoiled. I'm not used to being treated this way."

He smiled as he stood, but I noticed the smile didn't reach his eyes. I could see the guilt haunting him, and I decided to keep my trap shut. He was going out of his way to make it up to me, that I'd been hurt and he hadn't been able to stop it. Saying something stupid and screwing it up would ruin the moment, and would be about as kind as kicking a puppy. I decided to put the teasing into low gear for now.

I took advantage of a weak moment when the two of them weren't paying much attention to me to stand up slowly and walk to the kitchen for a soda. When I opened the freezer to get ice, I was stunned. He'd crammed every inch of my freezer with Ben and Jerry's ice cream. I figured I'd be in sugar shock by the end of the weekend if he kept it up. That and adding a few extra pounds I didn't need onto my butt, but Justin's attention to detail was positively overwhelming. I live for dessert, but wow.

Mom caught me staring at the smorgasbord of frozen dairy products and frowned, hands on her hips. "Young lady, we're here today, let us wait on you."

I tried to protest, but she steered me back to the couch, whispering in my ear, "I promise not to nag, but you need to take it easy. I'm going back to work tonight, but Justin's got the night off, so he's gonna be here if you need anything. That man really likes you. Give him a break and let him help you. Don't overdo it."

"Mom, I won't overdo it. You guys did great. Can you hand me the cat treats on the shelf? I should give Doyle some attention so he feels like the king of the house again."

She handed me the can, and spent the next few minutes fussing before she headed off to get some sleep before she went to work tonight. Justin hovered like a nervous cloud. Doyle, showing how grateful he was that I was home, alternated between licking my feet and bumping the top of his head against my hand for me to pet him.

Justin sat down in the chair opposite the couch when Mom left. I waited for Justin to say something. We sat in silence, staring at each other. And then the awkwardness set in.

"Okay, Justin, this isn't working," I started, but before I could add anything else, his face twisted, a look of raw fear around his eyes. He thought he'd screwed up, I thought. Jeez, he sure was strung tight today. I hurried to reassure him. "I'm not talking about what you did for me today. You did great. I'm talking about how you're treating me right now."

What I thought was fear on his face now looked like panic. Hey, no one ever accused me of being an expert on men. Nadia told me once that I was learning impaired when it came to figuring out the opposite sex. I never learned how to tell what was wrong with a relationship before it blew up in my face.

He stood up and walked over to the couch. I reached up with my good hand and grabbed the front of his shirt, forcing him to bend down to me. "Justin, I'm the same smartass you ride with every night. I want us to be together. I'm tired and sore, but I'm not made of glass, and I'm not mad at you. You couldn't have stopped it, and you're here to help me get over it. I appreciate everything, but don't treat me like I'll break. I won't."

He looked at me and nodded, getting up from the chair and crouching down in front of me to look me in the eye. "With work and all, we should make a decision on what to tell people before you go back, but we don't have to do that tonight. You're tired. Do you want me to go home and let you get some sleep?"

Tired as I was, and as much as I wanted to show Justin that I was okay, I felt panic at the idea of being alone. That was odd. I like being alone, but I didn't think I could handle it right now. I remembered feeling the same way this morning when I thought I was alone. "Let's take this one step at a time and see where we're at before I go back. Can we just curl up on the couch and watch a movie? That's the best thing we could do."

He picked up the bag of movies that Mom had left on the coffee table. Turns out he'd brought every buddy cop movie ever made, along with cop parodies, cop comedies and cop thrillers. I'd seen them, but they were mindless entertainment, nothing I'd feel bad about missing if I fell asleep. He started Police Academy, and I settled down with my head on his shoulder, bad arm resting on a pillow, smelling the soap and shaving cream he'd used that morning, and feeling that everything was right with the world. Just as Mahoney heard Jones making machine gun noises for the first time, I was asleep. Not a bad way to end a day. Now if things could just stay this way, I'd be happy.

I'm just not that lucky.

Chapter Ten

Logan walked into the barn looking for trouble. It didn't take long to find it.

"Hey, Max." He greeted the older man with a somber nod, showing deference to the pack leader before he said anything else. "Where's he at?"

Max tilted his dark head to indicate the room behind him, showing just a few grey hairs woven through his temples. "Leave him alone. I'm not sure any counseling's gonna fix what he's done this time."

"What do you mean?"

"He's getting worse. His screw ups pose a risk to the rest of us. It's reached the point that we risk exposure just by each contact he has with others outside the pack. We've tried drying him out. You've tried counseling. Adam's tried medical intervention. He's got no control, and now he's attacked someone. Someone we don't know yet will stand with us or against us."

Logan's eyebrows hit his hairline in surprise. "You're talking about killing him."

"Don't know that I got a choice." Max crossed his arms over his broad chest, deep in thought. "We've gone through alcohol and weed, and now he's into crack and pills. No control there and a great big pile of uncertainty. It's a weakness we can't afford. He gets busted, how long before he starts talking?"

A cold trickle of fear ran down the back of Logan's neck. If Max did this, there was no telling what he'd consider a threat later. Certainly the others he'd talked to about Max's behavior and ways of running the pack, the ones who'd said they'd stand by him if he made a move to get rid of Max, could be his next targets.

Clueless as to Logan's mental anguish, Max continued, staring off into space. "Only thing I can see to do, except maybe to take out that pretty little cop. Seems a shame to waste potential, but both of them pose a risk. Easiest thing is get rid of both of 'em."

"For something neither of them asked for, you're going to kill them. Stephen's not gonna say anything that could risk his ex and his kid. Why not wait and see what she'll do?"

"Can't risk it, boy. She opens her mouth and we're toast. Do you want to be the media darling on this? How about the military-testing guinea pig? Does that sound like fun?"

"I might be able to predict what she'll do before she does it." Careful, Logan thought. This delicate conversation could go so badly. He wondered why he put himself at risk for someone he didn't know, but he remembered the look on Sam's face. She saw him as a social worker, as someone who was supposed to help her. Hell, it was his job to help her. This wasn't the way he traditionally helped people but it was the biggest thing he could do at the moment.

"How do you plan to do that, hotshot? Got a magic eight ball in your pocket? Or are you thinking about taking a mate finally? You're the only one I've ever given permission to date within the pack, and you've never done anything about it. You're the best physical and mental specimen of the pack, and the only one I'd risk a born wolf from. She's a pretty little piece, and plenty of spit to her. I've got a hunch you might have an idea there that I'd get behind. If it got you on board, I'd agree to hanging on to her long enough to do what it takes."

Logan ignored that thought, even though his brain had no problem conjuring up the mental image of intimacy with Samantha. He'd turned down Max's request to start a breeding program a long time ago, and had no intention of participating in something like that. He had his eye on something bigger than being the pack stud. The idea appalled him. "I've already introduced myself as a trauma counselor. I've read her file, and offered my services through the police department. She's serious about being a cop. They're not gonna let her back on the force withoutdoing trauma counseling. I've got the contacts to make sure of that within the department. I give it two weeks before she calls. She'll do what it takes to go back."

"How does that help me?" Max narrowed his eyes.

"I'll know a good part of what she's thinking as things unfold. If it looks like it's going south, I can let you know. If it looks like she's on board, she's going to need us anyway, and having a cop in the pack, with their ears to the ground on the street can't be a bad thing."

Max chewed it over for a bit while Logan's heart pounded in his chest. He had no idea if Max had seen through him or not, but it was a risk worth taking. If Max said no, then Logan's own plans needed stepping up, and he'd have to do something soon.

One of the other pack members came out of the room Stephen Tipton was in, and Logan heard a whimper when the door opened. He wasn't sure he could save Stephen as well. Max wasn't wrong, he was getting worse. He felt bad at Stephen's downfall, a crash-and-burn that could be laid entirely at the feet of Max's grand plans for redesigned pack facilities. If Max hadn't been so eager...well, not much he could do about it now. "How sure are you that anyone has to be gotten rid of? Is there another way to handle this?"

Max looked disgusted. "You know, being soft and indecisive is one of the reasons why you haven't risen further in this pack. You know what it did to your dad."

It was an old wound, one that Max never failed to pour salt in. Logan knew from experience that Max wanted him to rise to the bait and issue a formal challenge to him, to show himself as a decisive leader that Max could groom to the top. He wasn't Max's lapdog. He was still a human, or at least mostly human, one that could think and reason, and make rational decisions. It might have worked on a boy of fourteen whose dad had committed suicide in front of him, but Logan was now an adult, and Max had been baiting him for years. The best way to deal with it was to ignore it.

"So, this time, instead of drying him out and throwing him back out there, let's hang on to him for a while. Maybe we moved him too fast back out into the real world once he was sober. Besides, how would you dispose of the body? It's only a matter of time until the police draw a line between him and the cop he attacked. If he turns up dead while they're looking for him, the investigation won't stop there. We don't want that kind of attention. Maybe he stays here at the barn for a while. There's always someone here to make sure he doesn't leave. Him turning up alive, or dead, would be bad if the cops are looking for him. Hanging on to him is smart, and hanging onto him alive smells less in a facility with no windows."

Max grinned, his white teeth gleaming. "That's good thinking, boy. Maybe I underestimated you. We'll lock him in and keep him here while you get him clean and sober. Then we'll see where we're at with the girl, and whether the police are looking for him."

Logan nodded. It was about as much as he could hope for at this point, but at least it gave him time to see how Sam would take the new twists and turns in her life.

He hoped she was limber enough to handle them all.

CHAPTER ELEVEN

I woke up later stiff and sore. I was alone, lying in my own bed. I had a moment's panic until I remembered Justin carrying me to bed and kissing my cheek before he left. Doyle licked the back of my hand and cried pitifully, as he always did when I slept past his scheduled feeding time. It hurt to sit up, but I felt okay once I was out of bed.

I stumbled into my bathrobe, and checked all the locks twice, uneasy about being alone. I even closed the latch on Doyle's cat door, so nothing could come in the house through that entrance. He whined at me again, but I ignored him. He'd just have to stay inside all day. I put a little extra food into his bowl to make up for it, but I wasn't taking any chances.

I found my gun in the hallway safe, loaded it, and engaged the safety before tucking it into the pocket of my bathrobe. I stopped in the kitchen to grab a soda and the chocolate covered potato chips, and then settled into the recliner to finish the movie I'd fallen asleep in front of last night. Drowning my fears in chocolate, grease, and comedy, couldn't be bad. If that didn't work, I had plenty of ice cream, and having my gun was a comfort better than any teddy bear. Doyle curled up in my lap and purred.

Five minutes into the movie, I fell asleep again, but this time it wasn't a restful sleep. I experienced the attack all over again in living color. Not exactly a restful visual effect.

I felt the hand on my arm and remembered how I'd felt when I couldn't shake it free. My ribs exploded with pain as they struck the brick wall and I fought to breathe. The ground rushed up and I saw stars when my head hit the edge of the curb.

The voice I'd heard that night sounded familiar, but I couldn't place it. It was too rough to be a normal voice. I'd smelled a wet dog when that voice spoke, but it was an outside dog. The odor was too ripe to be an indoor dog. Mom's pug Riley, who never went outside unless he was supervised, never smelled that bad. Come to think of it, the department K9 units didn't smell that bad. It had to be a stray dog. But then where did the voice come from?

I felt the teeth rip into my arm. Whoever bit me licked the bite. It burned, but it wasn't the bite itself that was the source of heat. The bite hurt, don't get me wrong, but it was the saliva itself that caused the sudden incineration.

It wasn't a fever, or the kind of heat one might feel in the pit of one's stomach when adrenaline hits in a stressful situation. Instead, I could trace it through each and every vein in my body. It was the scorching heat, rather than the head injury that had made me faint in the ambulance.

All of a sudden, the scene clicked in my mind like a remote control changing a television channel. I was in the woods, though I didn't know where. I ran joyously, following a smorgasbord of smells I'd never noticed before.

The colors were muted like a black and white photograph, but the smells were overwhelming. They were so sharp I could taste them as I ran. I could've navigated through the forest on smell alone. The air was crisp, and I smelled the trees, the grass, the wildflowers, and the dirt. The dirt smelled so clean, I couldn't help myself; I had to roll in it just to take the scent home with me.

"What?" I woke up with a start. My arm was sore, but I'd lifted it over my head when I'd woken up without realizing it. I took off the sling and sat up.

The phone rang again. I leaped out of the chair to grab it before I realized I shouldn't be able to move that fast with the broken ribs and the bum shoulder. "Hello?"

"Honey, I was just calling to check on you. How're you feeling?" It was Mom. "I stopped by yesterday after I got off work, and you were in bed. Your dad stopped by at noon, and Justin said you were asleep, so I waited to call you. Did you sleep okay?"

That's a joke, right? I'd slept just fine. "What time did you stop by?"

"Oh, it was early. I got off work at six, and came right over. I didn't expect you to be awake, but I was surprised you were sleeping when your dad stopped by."

"I'm sorry, Mom. Coming home took more out of me than I realized." I heard a hissing noise coming from under the couch, and went to investigate as Mom continued to talk. Doyle was hidden under the couch, hissing and spitting. I reached under the couch for him and he freaked, streaking out from under the couch and into the guest bedroom like a shot.

Mom continued, asking about my injuries, as I went in search of the cat. Doyle's never been afraid or aggressive with me. I wanted to make sure there was nothing physically wrong with him. I followed him into the guest room, answering Mom's questions as I went.

Mom tries hard not to worry about what I do for a living, but I know it gives her nightmares. I promised myself I would cut her some slack after what had happened and not get annoyed at the worry. Or, rather I should say woooo-orry, the way Mom always says it with something like fourteen syllables.

"I'm feeling good, Mom. I'll be bored silly before I can go back to work." Nothing doing, then; I tried the treats, a favorite toy, even catnip to lure Doyle out from under the bed. It hurt for him to react that way to me, but the only thing left to do was to let him just get over it. He'd come around eventually. I moved into the kitchen to make some coffee.

Mom can change topics with the speed of light. She was prattling on about how wonderful Justin was and how glad she was that he and I were dating. Thank goodness the coffee pot didn't take long to brew. I poured myself a cup of life-giving coffee, but the wake up jolt didn't come from caffeine. It came from looking at the digital clock on the wall and seeing the date, as well as the sunshine coming in the kitchen between the blinds on the sliding doors to my patio. I'd lost a day and a half to sleep, zonked out for twenty four hours straight in bed and another ten hours or so in the recliner.

No wonder I felt rested. I shook my head, and gulped coffee. Mom kept on. "Do you need anything? Have you had anything to eat except Justin's junk food? You really do need something more wholesome in your stomach with the painkillers they gave you."

"I'm fine, Mom, I promise." And I was, now that I had a bit of caffeine in my system. However, I felt sick to my stomach when I thought about actual food. I saw the box of chocolate covered potato chips with the lid askew on the table and quickly put them away. They weren't cheap, and the last thing I needed was for Doyle to get a taste for chocolate. It's toxic for cats. An unexpected and expensive run to the vet to pump his stomach was not on my agenda for the day. The thought of eating them myself had me ready to empty my stomach as well.

"Your dad will stop by tomorrow when he gets home, and Justin said he'd stop by after work tonight. Ooh, I just knew he liked you."

I swear I could hear her grin over the phone. She'd probably called all her girlfriends and crowed about having some unseen hand in finding me such a wonderful man and told them the story of him confessing his feelings to me. I wondered how much the story would grow in the telling. By the time it made the rounds, someone would probably hear that he'd dropped to one knee beside my bed as I was about to die, but the love he'd professed had made me fight for my life, or some other such nonsense. Gag me with a spoon.

She continued on, not interrupted by my internal monologue. "He's so nice and polite, and he'll be good for you. Oh, I'm so happy."

I smiled. There was no stopping the gossip machine. I'd laugh at the story even as I unraveled it all later. I was just glad there wouldn't be any awkward meet-the-family dinners. He knew everyone, and they liked him, if Mom's reaction was any indication. "Mom, we're just starting a relationship. It's not serious at this point, but I'm glad something good came out of all this."

"Samantha, you need to talk to someone, maybe get into counseling, about what happened before you go back to work. I've seen people get hurt and fall apart later. I know you think I worry too much, but it's better to be safe than sorry."

Of course she worried too much. She always had, but it occurred to me that Mom would nag until I agreed to talk to someone. I picked up Logan Boyd's card from the kitchen table and nodded. Please let him not be one of Mom's coffee buddies from the hospital.

"Mom I do have a name. You remember Logan Boyd, the guy who visited me?"

"I know the name and he's supposed to good. He works with the police departments. Justin said he taught hostage negotiation and mental health intervention at the police academy."

"I'll give him a call. I promise."

A few more minutes of assuring Mom that I was all right and I hung up the phone. I was tired again. I realized there wasn't enough caffeine on the planet to keep me upright and coherent for much longer. Who knew sleeping could be so exhausting? I left my mug on the counter and stumbled into my bedroom, where I was asleep almost before my head hit the pillow.

CHAPTER TWELVE

I spent the next couple of days asleep around the clock, waking up just long enough to shower, go to the bathroom, and eat a bite or two. I worried about it, especially since I relived the attack in my dreams over and over again. If it wasn't the attack, I ran through parks or drank from a stream, or chased something. Justin came over every night, and held me when I fell asleep. I hoped it would keep me from dreaming about the attack, but it didn't work. I wasn't going to complain about it not working, though. It made me feel safer to feel his arms around me.

He spent every moment that he wasn't at work or in court at my house. I was afraid when I was alone, but I didn't want my folks to worry, so I gave him a key. I was a clingy, needy mess. It was way out of character for me, and, much as I hated it, I couldn't seem to help myself.

About a week after the attack, I was able to stay awake more. Not a lot more, but enough to notice. I'd dropped fifteen pounds in four days from inactivity and sleeping through meals, and just generally not being hungry.

Justin was annoyed. We argued constantly about me not eating, and he told me my eyes looked hollow. A few days later, we found a middle ground. I could eat meat and protein, but anything else made me nauseous. Whether it was chicken, or steak, or pork chops, or sausage, I couldn't get enough meat. Seasoning wasn't important. Garnishes weren't necessary. I didn't even need it cooked all the way through. I just wanted meat in every flavor of the rainbow.

Once we'd reached that compromise, Justin outdid himself with takeout from the Greek restaurant down the street, to chicken places, hamburgers, and even brought over steaks to grill for me when he had the time. He seemed willing to let it go as long as I ate. After the initial meat argument, he kept his concerns to himself and let me set the tone and speed of conversation. That was a wise decision. I was irritable, cranky, and bored, but reluctant to leave the security of my home, especially after dark. I was also having trouble explaining why.

"Sam, you're looking better today," Justin said when I answered my door one morning after he'd been in court. When he smiled, I saw how tired he looked. I realized he'd hardly spent time at his own house. He'd run interference with parents and my friends, and gave me the space I needed to deal with what happened. I'd run him into the ground.

It was time to do something for him. "Can we go out to lunch?"

I don't think I could have surprised him more if I'd told him that little blue aliens had landed from Mars and were living inside my ears. His jaw dropped.

"You sure you're up to it? It would do you good to get out of the house."

I swallowed hard. He'd given me an out. I was terrified to leave the house, but I knew I needed to do this, if not for myself, then at least for him. He deserved it. "It's up to you, Justin. Where do you want to go?"

He looked at me skeptically. "How does sushi sound?"

As if on command, my stomach growled and my mouth watered. I smiled, and he laughed, that deep laugh that I loved.

"I guess that's a yes," he chuckled.

"Let me take a shower. I want to look a little more presentable. I guess you could say that this is our first official date."

A smile lit up his face and carried all the way to his eyes. He hadn't smiled like that in a long time. I wanted to try even if I fell asleep in my wasabi.

"Sure, Sam, it's no problem. I'll sit here and entertain Doyle while you shower. He's really taken to me lately."

I heard the reproach in his voice for ignoring my cat and cringed. I could've defended myself, but Doyle hadn't been acting like himself. One minute he'd curl up to me and the next he'd hiss and spit and bite. Justin headed toward the basket of cat toys while I headed for my bedroom. I heard a happy meow. Good, I thought. Even if I'd been a bad owner, at least he got attention and exercise.

I looked around the bedroom and sighed. Laundry wasn't done, and was all over the room. Figuring out something to wear that fit and was still comfortable with my injuries, but first date appropriate wouldn't be easy. I grabbed my robe and headed for the shower.

A shower is no mean feat with sore ribs and an aching shoulder. I'd noticed I had to get out the razor more often. It wasn't just that I had a man at the house. There was nothing happening that would have me worried he'd notice, but I was sprouting hair at an alarming rate. That made showering even more of a challenge with my injuries, but I was determined to treat this like a first date. That meant finding a way to shave my legs, no matter how sore I was. I chalked it up to stress. Obviously, if my sleep schedule and appetite were off, it made sense that other things would be off as well.

I pulled out a pair of slacks, boots, and a camisole, and then changed when nothing fit right. I kept the shirt but ended up in an older pair of jeans that had been too small just two weeks ago, and grabbed a button-up shirt to tie around my waist in case the air conditioning got cold at the restaurant. I took one look at the sling I'd stopped wearing the week before, and decided not to wear it. A sling is less than romantic on a first date.

I called Nadia, who I hadn't talked to since I left the hospital. I wanted her opinion about my clothes. To me, clothes were what a person wore so they weren't naked. I just didn't care about fashionable, but this was special. I really felt bad for how I'd treated Justin, so I wanted to be sure I looked nice. I hate shopping. Nadia and I used to share clothes all the time, so she knew everything in my closet, especially since it hadn't changed much in years. Once she approved the outfit, and I'd added a bit of makeup, I was good to go. I hate wearing makeup, but Justin was right. My eyes did look hollow.

It hurt to learn that my best friend had been reduced to calling Mom for information since Justin had run interference. He'd done the job a bit too well, if her account was to be believed. I resolved to call her more often, but it still took twenty minutes to get off the phone. I knew she'd call Mom right after I hung up. She'd been so happy to hear from me, she couldn't help smiling and laughing, and it was contagious. I was already in a better mood to deal with my fear of leaving the house.

I came out of the bedroom to see Justin sitting on the carpet with a can of cat treats in his hand, patiently teaching Doyle to "sit" when asked. The amazing thing was that

Doyle was doing exactly that. "Having fun turning my cat into a dog?" I asked.

He looked up at me. "We've been working on it for a while. You look nice."

"Thanks." I was glad I'd taken the time to worry over my appearance. Justin's reaction helped even more. He stood up and gave me a quick kiss, but he pulled back before it could go much further than that. I took a deep breath and forced myself to open the door and walk out to Justin's truck, even though I avoided looking out the windows as he pulled out of the driveway.

He drove to the Oregon District in downtown Dayton. Independent restaurants, antique stores, adult bookstores, coffee shops, and art galleries lined the cobble-stoned street, and for sushi, I knew he was headed for Thai 9, a restaurant and sushi bar at the edges of the district.

We went inside and got a table. Justin ordered an ocean's worth of fish and we talked about police gossip, my folks, his dad, and the cat. It was obvious that he avoided bringing up the attack. I was grateful. I was nervous being out of the house, but each minute got a bit easier, especially as we talked about simple things.

Our food came, and I was starving. Justin was still mixing up soy sauce and wasabi in a little dish when I swallowed my fourth piece of sushi. I couldn't get enough. Justin brought up the attack while I sucked down fish like a starving walrus.

"Sam, I'm worried about you." He put down his chopsticks as I put another piece of tuna in my mouth, leaving the rice beneath it on the plate.

I swallowed hard. "Oh no, not you, too."

"What do you mean?"

I guess my grace period was up. "I got the woooo-orried about you speech from Mom again today." Mom had called about twenty minutes before Justin got to my house. It was her phone call that woke me up before he arrived.

She'd taken to calling every day, and I got the same fourteen syllable warning every day. I took another bite. The fish tasted sweet and buttery as it filled my stomach and made me feel better.

"Sam, you scared everyone to death. Don't make a joke, I'm serious. You're sleeping too much. You've dropped a scary amount of weight. Please tell me you're going to talk to a counselor before you come back to work."

"Yes, *Mom*. I already promised her I would. I'm going to call Logan Boyd."

He grimaced, but pushed on. The man was like a terrier with a bone between his teeth, gnawing the very life out of it. "You're really going to call? You're not just saying that to get me to shut up?"

"I'll call him tomorrow, make an appointment. Can we talk about something else?"

He noticed the pile of rice on my plate, and the relief for my agreement to start counseling disappeared. "What the hell are you doing, Sam? Are you just eating the fish? Have you eaten anything but meat lately? I bought you some salad and stuff for while I was at work. Did you eat it?" He looked genuinely concerned.

I was genuinely pissed off. "You're gonna give me the starving children in Ethiopia speech? I don't want the rice. It doesn't taste right. Salad doesn't sit well on my stomach, either." I shrugged. I'd felt bad when he did my grocery shopping the other day. He'd spent money he didn't have to. Rabbit food wasn't going to get eaten no matter how much money he'd wasted.

"Damn it, Sam. There's nothing wrong with the rice. It's fine. You haven't touched anything with carrots or cucumber in it either. You didn't touch your salad before the fish came. No wonder you're losing weight." He leaned in closer to me, and I could tell he was trying not to yell, his eyes boring straight into me.

I leaned back and crossed my arms. "I thought you were my date, not my diet advisor. You're gonna ruin the whole day picking on everything I do or say. If I wanted a nurse, I'd call Mom. Then again, I don't think she'd bitch at me like this." I was vaguely aware that I was overreacting, but I didn't care. I was sick and tired of him asking about what I ate. I hated feeling scared all the time. I wanted to feel safe but didn't know how, so I decided to go with anger.

"I'm not picking on you. Like most people, I'm worried. Don't roll your eyes. I didn't want it to be like this. You're the one turning a simple question into an argument."

I ignored him and kept eating.

The waiter, of course, picked that moment to come up the steps with our bill. Justin snatched it up and ran down the stairs to the hostess stand, even though it was the kind of restaurant where customers paid the bill at the table.

When he returned, I took one look at his face and my temper exploded. The only reason I didn't scream right then was that I knew I shouldn't. This was a screaming match that wouldn't go over well in public, and could get us both in trouble for causing a scene, so I kept my mouth shut all the way back to his truck. Police officers shouldn't cause disturbances. It doesn't look good, and it certainly wouldn't help me get back to full duty.

He opened the door for me, and I sat down, slamming it behind me with a bang. I saw a red flush creep up his neck, and it made me feel better that I'd made him mad. He came around and started the engine, and yelled at me. I joined in. We continued to scream at each other the rest of the way back to my house.

"Samantha Jane, you are an ungrateful bitch. I've all but waited on you, hand and foot, over the last few days. Is it so much to ask for the two of us to have a nice normal first date? I know you were hurt, and I've tried hard to be whatever you wanted or needed, but I can't keep it up. You need help, and soon, or this isn't going to work. You're not the same woman you were two weeks ago, and even with the attack, this isn't right. I don't mind you venting, but you're either a walking zombie or a screaming maniac. I don't know where the real you went."

I was so angry I wanted to hit him, and I had an insane urge to bite him, but before I could respond, he kept going. I sat on my hands when he pulled into my driveway, trying not to reach out and smack the crap out of him.

"You're not wisecracking. You're not interested in anything other than sleeping, though you want me there to hold you every spare minute of the day. I feel more like a human teddy bear than your date. I understand you feel insecure and you're still healing, but this can't last forever. I don't want you at my back with a gun unless you get hold of yourself. You want comfort right now, and I'm happy to give it, but I'm not a walking security blanket, and you're not a weakling. You're jumping at shadows. Get help, or I'll call the sergeant and tell him you aren't fit to return to duty," he yelled. "It's the best way I can think to protect you."

I lost it. "How dare you! I don't even know what's in my own head right now. I'm still dealing with it myself. I'm dreaming about being attacked every night, so I'm exhausted all the time. My stomach hurts, and I feel like I'm coming right out of my skin. Justin, I was wearing Kevlar when this happened, and still got my ribs broken. I was armed to the teeth, and trained, and it wasn't my first night out on the street, and I still never saw it coming. I don't even know how to begin to describe it to a counselor when I can't even describe it to myself."

He ran his hands through his hair, gripped the steering wheel, then leaned forward and rested his head on his hands. "I know, Sam. I don't know how to handle it. I thought by treating you with kid gloves, you'd eventually snap out of it. You're trying so hard not to deal with what happened that you're fighting yourself, not me. After my mom dumped me and took off, it took someone who cared to tell me to snap out of it for me to see what I was doing to myself. I care, so I'm going to say it to you. I'm gonna call that social worker if you don't. Get help, Sam, or so help me, I will call everyone in the police department and tell them you aren't fit for duty."

"You fucking bastard, how dare you threaten my career." I jumped out and he tried to follow, but I was faster. It registered in the back of my mind that I shouldn't have been. "If you do anything to fuck up my career, I'll make you pay. Get out of my house and off my property, and don't you ever fucking come back, you sneaky, lying, controlling, manipulative son of a bitch." I wrenched my front door open.

The blood seemed to drain from his face when I said that. "Yeah, I'm a bastard. Yeah, my mom was a bitch. Those things are true, but Sam, you can't mean all of what you just said."

"The fuck I don't. Get the hell off my property," I screamed.

"I wouldn't have said that, except to make you see reason. You're killing yourself, and it's killing me to watch it. I'd rather you be pissed at me and getting help."

"No," I growled. I'm not kidding. I actually growled. If felt so good to make that noise between bared teeth, humming out of the back of my throat. "Get out of here."

"Call me anything you want. I'm calling that Boyd guy on Friday. That gives you two days. If you haven't made an appointment by then, I'll make one for you and I will, by God, bodily drag you in there kicking and screaming if I have to."

I slammed the front door hard enough to rattle the doorframe and heard him slam his truck door. A big part of me knew this was my fault. I was being a complete bitch. Another part of me was excited by the fight. If Justin had knocked on the door at that moment, I'm not sure I'd be able to control myself. I'd have flung myself at him and showed him that he was way more than a walking security blanket, busted ribs and bum shoulder be damned. I guess I'd never get that chance now, since I'd tossed away my only opportunity at having a relationship with him. Good riddance.

Wait a minute. This is the man I've wanted ever since I met him. He's the guy I trust with all things, including my life. He's the man that I...oh, God. What had I just done? I collapsed against the inside of the front door, wailing and crying until my ribs hurt and my head ached and I whimpered under the emotional pain of my own stupidity.

Chapter Thirteen

Since Justin and I had gone for a very late lunch on our first, and at this point, likely last, date, it was only four o'clock in the afternoon when I slammed the door. When I stopped crying, I wiped my eyes and stumbled into the kitchen. I plucked Loan Boyd's card off the refrigerator where it hung beneath a police union magnet and dialed.

I didn't doubt Justin. He'd do what he said, whether I apologized or not. I also knew that my behavior today was not normal. I have a temper, there's no question of that, but I usually build up slowly, and explode, get over it and move on. I didn't want to lose him, regardless of what I'd said. As much as I hated to admit it, there was something wrong with me.

Logan answered on the first ring.

"Mr. Boyd, this is Samantha Hochenwalt. You spoke to me at the hospital last week?"

"Yes, Samantha, or is it Sam? How're things going? I heard you'd improved and went home before I had a chance to come talk to you again. How's life treating you?"

"Things aren't so good. I think I better start talking to someone about what happened." I was close to tears again. I could feel them sting the inside of my eyelids, and swallowed hard.

"Are you okay?" He had a gentle, caring voice.

"God, if I had a dollar for every time someone asked me that question over the past week, I'd be a millionaire." I laughed as I fought back a sob. Even to me it sounded harsh and critical. Then a dam burst, and I cried.

When I say that I cried, I don't mean that tears escaped the corners of my eyes and trickled down my cheeks. I was blubbering. My nose ran and I couldn't see to sit down at the table. I cried for five minutes while Logan sat silently and waited for me to compose myself.

When I finally got control of myself, Logan asked, "Is that the first time you've cried?"

"No, I cried when I broke my finger when I was four. Of course it's not the first time."

He sighed. I had a feeling he'd be doing that a lot. "You know what I mean, Sam. Is that the first time you've cried since the attack?"

I nodded and realized, like a moron, that he couldn't hear me nod over the phone. "Yes."

"It's okay. You need to cry. If you don't let some of this emotion out, it'll overwhelm you. I'm surprised you haven't broken down sooner. Let me guess, you've been ping-ponging between extreme moods and losing your temper on a whim?"

I nodded, miserable, and whispered that it was true.

"You've been crying at the drop of a hat, tired and lethargic? Are you afraid to leave the house? Are you having nightmares? Experiencing flashbacks to the attack?"

"Yes."

He continued. "I have your address from the hospital file. You need to talk, and now is as good a time as any. I just finished up my last meeting, so I'll be there in twenty minutes. You okay until I can get there?"

"Yeah, I think so," I sniffled, and took a deep breath. "I'll be fine. You sure you want to do this now? I'm okay to wait for an appointment. I don't know what came over me. It's just an overreaction. I've just pushed myself too hard."

"I'm sure. You'd be more comfortable not having this conversation on the phone. In your case, I think it might be imperative that we do this right now."

I wasn't so sure about that, but hey, I needed therapy. Justin wanted me to get involved in therapy. Mom wanted me to do it. They'd be happy at how fast I'd done it. I still didn't want to do it, but preventing the whole dragging me kicking and screaming as Justin had threatened was a nice side effect. "Okay, if you're sure, come on over."

I picked up a paper towel to wipe my nose. Justin must have put them on the holder. I never remembered. Something clenched tightly in my chest, and I sniffed back another round of tears and tried to ignore that small reminder of Justin's presence.

"I'm on my way to my car. We'll talk about any other symptoms you have." He hung up.

I puzzled over what he'd said. What in the world did was wrong with me? There were things I'd noticed that were odd, like my recent eating and sleeping habits, craving for meat and sudden acceleration of body hair, but I didn't plan to tell him about my hairy yeti legs. That was a bit too personal. I hardly knew the man.

I figured he'd tell me what he meant when he showed up. Coffee, then, while I waited, would keep me awake until he got here. I looked around and realized I had nothing to serve a guest, other than Justin's junk food and wilting salad. Better make cookies then. The activity would keep me awake, and Mom would be proud of my sudden hostess-like urges.

There's nothing like the smell of warm cookies in the air to calm my frazzled nerves. I sometimes think we should give out homemade baked goods instead of Prozac for the emotionally disturbed. It just feels that good to have a warm, yummy kitchen.

He rang the doorbell just as I put the first pan of cookies in the oven. It took a few minutes before I answered the door, since I had to set the timer and take off the oven mitt. I remembered that he was blond and good-looking, but I couldn't help comparing him to Justin. Logan's nose was crooked, like it had been broken in the past, but he had a kind and intelligent face. Justin's face was more refined, like his features fit together perfectly. Logan seemed like a collection of different features that shouldn't go together, but worked well as a whole. I caught the same earthy, forest smell I'd caught on him at the hospital and it eased something in my shoulders. That confused me.

"Sam?"

I blinked, nodded, and let him in, then walked back to the kitchen. "Sorry. I had a bunch of nervous energy all of a sudden, so I thought I'd bake some cookies. Let's go sit in the kitchen so I can hear the timer."

"Is that butterscotch?" He sniffed the air with relish, and, I noticed, a bit of relief. That was odd. I didn't expect relief. I was the one who needed to learn how to deal with stress and anxiety. Maybe he just hadn't eaten anything all day.

"Butterscotch oatmeal cookies are in the oven."

"Okay, now I'm happy I came on out here tonight. I haven't eaten anything since breakfast. Those smell amazing. Got extras?"

"Sure, once I've finished baking them, you can have as many as you want. I started baking to keep from falling asleep while you were on your way over. I probably won't eat them, but it made me feel better to make them."

"Oh." His face fell.

Why would he care if I didn't eat the damn cookies?

He came into the kitchen and sat down at the table. Out of his briefcase came his leather bound portfolio. "Do you mind if I take notes?"

Keep it light, I thought. Keep him smiling, and concentrate on the cookies. The timer will go off every ten minutes to change the pan, so I've got a ready-made excuse if I want to change the subject. "Is that normal? I've never been in counseling before."

He nodded at the offer of coffee, so I got out a mug and filled it to the brim. He took a sip before he spoke. "I try not to take notes, but sometimes I hear something I don't want to forget. I talk to a lot of people in a day. I don't want to mistake something you say for something someone else might say, and confuse things. That's embarrassing, and a problem. The only person who sees my notes is me. They're completely confidential."

"Long as you're not stealing my cookie recipe, I guess I don't have a problem with it." I saw the hint of a smile around the edges of his mouth, but he moved right into the business at hand. I guessed he'd be harder to distract than I'd hoped.

"So, what brought on the crying today?" He removed the cap from a cheap pen and wrote down the date and time at the top of a legal pad, and noted my address and name.

"Just like that, huh? No lie down on the couch and tell you about how I want to kill my mother and sleep with my father and no one ever loved me? No dumb theories about not being loved enough as a kid or that I was abused because I had to take the trash out?" I had to find out what made this man laugh. Otherwise we'd shovel emotional crap forever. That's no fun.

He grinned, and set down the pen. "No. That's a really bad stereotype. Basically, we're gonna talk about what's been going on in your head as it pertains to your attack, and the reactions you've had. We'll sometimes go a little beyond that, because I might need context to what you're saying. I might see connections that you don't. For example, how've you been sleeping since you got home from the hospital?"

"A lot. Almost too much. I'm tired all the time, though I'm pretty keyed up right now. That's a first since the attack."

"What's a lot?"

"Twenty hours or so a day, with naps in between, of course."

"I think we can qualify that as 'a lot'." He smiled, to take the sting out of the comment. Good, another smartass. He'd get my off-hand comments without thinking I was hiding from my true feelings or some stupid shit like that. I can do smartass humor all day.

"Look, I was overstressed and overworked before this happened. I've been working overtime and I haven't taken any time off work for vacation yet. I just became eligible to use vacation days last month. My mom, who's a nurse, says sleep is the body's way of healing itself. So I've slept a lot, but I feel a lot better. Maybe it'll let up now that I've had a break from work."

"Yeah, maybe it will. On the other hand, maybe it won't. Are you dreaming at all?" He noted the amount of sleep I'd confessed to on his legal pad. So far he hadn't written down anything I had a problem with. Of course, we hadn't talked about anything I had a problem with yet, either, though I had a feeling we'd get there eventually. I really didn't want to talk about my dreams of the attack. It was one thing to accidentally live through it while I was asleep. I had no desire to relive it on purpose while I was awake. Once was enough for that. Nope, didn't want to go there. No, thank you.

"Oh, so we are talking about dreams? Like the sheep in the corner of my closet waving at me is really my desire for a new mattress?"

He laughed. "I see you've had a Psych 101 class somewhere, and read a bit about dream interpretation and Freud and all that, right?"

I grinned and nodded. Seemed like most majors in college had to take a Psych 101 class, and since I couldn't go straight into the police department out of high school, I'd headed to college for a criminal justice degree. Stupid age requirement to be a cop was twenty-one. I turned twenty-one just before I started my senior year. Mom and Dad made me finish since they paid for it, but I signed up for the police academy the day after graduation. The classes in my major were cool, but I had to take a lot of weird classes to fulfill the general requirements.

Logan continued, "Well, a lot of what Freud said and did was utter bullshit. Remember he was the man who thought cocaine was the new wonder drug. It's crap. I mean, he even got addicted to it before he realized it wasn't what he thought it was. But he was right that our subconscious at times forces us to deal with things that our conscious mind doesn't want to deal with, and it comes out in our dreams. What are you dreaming about?"

No avoiding it, then. I'd have to talk about it. "Okay, yeah, I'm dreaming about the attack, but I'm having other dreams as well."

"Like what?"

"I'm running through the forest, almost like I'm in a black and white movie. I'm running and I wallow in all the smells around me so I can take them home and sort them out later. I'm chasing something, and it feels so good to stretch out and run. I'm not sure what I'm chasing, but whatever it is, I can't quite catch it."

Logan looked horrified. He hid it quickly under a mask of professionalism, putting down his pen and his coffee cup, and taking a deep breath before he continued. I felt a sudden urge to smack him. I turned away and replaced the cookies in the oven with the next pan. "Sam, let me make sure I've got this right. One of your injuries was a bite, wasn't it?"

"Yeah, it was inside the bend of my right elbow. I go to the doctor in a couple of days to get all the stitches out."

"How many stitches did you have?"

"Forty-six stitches and a shot of antibiotics, and they gave me the first set of rabies shots because they weren't sure what bit me. I'm glad I was unconscious, because I've heard that those really hurt."

He let out a short bark of angry laughter. "Yeah, of course they would."

I couldn't figure out why that mattered. "Why do you ask?" When in doubt, ask questions. It gets the focus off you and sometimes teaches you stuff.

It didn't work. "Are you having any other odd physical symptoms?"

"Like what?"

He crossed his arms over his chest, impatient. "Come on, Sam, you know what I mean. Are you quicker to lose your temper? Having mood swings? Have your eating habits changed? Are you losing weight? Having flashbacks?"

I was surprised at him. He'd catalogued everything that happened since the attack. "Yes to all of the above. I blew up at the guy I'm dating when he tried to take me out to lunch. The whole thing started with him upset at me for not taking care of myself. I'm not even sure why I lost it so bad. I know I need to apologize."

"Did you eat lunch?"

Rage swirled through me. "Yeah, I did. I wish everyone would stop fucking picking on me for what I eat or don't eat. It's annoying. I'm not a damn kid."

"What did you eat, Sam?"

"Sushi."

"Anything taste funny to you?" He was upset. I could see it in his face. What did it matter that nothing tasted right?

"Yeah, everything tastes funny. I haven't had a taste for anything but meat, though fish works too. If it's got protein, I'll eat as much as I can get my hands on. I've been cooking it rarer than normal. The sushi today tasted great, but the rice tasted bad. I normally love fresh vegetables, and I can't stand them lately. They taste like cardboard."

He had an odd look on his face. It was a strange mix of horror, revulsion and hope. "Sam, are you having any other symptoms? Restlessness, agitation, increased skin sensitivity, increased body hair growth?"

I looked at him in shock. "What does my being attacked have anything to do with shaving my legs more often?"

"Humor me." He wasn't laughing.

"Yeah, okay, I've had all those things. If I'm not sleeping, I'm on a roller coaster of emotion, worse than it's ever been in my life. I've noticed that I need a haircut soon, though I just had my hair cut about two weeks ago. I'm shaving more often. I feel like my arms and legs want to jump out of my skin, like there are ants just below the surface. I'm a ball of nervous energy that has to keep moving. This only happens when I'm awake, but I'm exhausted easy, and I fall asleep at the drop of a hat. What does that have to do with what happened?"

He sighed. "Sam, as a police officer, have you ever seen anything that just seemed wrong? It just didn't fit any rational explanation you were able to find?"

"Yeah, and then we get a report back from the crime lab, or someone turns up a witness, or something, and it fits a rational explanation."

He rubbed his hands on the legs of his pants and stood up. "I think there's more going on here. Do you mind if I make a phone call?"

What the fuck? This guy came in and made a big deal about my hairy yeti legs and oversleeping and my recent love affair with all things meat and says something like that and doesn't explain it? What an asshole. I don't care if he is a cute blond, that's downright rude. "You're going to make a phone call before telling me what you mean?"

"Yeah, I really hate to, but this is a little beyond my capability to tell you this without higher authority, so I need to make a quick call to verify something."

"Fine. Whatever." I waved toward the patio that sat just outside my kitchen, beyond a set of sliding glass doors that led out to the backyard. "If you want some privacy, help yourself." Part of me wanted to tell him to keep walking when he hit the door, but curiosity got the better of me and I kept my mouth shut. I wanted to know what he was talking about.

"Thanks." With that, the jerk stepped outside and made his stupid phone call with his cell phone. I was pissed off all over again. I switched out the cookies in the oven, and set the timer. On the upside, the anger kept me from falling asleep. Too bad I wouldn't eat the cookies. Maybe I could wrap them up for Justin as an apology gift. Goodness knows I needed to apologize to him. Then again, maybe I just needed to stay mad to stay awake. That would suck.

Logan came back in and asked if the cookies were done.

After I gave him an incredulous look, I told him I was on the last pan, and would be done in ten minutes. "Why?"

"I hate to say this, but you aren't going to believe me unless I show you. I can't show you here. It's just not safe. There are too many neighbors who could see something. That's the last kind of attention you want right now."

"Okay, now you're being cryptic. That's not cool, especially when I was going to offer you cookies fresh from the oven." I was partly teasing, but I wanted to guilt him into spilling the beans. If all else fails, blackmail with warm baked goods felt like an appropriate bribe. If he could refuse that, I'd believe he wasn't human and would ask him to take me to his leader.

"Sam, if I told you, you wouldn't believe me. I can promise you right now that you're going to need me in the next couple of months. I really hoped this wouldn't happen to you."

I sat down and stared at him. The buzzer dinged for the cookies just as my butt hit the chair, and I stood up to rescue them from the oven. "What wouldn't happen to me?"

He stood there, silent.

"I'm not kidding, Logan. I'm not just going somewhere nonspecific with someone I don't know to do something I'm not prepared for. I'm not stupid."

"No one said you were."

"But you're still not going to tell me?"

"I'd tell you if I could. I need you to trust me. All your questions will be answered, and by people who have been where you are now. It couldn't hurt to talk to others who've been in your position, would it?"

"Why's it so important to do it now?"

"Because I think some of your symptoms could get worse over the next few months before they get better. Better to be prepared, right? You'll believe it better coming from someone who's been there. Besides, if you've made the decision to start counseling, why not get a good idea of what you'll be facing?"

Months? I'd have to do this for months? I shrugged off my concerns. If that was true, then I'd better get started. I'm a cop. I can take care of myself. "Fine. Where are we going?"

"I'll drive. You'll see when we get there. You won't believe it at first. It's both amazing and terrifying. Can we take some of the cookies with us?" He smiled.

I grumbled as I put a few in a bag for him. Oh goody. That's just what I need now, more complications in my life.

But if I went with him, I could at least tell Mom and Logan that I had taken their request to start counseling seriously. I made an excuse and slipped into my bedroom before we left to try to hide my gun in a holster at the small of my back. Hey, I was still a cop, and I planned to be prepared if he was going to go all cryptic on me.

CHAPTER FOURTEEN

Nadia hung up her cell phone, grinning at Sam's nervousness as she went about her errands for the afternoon. Leave it to Sam to have to work up the courage to go on a date with a gorgeous man who was nuts about her. She shook her head.

At least some things were getting back to normal. Justin had been as protective as a pit bull over Sam, keeping anyone else from bothering her. Nadia remembered the devastation on his face at the hospital and felt bad for him, even though she'd been annoyed at being shut out from Sam. Even Sam's mom, Kathy, had started to worry that Sam wasn't bouncing back fast enough. Leaving the house was a good sign. Sam's desire to impress Justin was another, and Nadia was happy to approve the outfit Sam suggested.

She stopped by Sam's parents' house to give them the good news and headed to the county animal shelter. Going back to vet school in the fall made it hard to find a paying job that would also put experience on her resume, so she volunteered at the animal shelter when she wasn't hawking ridiculously expensive body lotions at the mall.

It was an internship made in heaven. Nadia wanted nothing more than to work with an animal shelter or rescue society when she finished her degree. She treasured each moment that a fully healed and happy animal found a forever home. Seeing the before and after adoptions filled her with a sense of accomplishment and satisfaction that she hadn't found anywhere else. She wanted to spend her time with animals in need of homes, rather than pampering exotic animals with hypochondriac owners, like she'd seen at the frou-frou vet service she'd done an

internship at a year ago. The shelter was happy for the help. There were always more animals than hours in the day for their dedicated staff.

She walked into the shelter's new facilities and the receptionist greeted her at the door. "We're glad to see you today, Nadia. The vet's got her hands full."

"What, did Kong get out of his cage again?" They'd had problems with an overeager boxer mix that had learned how to open the door to his kennel. Kong wanted to greet everyone, which generally meant knocking people to the ground and enthusiastically licking faces until he was forced to stop. Everyone liked him, but over a hundred pounds of puppy love is hard to handle for anyone.

"Kong's fine. I think we finally found the gate that could hold him. Dr. Anderson's got her hands full, though, even without Kong's antics. The Dayton police busted another dog fighting ring."

Nadia groaned. No one liked dealing with dogs that'd been born, bred, and groomed to fight. They were a menace to staff, biting and snapping, and destroyed their surroundings. She hated having dogs like that around, because they traumatized other dogs in the facility, and scared her half to death. "How many pit bulls did they get this time?"

"None. This time, all they found were a couple of dogs who are at least part wolf. They're huge. The good news is that they aren't acting all that vicious. They're cooperating with the vet, but they're pretty bad off. One has infected bites on its muzzle, and we're not sure we'll be able to save him."

"Wolves? I didn't even know there were wolves in this area."

The secretary nodded, pointing toward the back examination room. "Well, they're certainly here now."

Nadia pushed past her and headed straight into the vet clinic, where one of the animal control officers was trying to assist the vet. Gaping wounds on one side of the poor animal's muzzle caused her stomach to clench. The idea that any human could do this to an animal, or force them to do this to each other pissed her off. She immediately jumped in to help, channeling her frustration into the long hard fight ahead.

Four hours later, she stepped back and stretched. Both animals were back in their cages, resting comfortably, at least for now. It had taken human sized doses of painkillers to give them relief. The two animals had four hundred stitches, sixteen staples, several doses of antibiotics, and a splint between them. She hoped the one dog didn't lose his eye. They'd done everything they could think of to save it.

Dr. Anderson raised her arms over her head to stretch. "Nadia, I really appreciate your help today. I'm not sure I could have done all this without you."

"No problem. I just hope we're able to find the people responsible."

"You know, there's something odd about these two. Most dogs from that kind of situation can't stop snapping at each other long enough to be treated, and try to start fights even while we're trying to help them. These two seemed like they knew we were helping, and didn't really snap at each other. I hope that's not because they were torn up too badly to be aggressive. We'll have a specialist take a look at them when they've recovered a bit, but there might be hope that we don't have to put these two down."

"Really? I thought all dogs recovered from these operations were put down."

"Generally they are, but we assess each dog's behavior separately. I don't think we've had one yet that's able to recover enough from being a part of this to become a pet. These two might have a chance for a normal life. I hope the part-wolf thing doesn't prevent them from being adopted. I'm going to talk to the shelter director about it in the morning. Either way, they're no longer hurting. We've given them some relief for now."

Nadia smiled. The two dogs had been reasonable to deal with. She was glad that there weren't more of them. Maybe it was that they'd been better behaved than most abused animals when they came into the shelter. She'd watch them over the next couple of days.

It was a day for hope. Two dogs had escaped hell on earth to get veterinary treatment and possible homes, and her best friend was starting to recover from her own hell. It was time to head home and kick back to enjoy her evening. She hoped Sam would call her later to fill her in on the dishy details of her first date with Justin, so she could share her own good day. Sam would argue with her about whether the dogs could be rehabilitated, but she didn't care. She looked forward to having her old friend back.

CHAPTER FIFTEEN

I wasn't acting like myself. Something had to be wrong, but I couldn't stop myself. I wanted to know what was wrong with me. I kept thinking that we must be headed for some kind of support group meeting. As much as I really didn't want to go, I was curious, so I didn't question him. And that was definitely not in my character. I question everything.

We got into Logan's car, a vintage Mustang, but I couldn't shut off the worried part of my brain. What am I doing getting into a car with a guy I don't know? I did have my gun. Of course, carrying a gun hadn't stopped me from getting hurt. I have no idea where he's taking me, and we've left the city limits. I didn't even grab my cell phone. What in the world was going on here? Had I lost what was left of my mind? And yet, no matter how many questions I asked myself, I didn't stop what I was doing, and I didn't ask.

The old Sam would have demanded answers, and thrown a temper tantrum until she got them. I wasn't angry anymore, merely annoyed. I wanted answers, and I was afraid I wouldn't get them if I threw a fit. Instead I found myself getting nervous. It couldn't be good if I had to go this far from home to find out the truth.

We drove for about twenty minutes, as Logan plowed his way through the cookies I'd wrapped up before we left. He complimented my baking until I told him to shut the hell up. I recognized the road signs, and realized we were headed for Yellow Springs.

Yellow Springs is a town that's sometimes hard to describe. The site for a liberal arts college and a quirky shopping district, it's a quintessential college town. An oasis of liberal thought in the middle of a conservative area of the state, Yellow Springs has a feeling of individuality in every stone and plank and blade of grass. It's a small town, surrounded by farmland, and I always thought of it as Greenwich Village meets Green Acres. It's the only place on earth that I know of where aging hippies and salt-of-the-earth farmers would think nothing of being next door neighbors. I love everything about it.

We drove through Yellow Springs into the countryside. By the time Logan pulled onto a country road and we passed John Bryan State Park, my heart was in my throat, and I could taste metal on the back of my tongue. I tried not to let on how scared I was, but I failed.

"Sam, you need to tone down the fear level before we get there. They'll know if you're that scared."

I couldn't hold in the questions anymore. "Who are they? Where are we going? I wouldn't be so scared if I knew a little more about what's going on."

"If I had the authority to tell you, I would. It's not as bad as you think. The people we're meeting will have a few more answers for you than I can give."

How did he know how scared I was? What was he, some kind of mind reader? The anger started building and helped chase away the fear. He turned and grinned at me, and then turned up the radio. Music reverberated through the car, and I lost myself in my thoughts again. It was clear he wouldn't give me any more answers than he'd already given. I could be a brat and keep pestering him, or I could shut up. If they would really have a problem with me afraid, then I needed to calm down. Bugging Logan wouldn't help me do that.

I took a deep breath and closed my eyes, trying to relax. While I wasn't calm, I was less on edge just because I'd made the effort. I repeated the move a couple of times. When it stopped working, I stopped doing it. It didn't take long to stop working.

He pulled into a wooded drive with a sign marked 'private'. At the end of the drive, there was a deserted barn. I couldn't see anything moving, but I felt that there were others nearby. The hairs on the back of my neck stood up on end. He should have at least told me what to expect. Damn him.

Logan hit a garage door opener. A door opened in the barn in front of us. We pulled into the barn in the dark, with only the headlights to show me that we were on some sort of pneumatic lift that gently lowered us into a basement. Logan drove off the lift and parked beside six or seven other cars.

"There aren't that many people here tonight. That's a good thing." He seemed to have an odd set to his jaw. "We've fit as many as twenty cars down here at once and still had room for more. Max knew what he was about when he came up with the idea for the place."

I stopped dead in my tracks. That was it. The temper tantrum I'd been wondering at was now ready to erupt. "Max? Who's Max? And what the hell is this place? I'm not going any further until you tell me why you brought me here. I have no idea what any of this has to do with me." I stood my ground, but I was keyed up and ready to run. The problem was that in the dim light, I could hardly see three feet in front of my face, much less how I'd get out if I did run. Places like this didn't exactly come with fire escapes with lighted exit signs. Oh well, sometimes a good bluff works wonders.

"We're meeting some people who've been where you are now. I need to show you what's happening to you. I need you to understand why we fight so hard to keep this hidden. If people knew our secret, they wouldn't accept it. Many wouldn't believe it. Others would use it as a reason to hurt us, to shame us, and to hunt us down. We're terrified of the reprisals that could and would happen if this became public knowledge. We'll be here to help you through it, but you need to understand the importance of secrecy."

"As long as you're not breaking a law, I don't see why I have to tell anyone. If someone's committing a crime, I'm not sure how I could keep that a secret."

Logan shook his head and held up one hand to top me. "Don't give me an answer now. I want you to see and understand and then we'll talk." He walked away before I could come up with another comment. I hurried to follow since he seemed to know his way around and I couldn't see a damn thing.

He punched a key code into a panel that I hadn't seen. These people took their security seriously. It must be one hell of a secret. I recognized the model of the security system on the panel, and knew it to have a good reputation, as well as being fairly expensive. The fact that they had an alarm system made me feel better about being here. Such systems always had a panic button that dialed directly into 911. If something weird happened and I felt uncomfortable, I'd just have to get to the nearest panel and hit the right button. I felt better knowing that the cavalry was only a button away.

SHADES OF GRAY • 101

"Samantha?" A man approached us. I didn't recognize him, but his face did look vaguely familiar. It was one of those faces I knew I'd remember at two o'clock in the morning and feel like an idiot for not making the connection before.

"I'm Sam." I realized I stood in a bladed stance as I reached to shake his hand, the stance that all officers are taught to assume in a threatening situation. I stood slightly sideways with the hip that should have carried my gun away from the person in front of me. As a police officer, it also was also a defensive stance, and gives you an advantage if someone comes at you aggressively. It didn't actually protect my gun side as well as it would have if I'd been in uniform, since the gun was resting at the small of my back instead of on one hip, but it was an automatic defensive stance for a cop unsure of their safety.

The man looked me up and down, and nodded, a sly smile spreading across his face. "She'll do." He walked away, and opened a door. Inside a sparsely decorated room with card tables and folding chairs off to the right, others stood around a conference table to the left of the door, sipping cups of coffee. They had been looking at a set of blueprints, which got rolled up quickly and spirited away as we came into the room.

The man who'd approached us introduced himself. His name was Max, and he called himself the 'Alpha', as if it was supposed to be capitalized. This must have been the "Max" that Logan had spoken of in the car. I wondered who he thought he was. It seemed pretentious and stupid. I guessed his age in his late forties, maybe in his early fifties, with black hair in a ponytail, going gray at the temples. He wasn't a large man, but there was no doubt he was in charge. Good. Maybe I'd get some answers.

One of the men at the table asked me to have a seat, and offered me a cup of coffee. I accepted, more out of having something in my hands than the need for caffeine.

Logan didn't sit down. Rather, he took a position slightly behind and to the right of me. I really didn't like having him behind me, but I guessed it was better that it was him than one of the others. After all, even Justin vouched for him before I'd invited him over.

"Sam, Logan called us from your house. You've exhibited some symptoms that have us concerned, and now that we have you sitting in front of us, we can smell it on you." Max started.

I was offended. "Smell it on me? I just took a shower three hours ago. That's not cool. You don't bring a woman into a strange place with no explanation and then tell her that she smells. That's not very polite." Besides which, I hadn't done anything more strenuous than gorging myself on sushi and baking cookies. Oh, yeah, and having a screaming match with Justin. That hurt.

Max chuckled. "There's no good way to tell you this. We believe that you were attacked by a member, a person who runs in our pack, so to speak."

"Pack? What the hell is going on here?" I started to stand up, only to find Logan's hand on my shoulder, pushing me back down. Anger welled up inside me, and that same growling noise I'd made at Justin earlier came out of my mouth. It felt good. It felt like I was about to have a good old-fashioned Samantha Hochenwalt meltdown, and I welcomed it.

Logan whispered, "You don't stand if the Alpha is talking unless he gives you leave. Trust me. You don't want to get off on the wrong foot here. Sit down, Sam. Please."

It took more courage than was pretty to relax back into my chair. "Someone tell me what's going on. The suspense isn't necessary."

"We're not sure yet who did this, but we are looking into it. However, we must ask that you not go to the authorities until we've had a chance to discuss this." Max, again.

"You're asking too much. I was attacked. I want that person, whoever he is, to face justice. I spend my time making sure that people who attack others face justice, is it wrong to want the same for myself?"

"No, Sam. It isn't, but there are extenuating circumstances here. You see, you're exhibiting all the symptoms of someone who is going to turn."

"Turn?"

"Change."

"I don't get it."

"You're becoming a werewolf, Sam. That's what we all are. That's what you'll become. And that's what the person who attacked you is."

It seemed like all the air in my lungs disappeared in a giant rush. I shook my head, and tried to augh. "Bullshit. Not possible. Werewolves are stuff in books, movies, and videogames. They aren't real. Where're the hidden cameras? Did the guys at the station put you up to this? Isn't that one goofy looking guy gonna jump out with a camera crew and tell me I've been the butt of a bad joke?"

"It's not a joke." Max crossed his arms over his chest, and watched my face.

"I don't believe you." I matched his action by crossing my own arms.

"We can prove it."

"Call me a Doubting Thomas, then. Prove it." Just because I had yeti legs did not make my life a Lon Chaney movie. Not even remotely possible.

A middle-aged man with a buzz cut who had been sitting off to my right stood up and walked away from the table. Someone hit a switch, and a light came on in front of him. He unbuttoned his shirt, and took off his pants in front of everyone.

I was the only woman there. I was surrounded by guys, and watching a guy old enough to be my dad strip down to his jockeys. I see streakers and flashers all the time at work and laugh about it, but still. I was horrified. I wasn't in the mood, and so didn't want to see his old, wrinkly, naked ass. "Not funny. Tell him to put his clothes back on."

"If he does this with his clothes on, he'll tear them and have nothing to wear home. Human clothing doesn't fit well on a wolf."

I felt something on my skin, like a spark of power on the air. The others watched with a bored look on their faces, as if they'd seen the show before. My mind couldn't make sense of what I saw, but I couldn't look away.

Hair began to sprout on his face. His skin rippled as if something was moving beneath it. His mouth and nose lengthened, and he doubled over onto all fours with a cry. Slowly, he gained more hair on his arms and over his spine, his teeth growing and his hands and feet shrinking.

I stared at him in gape-jawed horror. This couldn't be right. Someone was projecting a hologram into the room. I looked around for the trick, but I found no beam of light from a projector. I couldn't see computers nearby. The only light was a plain naked bulb over his head.

It was true. There really were werewolves. It took ten minutes for him to complete the change into a lean and fully formed brown and white wolf. He threw back his head and howled.

"No." I said, ignoring Logan's earlier instruction not to stand without permission. I backed away from everyone. "It's not possible."

Logan and Max walked toward me, with the wolf not far behind.

"No." I was breathing hard, denying with my mouth what my mind already knew.

Logan reached out a hand for me.

"No." Now I knew how an asthmatic felt. I couldn't get air. I panicked, repeating myself over and over. "No."

Max leaned over. "Yes."

No. I didn't want to accept it. I couldn't accept it. The wolf came up and rubbed my hand with his muzzle, and my butt hit the concrete wall at the edge of the room. I felt the coarse hair of the wolf's muzzle and the last shred of doubt disappeared. My sight went dark with the lack of oxygen. No doubt about it, then. It was real.

CHAPTER SIXTEEN

I slowly opened my eyes. Please let it be another one of those weird dreams I'd had since the attack. I'd even relive the attack again to make this not real.

No such luck. A brown and white wolf curled up beside me as I sat against the wall with my feet straight out in front of me. I must have been out for only a minute or so. I felt someone take my hand. Logan had his hand on the back on my forehead, and another man, younger than I was, had his fingers on my wrist, taking my pulse.

Max's face came into view. "You okay?"

"Good question. Here's another one. Why? Assuming it was one of you guys, why would you do this to me? Why would you do this to anyone?" Hot, angry tears flowed down my face.

"Believe me when I say that no one planned to do this to you. We're still looking into what happened. There was no plan, no conspiracy against you."

I cocked an eyebrow at him. "If you were in my shoes, would you believe it?"

"I've been in your shoes. And I haven't lied to you yet."

"You tell me I was attacked by a monster. Because of the attack I'm going to become one. You tell me that you're the same kind of monster. And then you tell me to trust you? I don't trust monsters. I put them in jail."

"Everyone in this room has been where you are right now. That gives you a certain amount of latitude and understanding. Don't push it too far. Whether you believe us or not, you will need our help in the coming weeks. Hear us out before you say no."

"Why? Why would I accept it? Why would I want to be indebted to monsters?"

Max stood up and walked away, taking everyone but Logan to the far side of the room to speak in whispers. When I was a kid, Nadia and I teased little girls who whispered in the playground by telling them that all secrets were lies. It was odd that I remembered that now. I didn't know who was telling the truth. I wasn't even sure that I believed Logan.

He waited until the others stepped away, and whispered, "Are you all right?"

"I really don't know. I guess you were right. I did need to see it before I could believe it." The wolf's pile of clothing in the corner caught my eye. If I'd needed further proof that what I'd seen was real, that sad little pile of denim and flannel clinched it. "So, okay, I believe now that werewolves really do exist. I can't believe I'm saying it, but after that little demonstration, I'm having a hard time not believing it. This is going to happen to me?"

He nodded. Nothing in his expression gave me any hope that I'd escape this. "Yeah, Sam, it will. That's why

I approached you in the hospital. That's why I gave you my card with my home and cell numbers. Most counselors don't do that. It's why I was willing to come to your house tonight rather than making an appointment later on. It's why I brought you here tonight. You have all the symptoms. We'd rather help you through this transition than force you to deal with it alone."

"Logan." Max issued a quiet command. To me, Max looked like the kind of guy who would be more at ease with a suit and tie than in the faded jeans and old polo shirt he wore. I was surprised to see Logan dip his head in deference as he got up to walk toward the group of men. It seemed so subservient for a guy who'd been forceful enough to talk me into going out in the middle of nowhere with him. I could feel the gun digging into my back under my waistband and felt reassured.

Logan bowed his head as Max gave quiet directions to him. I remained seated, watching the interaction between all of them. The others adopted the same posture that Logan had, with their hand clasped behind their backs, head bowed.

As they talked, I rose to my feet. Max finished talking and everyone but he and Logan left. The two of them walked over to me. I looked up at him and could see the intelligence in Max's eyes. This guy was no fool. He looked like he could read my mind and predict what I was about to do before I even knew. Something about him made me uneasy. Maybe it was just the request to trust him. It might be the feeling that I'd seen his face before. I wasn't sure what it was. All my training as a police officer told me not to ignore my instincts, but, of course, my mother also trained me to be polite when I was in someone else's, well, place.

"So, it's Max, right? And you're the leader here? Anything else I need to know?" I wasn't happy at being out of my element and I wanted to go home. I didn't want him to think of me as rude or afraid, especially since they'd been able to smell something about me earlier, and Logan had made comments about knowing I was scared.

"Okay, look, the name's really Maximillion Ignatius Howard. You could say that Max was about the best I was gonna get out of that mouthful." He smiled, a big toothy smile, and all I could think of was Little Red Riding Hood and the Big Bad Wolf. I shook my head to get rid of the mental image.

He continued talking, oblivious to my irreverent thought. "Logan will be your guide for the next month. From what we know and can sense about you, you'll likely have your first change in that time. Don't be afraid to call Logan for advice if you feel it start to happen at work. Unlike what you read or see on TV and in the movies, we aren't compelled to turn at the full moon, but we do have to change on a regular basis or the wolf will pick the time for us. There are ways of delaying the change. Logan can help you with that."

I nodded. I felt like I should be taking notes.

He continued. "This is always a safe place to change. We have quite a bit of land here, and we have sentries posted around the property to keep trespassers away. However, it's not a place that you will have unlimited access to until Logan has introduced you to all of our customs. It wouldn't do for you to cause a problem with another of our members without knowing the proper etiquette, greeting, and other issues. He'll help you with what you need to learn."

Logan nodded at me, as if he'd expected it.

Max kept talking, giving instructions and making plans. I tuned him out and my brain asked a million questions all at once. I pushed them away. For some reason, I felt like I'd get better answers out of Logan than I would out of Max. I just didn't trust him. Not that I trusted Logan, but something about Max just had me on edge. Since Logan was the one showing me around, I figured I'd get a chance to ask later, and tuned back in to Max's directions.

"Logan will be available to you on-call pretty much any time of day or night while we help you through this transition. Do you have any questions?"

"I'm sure at some point I'll have a ton of questions, but I'm not sure where to begin." I didn't want to ask Logan questions with Max breathing down his throat, and I didn't want to ask Max anything if someone else could overhear. It might be a good idea to question them both, on their own, and compare it for later, to see if my instincts were right about them.

"That's understandable. Logan, why don't you show her around, maybe acquaint her with how we work?"

I nodded, and Logan took my arm. I wasn't sure if he was trying to be chivalrous or to control where I went, but I didn't like it. I tried so hard to be polite that my back teeth hurt. I let him drag me away and down a short hallway.

When we were out of sight, I yanked my arm back. He made a face at me, so I explained. "Sorry, Logan. I'm just a bit touchy about being grabbed right now, and I really don't want to be grabbed on my only good arm."

"Oh, I'm sorry. I should have realized." Logan seemed apologetic, but I had this strange feeling that there was something else going on here that I couldn't quite put my finger on. Yeah, I'm a cop. I like a good mystery, unless it involves my own well-being. And this definitely had the hairs on the back of my neck standing at attention.

I was determined to figure out what the hell was going on. My instincts are pretty good. Max wasn't telling me everything. If he was, I'd eat my hat.

Chapter Seventeen

Stephen Tipton looked up at Adam Winters, and asked again, "So, have we heard whether or not she's going to become one of us?"

"Are you really sure you want to ask that question, Stephen? Max could ask that both of you be executed. And how could you purposely do this to someone else after all that you've been through? I just don't understand." Adam, the man who'd checked Sam's pulse when she fainted earlier, put the stethoscope to Stephen's chest. "How could you put someone through this? Isn't it hard enough that we have to deal with it?"

"You don't understand." Stephen looked at the ground.

"You're right. I don't understand. Max will use her for his own purposes. And she's a young girl. You know how he's been on and on to Logan about finding someone strong and young enough to start trying to get a born wolf. We have no other female pack members young enough to handle it. And you go out and get him a perfect physical specimen. I've seen her medical charts. Why would you give him that kind of power over any woman?"

Tears spilled out of Stephen's eyes. He hadn't even thought of that. It was true. Breeding and producing a born wolf had been a dream that Max often spoke of. He'd forbidden most of the men in the pack from having children. Logan was the only exception, the only one with permission to find a mate and have a child. It was one of the things that he and his wife had fought about before the divorce. She'd wanted another child, and as much as Stephen wanted one as well, he couldn't risk her life for Max's plans, or risk Max's anger for disobeying him. Funny that he'd forgotten all of that in his grand chemically induced plan to protect his ex-wife and daughter with the pretty young cop.

Adam shook his head as he put the stethoscope away, and reached for the blood pressure cuff. "Most of the physical symptoms of withdrawal should have passed by now. You just have to get through the emotional and mental withdrawal. You've been here before, and it hasn't worked. What are you going to do different this time?"

"Does it really matter?" Stephen asked. "Even if I wanted to leave, I can't. Max has guards on me all the time. I don't have access to cash, so I couldn't try to bribe them even if I wanted to. They're not going to bring me drugs. I couldn't even get them to go to my house to bring me a picture of my kid. I never even thought about Max's breeding plans. I was just thinking that she always protected Jenna and Rory, so she'd protect them from Max once she knew the truth. I know. It was stupid." He hung his head. "I just got so angry at her for always taking me away from them, and I wanted her to understand that Max was the real threat."

"It was incredibly stupid." Adam rubbed his hands over his face. "I'm just glad that Logan's the one he's focused on. I would hate for Max to start thinking of me as potential breeding stock. I'm no one's lab rat."

"You're actually younger than Logan, aren't you?" Stephen asked. "Are you telling me that you don't date?"

"No. I date. I'm just very discrete and very careful. Yes, I'm younger than Logan, but Max knows I'm also the only wolf with a medical degree. He doesn't want to jeopardize that. And he knows that there isn't much he could do to threaten me. I just stay out of his way as much as I can."

"But, your parents? Could he go after them?" Stephen had always followed Max's lead because of the threats against his own family.

"They're very active in the community, and an attack on them would bring the media out in force. Dad's a writer and professor at the university and Mom's a judge. It's hard to threaten either one of them without the threat of exposure, so he hasn't done it. Doesn't mean he won't, but I think he's as terrified of exposure as the rest of us are, if not more so."

Stephen felt helpless. He didn't have any big shot family members. He was nobody. "I don't get why the obsession with a born wolf, though. He talks about it all the time. If that's what he wants, then why can't we have kids ourselves? Why's he limiting it?"

"I don't know why he wants it. I've heard him talking to some of the others, though. I think it's possible for us to have kids with a normal woman, at least theoretically. There might be a higher miscarriage rate, but it is possible."

"Why do you say that?" Stephen wondered if his marriage might have been saved if he had gone ahead with his wife's plan to have more kids. It was yet another what if question to torture himself with at night.

"We've learned that our condition is a disease, that's to be maintained and controlled with constant changes, much like a diabetic maintains their blood sugar with insulin, right?"

"Yeah. I've heard you say that."

"Gary and James have been sneaking samples over to the hospital labs for analysis, and we've been studying them whenever we've been able to get away from work. Max doesn't even know about all our findings. You ever changed when you weren't upset or angry or scared?"

"No. I don't think I have." Stephen's self-loathing gave way to interest at Adam's simple explanations. Maybe here was information that he could use to prove to his ex-wife that he wasn't a danger to his daughter.

"It's about regulating the adrenaline in our systems. Like a diabetic can't handle too much sugar, we can't handle too much adrenaline. Adrenaline builds up in our bodies, forcing us to an eventual change. But we've found that it's not adrenaline itself, but a chemical within our own bodies that builds up with an adrenaline rush. We haven't identified that chemical yet." Adam sat down, making notes on a chart for Max's inspection later.

Stephen understood that Adam had work to do for Max, documenting his treatment, but the current conversation was more interesting than his own recovery or his own problems. "Wait a minute. Most of us can change whenever we want to. That doesn't make sense that we have to wait for a buildup of some chemical."

"No. You missed my point, Stephen. It takes very little of that chemical to allow us to change. The point is that we can't let it build up forever without changing."

"What are you saying?" He didn't dare hope that Adam, brilliant doctor that he was, had some solution to the mess his life had become.

"I'm saying that once we identify the chemical that's causing the change we might be able to lead completely normal lives."

Stephen stared at him in amazement. A normal life was all he'd ever wanted. He'd do quite a bit to have that chance back. "What can I do to help?"

"You can answer some questions for me about your drug use and the effects of the drugs you took on the changes you had. We obviously can't experiment on anyone. I'm not going around pumping drugs into other wolves just to test their change reactions. Anything on that scale would tip off Max. But sitting in front of me is someone who is intimately familiar with how different drugs affect the change."

"How can that help?"

"It'll give me an idea of what to look for. If the only way to stop this is a large number of sleeping pills, I'm not sure anyone would want that. None of us wants to be turned into a living zombie. If, however, there's some way of suppressing a person's change, then we might be able to give werewolf women a chance to carry a healthy baby to term without worrying about their changes. I don't know what that would do to a fetus. That's what I'll tell Max if he finds out. The truth is that I'm looking for a way for all of us to walk away from this."

"Truly? Do you think it's possible?"

"Seventy years ago, people thought going to the moon was impossible. They thought all cancer was an automatic death sentence, and that there was no cure for polio. We've proven different. Why can't we do it here?"

Stephen felt odd, a vaguely euphoric feeling rising from his toes into his belly. Tears started again, and he dropped his head to cover it. Was he being given a purpose? A way to redeem his stupidity? He'd do a lot to prove to everyone that he was worth saving.

"Stephen, I'm asking you to help me. Help me find a cure. Help me find a way of fighting this. Can you do this?"

He nodded as he recognized the feeling that had leaped through his body. It had been a lifetime since he'd felt it. It was hope.

CHAPTER EIGHTEEN

L ogan showed me around the underground maze, giving me the nickel tour. It was mostly deserted, but every once in a while, Logan would nod or smile or say hello to someone. It annoyed me that he didn't introduce me to any of them, so after the third time it happened, I mentioned it to him.

"Sam, we just don't do that right away. We've got a pretty secure set up here, but you're still a stranger to everyone. Most people here are terrified that the secret would get out."

"I understand wanting privacy. I know no one asked for this, but it just seems paranoid. I mean, we're all in the same boat, right? What could happen?"

"If it got out to the public that we exist, marriages could break up. Jobs could be lost. All kinds of discrimination could happen. Think about it, Sam. This is a disease, a condition that is contagious, and is passed through bodily fluids and saliva. Have you ever read any reports about the kind of discrimination that the first AIDS victims faced? They couldn't get housing, they lost their jobs, and others treated them very badly. Public opinion alone could be disastrous. Remember the Ebola scares here recently? That wasn't much better."

"What do you mean?" I leaned up against the concrete wall of the hallway and crossed my arms to wait for his answer.

"Do you want to receive medical treatment from someone with a contagious disease? Do you want them preparing your food or cleaning you teeth? You can't catch this from those activities, or at least, we've never seen it happen. There's no reason to believe that it's even possible. Will the public believe that? Will people hunt us down to protect themselves? Are we to be animals with no rights? And what would the government do?"

I couldn't fault them for being afraid. I'd never thought about it, but all of those things were a definite possibility. It took brave people to get the information about AIDS out in the open, and the public is safer for it. Maybe the same thing was necessary here. "But, Logan, those fears will never get addressed if no one steps up and sees what actually does happen. We can be scared of what could happen, but we don't know what will happen."

He slapped a hand on the concrete wall just over my right shoulder. "Are you volunteering to be the guinea pig for that little experiment? You want to put yourself on the chopping block of public opinion? I sure don't. Are we a bit paranoid? Yes. Are we overreacting? Probably. But until you're willing to do it yourself, you can't ask someone else to do it either." He pulled his hand back, and ran it through his hair. "I'm sorry Sam. I know you have questions, but some of them have hard answers. It's not that we would always keep it a secret, but that's part of why we're trying to find out everything we can before we make that kind of decision."

"What do you mean?"

"Well, that's why we're putting together this facility." He walked on down the hallway, and opened a door to a room filled with beakers and Bunsen burners and test tubes. "We're going to try to find out what causes this. So far we've learned that this is a virus. We're learning more and more about it every day."

"Is there a cure?"

"No. There is no cure. We haven't been able to find one yet. I'm not sure if we ever will, but we are looking for one. Max doesn't let us speculate on it, and until they have a definitive answer we don't want to get anyone's hopes up.

"Until then, we're also looking for ways to help us control it better. We want to know if there's a drug we can take to keep it at bay. There's been some success, but it's hard. Do you test something like that on yourself? How can you ask others to test it out for you? It's the same problem, but until they tell me there's no hope, it's not out of the question. Max is working on it. He wants us to be proactive."

"Well, by all means, then. If Max decrees that it's done, then onward and upward to the answers, my good sir." I gave him a mock curtsy.

"Sam, that sharp tongue is fine when it's you and me, but you don't want to piss anyone off until you know more about what's going on. That'll take time. For now, stop it." He grinned at me anyway, and I saw that he enjoyed my sarcastic humor even as he warned me against it.

I decided to lay off a bit until I knew more, so I nodded. I was happy that they weren't just sitting idly by, but they were doing something to make their lives better. "I can understand that. Who does the research?"

"We have a couple of pack members who do this kind of research in chemistry, genetics, and biology. They've been the ones to set up the tests. However, they also have families to feed, and full time jobs, so it doesn't happen fast. We also have offices for those with historical research backgrounds to comb through folklore and historical references to such things. The hope is that something in a historical reference might spark an idea for scientific development."

I was impressed. "What else goes on down here?"

He closed the door, and walked down the hall. The walls in the hallway were unfinished concrete blocks, with no paint and no drywall. The hallway was lit with single bare light bulbs hanging from the ceiling. "We've got a weight room here, as well as a dormitory. It's a place to go when you're worried about your change or you can't control it. It's a safe place for us."

He showed me the dormitory, (which worried me that people might be using it to hide from warrants, but Logan assured me that that hadn't happened) and the shower facilities (for cleaning up after a run), and went on with the tour. Some of the rooms were finished and painted. Others were still a work in progress. We walked into one room where two people were painting with ventilation masks over their faces. Logan shut the door, but I still smelled paint fumes.

"How in the world did you guys build this place without anyone noticing a construction site?" I wondered aloud.

"Very carefully. It wasn't something we wanted advertised. You can see that we're still working on it. Our pack has around fifty members. Some of them are in the construction and excavation business. Everyone pitched in. If someone didn't have any skill at building, then they carried or dug or otherwise did grunt work. Some people hung dry wall, others ran electrical wires, or did plumbing. There were a lot of weekends and long evenings that were spent as a pack, doing this. It really lent us a sense of community, and brought us all together."

"I can see that. It's impressive."

We kept walking, and he showed me more rooms. He showed me the security offices where one man watched the camera feeds from different locations around the barn. Nothing was happening on screen, so we left. I noticed that there were quite a few cameras, and it seemed like a very secure set up. They seemed obsessed with security. And when I say obsessed, I mean paranoid. These guys had top of the line security equipment. The only thing I didn't know was how they expected to get out if something got in. I had a moment or two of panic, and had to fight against it. Nobody had threatened me; it had to be the paranoia I'd suffered over the last couple of weeks that was getting to me.

We ended up in the last room to see, which Logan called the "Lounge" as if it was supposed to be capitalized.

"What's this?"

"It's a place for us to hang out. It's also a library, and we do have satellite TV down here. Max is going to meet us here to answer any questions you might still have."

Good. I still felt like there was more I needed to know.

CHAPTER NINETEEN

I walked into the room that Logan had called the Lounge, and was pleasantly surprised. The room was furnished with cushy leather couches and overstuffed reading chairs. The walls were lined with dark wood paneling and bookshelves crammed full from floor to ceiling with papers, books, scrolls and other research materials. There was also a large flat screen television at one end of the room.

Logan plopped down in the leather couch, as if he'd done it a million times before, his long legs sprawled across the cushions. I sat down in a chair facing him. "So, okay, I've seen the digs. I've met the leader. What you haven't told me is what it's like to be a werewolf. As much as I don't want this, I need to ask. Am I going to kill everyone I love on the night of the full moon? Will I break laws, chase cars, or become a serial killer? Would I be strong enough to bench press a school bus? Do I have to howl at the moon?"

He chuckled at my ignorance. "Look, Hollywood has done a real number on us. There's a kernel of truth in most of the legends, myths, and rumors you hear, and in the things that have happened to you."

"Like what?"

"Well, your head injury after the attack would have put a normal human into a coma, if it hadn't killed them outright. You might be relearning how to walk, or talk. Instead, the virus that causes us to change acted in your bloodstream almost immediately. It helped you to recover. Your ribs and shoulders are also healing faster than they should have."

"So, what, I can heal all injuries unless they're caused by a silver bullet?"

"Not quite. The catch, as we've found, is that something that could slowly kill a human, we can recover from but we're not invincible. An immediate killing blow can still take us out. For example, you might heal a gunshot wound to your stomach with the help of medical intervention where a human might bleed out. A bullet to the head, however, is still a bullet to the head. It would kill you on the spot. You could take a hell of a beating, but falling off the Empire State Building is still going to kill you. Oh, and the whole silver thing is total crap. I wouldn't even know where to find a silver bullet."

"You're kidding! That's the one thing I'd have put money on to be true." I sat forward in my seat. This kind of information could be important. And it was interesting.

"It all got started in Europe a couple hundred years ago. Some priest told a hunter that werewolves could be killed by a blessed or inherited silver bullet. It worked for the priest when he killed werewolves, so he spread the word. Hollywood ran with it. The truth was that it was the bullet that killed them, not the silver itself. Old fashioned bullets exploded and left big holes. Explode someone's heart or brain and they're going to die, regardless of whether they have a genetic or viral advantage to their healing capabilities. Has nothing to do with what the actual bullet was made of."

"Why would that priest use silver bullets in the first place? I'd think that'd be expensive."

"Sure it would, but how well do you know your history? Some of the richest people at the time were the clergy. That priest was the kind of guy who had his old silver jewelry melted down for bullets because he wore only gold, and was the kind of jerk that had his bullets blessed to give him an edge over others when he went out hunting. It had nothing to do with the kind of metal, whether it had holy blessings, or whether it was left by an old relative."

"Good to know. What about scarring? Do we scar like a human, or does that heal?"

"Most wounds we heal pretty well and we don't scar as badly as a human. Scars you had before you were bit will never go away. Some wounds after you were bit, if they were bad enough, will leave a scar. Mostly, our wounds just heal faster, so there's much less scarring. It's not a bad thing, when we all hide what we are."

"It would be hard to explain scars that happened when you were in wolf form to people outside of the pack." It made sense, but it was too bad. I had hoped the scar on my knee from falling out of my tree house when I was eight would go away. That wouldn't be a bad side effect. Too bad he was telling me it wouldn't work.

Max slid into the room, as Logan kept talking. I wished I'd paid more attention in my college history classes. He hit lecture mode as Max watched. "In the Middle Ages, there were a lot of people who were burned, tortured, or executed because they claimed to be werewolves. Most of them never were. They were mentally ill, or were hallucinating from bad food or medicines. Some embraced the hallucination, and started wearing belts they told others contained the power to be wolves. The truth is that real werewolves followed the accounts of the executions and torture with horror. They were terrified someone would find out they were real and suffer the same fate as the unfortunates that were caught up in the Inquisition."

Max stepped in at that point, and sat down in the chair beside mine and joined the conversation. "Here's the thing: even when the Inquisition ended, that air of terror remained. No one trusted that the pendulum wouldn't swing back to such a time. Man has found reason to target and condemn people of different ethnic backgrounds, racial backgrounds, religions, beliefs, ideals, politics, and sexual orientation. From the Inquisition to slavery to the Holocaust to the civil rights movement, such a concern has been paramount in the minds of werewolves that we could be next. We don't want to be scientific guinea pigs or the military's newest weapon. We want to live normal, everyday lives, at least as much as we're able."

"I get it. But there may come a time when you can't put your head in the sand and hope things will get better."

Max didn't look happy at my statement. I realized he didn't like living in the shadows either. He was a man of action, but he was toeing the party line of paranoia and fear. Interesting, I thought, considering he was advocating hiding his head in the sand.

I looked back to Logan to ask another question. "So, um, do I have to take the full moon off work every month? I'm not sure I have that much leave time, and it looks suspicious."

Max continued with the death stare. I could feel his eyes on the side of my head, but I refused to give in to him. Logan sat up on the couch to answer. "No, that's Hollywood crap, although the added light from the full moon makes it an ideal night for a hunt."

I ignored Max. Instead, I peppered Logan with questions regarding the truth rather than the myths of being a werewolf. I was kind of amazed that I had so much random knowledge about werewolves. I must be spending too much time watching cheesy horror movies. "So, you didn't answer me before. Am I going on a murder spree and kill my loved ones?"

Logan continued. "Wolves don't go on random murder sprees, only humans do. Wolves only kill to defend their territory or for food or for protecting their pack or their young. Werewolves don't commit murder on an uncontrollable impulse any more than the general population, and then only because they are also people. Evil people make evil werewolves."

Go figure. I wondered if they were referring to someone in particular when they spoke of an evil werewolf. Oh, yeah, of course they were. The one who did this to me had to be evil. That sure would fit the bill.

CHAPTER TWENTY

The three of us spent the next hour detailing the physical changes that would happen, and what I could do to make my life a little easier. While I couldn't argue that the symptoms they listed were true, or that werewolves existed, I still had a hard time believing it.

Max advised me that my diet would make some subtle changes. He'd loosened up a bit, but still looked at me like a recruit rather than a victim. I didn't like it, but kept watching him while he and Logan answered my questions.

"There's nothing subtle about my current meat obsession." I deadpanned.

Max laughed. "As carnivores in the wild, wolves eat mostly meat, and need large amounts of protein, although they have needs for vegetation and carbs as well."

Logan jumped in. "It'll taper off, but your body needs the increased protein right now to deal with the physical changes you're undergoing. You might not be aware of it at the moment, but you're healing from the attack, as well as growing new tissue. Your metabolism is going to speed up, so you'll need more fuel to keep going, which means eating well and often. You'll hit some mood swings until you get used to the adrenaline, as well."

"When do I know for sure? No one's done a blood test. This could be for nothing."

Max growled at me. "There's no doubt. Deal with it."

Before I could snark back, Logan jumped in to defuse the situation. "Sam, I know you don't want to believe this. You have some time to process it, but you need to take in what we're saying and accept it so you can be prepared."

It made sense. I didn't want him to make sense. I knew I'd seen the guy change into a wolf earlier, and I believed that werewolves existed, but we'd gone from the abstract, where I believed it was possible, to embracing that it would happen to me. I just couldn't get there.

Wait. Max had growled. I'd made that exact noise at Justin earlier. I dropped my head in my hands. That was the clincher for me. Once that light bulb went on in my brain, there was no more doubt. It was true. I started crying softly, and hated myself for it.

Logan and Max sat and waited for me to pull myself together. Neither one of them offered comfort. It pissed me off, but also helped me to get back on track. Anger was the key, yet again, to keeping my emotions in check. Yeah, that was gonna suck.

I sat up and wiped a tear out of the corner of my eye, and sniffed. "I'm sorry. I don't know what came over me."

Logan's face softened as he watched me. Max looked at him and then looked at me, and nodded. I didn't like what I saw on his face, but he stood up to leave, and I didn't have any objection to that. "I can see that we're into counseling mode. That's more Logan's department than mine, so I'll let you two alone to talk. The only thing I ask, Sam, is that you be very careful about what you say about all this outside the barn and outside the pack."

I nodded. What else could I do? It wasn't like anyone would believe me anyway.

Logan waited for Max to get up and walk out, closing the door behind him, before we continued sifting through practical questions about life as a werewolf. Logan gave me more advice, and again I felt like I should be taking notes. When I asked, he refused, telling me that he'd rather I call and ask him a second or third or tenth time, even in the middle of the night, before someone else found notes like this lying around.

Of course, he wouldn't let me leave without making sure I knew that the name of the game was control. He told me that it'd probably be once a week or so in the beginning, but later I'd be able to hold off further to the point of only changing once or twice a month.

Changing is related to emotions. I must have given him a skeptical look when he said it, because he grinned. "I'm really not kidding. You told me you caught yourself growling when you were angry at Justin. It comes out in times of stress and anger and fear. My degrees are in psychology and counseling. I'm not a medical or scientific expert, but it's similar to a fight or flight reaction. It's all to do with excess adrenaline, and that pumped up feeling you get from stressful situations. Stress management is the key."

"So I have to avoid stress to prevent becoming a werewolf? Um, I'm a cop. I can't avoid stress. Or stressful situations. And I'm not giving up my job. I worked too hard to get it."

"No one can completely avoid stress. You're becoming a werewolf, no matter how calm you try to be. The physical reaction to stress, however, can trigger the change. As a police officer, you're going to be faced with a lot of stressful situations. I won't try to tell you to give up your job, but it won't be easy. The trick's going to be in scheduling times for yourself to change and satisfy that need before you get into a bind at work. You'll have to have frequent changes while you're off-duty to prevent an unavoidable change while you're on duty. It can be done, Sam. It won't be easy, but it is possible."

"Is there anything I can do to prevent having to go through this? No offense, Logan, but I'd give just about anything to prevent this."

"It's not possible. You can't prevent it. The only thing you can do is control it before it controls you. Think of it like diabetes. You have to eat regularly, and maintain your weight, and take insulin, and check your blood sugar if you're diabetic in order to stay healthy. Well, werewolves have to schedule regular changes to stay in control. It's the same kind of thing."

Me. He wants me not to get revved up at work. Yeah, like that's gonna work. That's the part of the job I live for. It's the high of doing the job and the triumph of doing it well. And he wants me not to lose my temper? Yeah, right. I realized that there was a reason for all these guidelines, but damn it, I didn't want this.

"Okay, I can handle that." I was amazed as the words came out of my mouth. Huh? This wasn't me. I don't just fall in line. But he made it sound reasonable, like I could handle it. A part of me wanted to prove that I could.

"You seem to be taking this in stride."

"Believe me, on the inside, it's anything but 'in stride'. I am shocked, amazed, sickened, scared, dumbfounded and shell-shocked all in less than a minute. I don't really know how to react to this. I guess you could say I'm reserving judgment pending further information."

"Sam, you can't bargain your way out of it. It will happen to you. I wish I wasn't so sure. I wouldn't wish this on anyone."

I wasn't getting anywhere; he was starting to repeat himself. It was time for a change of subject. "What is the book over there, the one on the stand with the gorgeous antique leather binding? And why is it covered by a locked glass case?"

"That's a book that belongs to the Alpha and he's the only one allowed to look at it. It contains a history of werewolves. He consults it from time to time for guidance."

"More rules of the pack that I'll understand in time?"

He nodded and I was struck by the individuality in his face, even as he seemed to give lip service to the party line. He looked me in the face and gave me a small smile. "I'm impressed. It's been my unfortunate duty to counsel people when they face what you're going through. You've had a few moments of denial, but you're holding it together well."

If he was impressed, then maybe it was time for me to bow out and ask for a ride home. I was all out of patience for new revelations. If he told me about one more rule or requirement, I would lose it. "Logan, I'm exhausted. Can you take me home now?" I looked at him, begging with my eyes. "Please?" No harm in being polite.

"No problem, Sam. You should go home and take some time to absorb all of this. Please call me immediately, though, if you feel like you're about to change. It's a little scary that first time, and a little daunting. I can help you through it, if you'll let me."

I nodded. I'd have agreed to just about anything. I just wanted to go home.

We stood up and walked back to Logan's car. I could hear an argument start up as we walked out of the conference area where the guy had changed into a wolf. I didn't even look behind me once I heard others intervene. I didn't really want to learn how werewolves solved a disagreement at the moment.

It was one of those days that I wanted to go home and cuddle up with Doyle, where I couldn't learn new and bigger and badder things. I wanted to call Justin and apologize, and beg him to come over and give me a hug. None of those things were going to make this go away, but they might make me feel a little better.

I was lost in thought as Logan started up the car. We drove back to Dayton in silence, and he left another card with me with all his numbers on it. I wondered if he'd bought stock in a stationary company the way he handed them out.

"I'll check on you daily for the next week or so. If I don't miss my guess, that's when your first change will be," he said to me, as I got out of the car a block away from my house.

Yeah. That'll make things all better. Trying to fix my relationship with Justin will go oh so well with Logan hanging out and waiting for me to grow hair and fangs. And if you believe that, I'll sell you a snow cone franchise in hell.

Chapter Twenty One

No one answered the door when Justin rang the bell. He rang it again, and then knocked when no one came to the door. He saw Doyle climb into the front windowsill but there was no other movement inside.

He wondered for a brief minute if Sam had fallen asleep after he'd left. She'd certainly been sleeping a lot, and today's fight at the restaurant was more activity than she'd seen since the attack. In fact, her sleeping habits had led to him getting a key to her house so he could let himself in to feed Doyle and start dinner without bothering her. He toyed with the key in his hand and wondered if he should go in and check on her.

She couldn't be asleep. Not after the screaming match they'd had earlier. He felt bad enough about their earlier conversation. Not that he was wrong; he wasn't. He thought he might have pushed her too far, too fast, though. No matter. He stepped away from the door. She wouldn't thank him for waking her up, and he didn't really want a repeat of the earlier fight.

Justin stepped off the porch and walked to his pickup truck, fully meaning to leave her alone for the evening. As he opened the door to get in the truck and leave, he felt the hairs on the back of his neck stand at attention. Something just wasn't right. He tried to ignore it, move past it, blame his own churned up emotions from the fight earlier, but whatever had set off the cop antennae in his head refused to quiet down.

He grabbed his gun out of the glove compartment, and fished a clip out of the gym bag he used to haul his equipment back and forth to work, feeling better when he heard the clip slide home. He chambered a round and held the gun out in front of himself with both hands, pointed toward the grass, as he edged around the brick corner of her house into the backyard.

He heard a noise coming from down the street. It sounded like a dog barking, and he headed in that direction. If someone was cutting through backyards to break into houses, any dog would bark at the intrusion, and cause a commotion.

No dogs in the yard next door. That was odd, he thought. Then he heard it again, coming from the opposite direction. An intruder had gotten past him, and into the neighbor's yard on the other side of Sam's house? He didn't think so, but he moved to check. There was still no movement from inside her house.

He saw the German shepherd in her neighbor's yard, yapping its head off, but it wasn't the same bark he'd heard. There was nothing in the backyard, so he moved around the house to the opposite side and hugged the wall as he inched his way back to the front yard.

Across the road were two men getting into a dark van. One was just slipping into a leather jacket. They weren't carrying anything, but Justin aimed the gun at them and shouted, "Stop, police!"

The two of them stopped. He held out his badge for them to see as they raised their hands above their heads, thankful that he always carried it in his pocket when he was off duty. "Whoa, what's going on here?" the big one asked.

Justin saw the smaller one holding a map. He quickly patted the two of them down one-handed, and didn't find any weapons. "What are you guys doing here?"

"We're lost is what we is." The smaller one with the leather jacket piped up. "We're tryin' to get to the Air Force Museum, and we took a wrong turn. We can't find Springfield Street." He held up the map to illustrate.

"Museum closes at five. That was three hours ago. What are you guys doing? How long have you been sitting here?" Justin asked. He knew he could detain them for a cruiser to respond on suspicion of trespassing and attempted breaking and entering, but there could be a legitimate reason for being in the neighborhood. Besides, they might have had nothing to do with the barking dogs. Or the creepy feeling on the back of his neck. It was hard to make 'creepy' fit any definition of probable cause he could think of for an arrest, but he wanted to check. The museum was only ten minutes or so drive away. He couldn't imagine anyone getting so lost they'd be three hours late for closing when they were that close.

"'Bout ten minutes or so we've been sittin' here. We got turned around in Cincinnati, and got here too late, so we thought we'd try to find it tonight so we could get a hotel room and visit in the morning. We've been driving around for an hour, and we keep seeing signs for it but we never actually found it. We stopped to try to knock on someone's door to get directions." The big one added, still keeping his hands in front of him where Justin could see them.

The knocking could have easily set off the neighborhood dogs. He grimaced as he finished checking them for weapons. Once he was satisfied that they weren't armed, he shoved his gun in the waistband at the back of his jeans, and put his badge back in his pocket. They showed him their driver's licenses and VFW membership cards, and a pamphlet for the Air Force Museum. Justin was satisfied they weren't committing any crimes, but he was still suspicious.

"Naw, nothing strange, but there was a couple o' dogs that didn't like us knocking on doors and they started barking pretty fierce." The taller one answered his question.

Justin felt like an absolute fool. What else was new? He'd felt like that a lot lately. "Sorry, fellas. Didn't mean to scare you. It sounded like someone was trying to break into a house when I showed up to visit a friend, so I figured I'd better check it out." He gave them directions to get back to Woodman Drive and head toward the Museum.

They drove off just as Sam walked up. He stood on the sidewalk just looking at her as she approached. She had an air of confusion about her, as well as a more determined step to her walk as she approached him. In fact, she looked more like her normal self, even though there was a question on her face.

"What's going on, Justin?"

"Nothing. I stopped by to check on you, and heard noises when I was knocking on the door that sounded like someone trying to break in, but the guys in that van were knocking on doors to get directions."

She nodded, watching the van turn at the stop sign at the end of her street. "I'm glad you were here to check."

He nodded. "Are you okay?"

"Yeah. I've had a couple of hours to think. I took a walk."

He had no idea he'd been holding his breath until then. Taking a walk was a good sign. She was out of the house, and she looked better, more solid and grounded, than she had in a long time. Her hair was a riotous mess, and she still looked tired, but she was outside, moving around, awake, and in one piece. He'd take it.

They stood side by side, watching the quiet neighborhood for several minutes, until Sam broke the silence. "I called Logan Boyd."

"You did?"

"Yes. And he came over to talk to me about how I've been handling all this."

"He came over to your house for a private session? That doesn't sound real professional." He could have kicked himself. He'd all but forced her to counseling, and now he was so jealous he could taste the bile in the back of his throat. Another man showed up at a moment's notice and sat in her house with her, and she'd confided in them. Not her partner, not her friend, or even her boyfriend, but some stranger, after all he'd done since she'd come home. He swallowed hard and hoped she didn't notice.

"I was surprised, myself, but I needed it more than I thought. I think counseling's going to help." She smiled.

He fought back the jealousy as it threatened to open his mouth and start an argument. It wouldn't be fair, he thought, especially if she was smiling. He'd do a lot to keep her smiling. "Sam, I'm sorry I yelled. I don't regret asking you to get into therapy, but I shouldn't have handled it like that."

"I shouldn't have yelled either." She hugged him around the waist, settling her cheek against his chest.

He wrapped his arms around her shoulders and kissed the top of her head. "We'll figure it all out, Sam. I promise."

CHAPTER TWENTY TWO

The next few days, I forced myself out of the house more. I went to a doctor's appointment for a check-up and learned I was healing at a rapid pace. However, doctors are never satisfied. They were concerned that the quick healing was deceptive and masking more problems, but I begged to go back to work. The doctor agreed to let me go back, but only if I went back to light duty for the next month. He told me I would re-injure myself if I wasn't careful.

I also got official permission to stop wearing the sling. Glad they approved, because the thing drove me nuts, and I hadn't worn it since I'd come home from the hospital.

Justin and I were able to go out to dinner without a fight. We started meeting outside the house more, since Logan stopped by on a daily basis to check up on me. Justin was the one who'd forced me into counseling. He fought not to comment about Logan coming over all the time, but I could tell it bothered him. It was ironic that he was jealous over Logan when counseling was his idea in the first place. Yeah, life was getting back to normal, and I forgot about the whole thing for hours until Logan showed up for another counseling "session".

When I reported to my sergeant with the news that I could come back to light duty, I was assigned to the information desk at the Safety Building, the police headquarters downtown. While it was nice to wear civilian clothing, I'd spend my day doing paperwork and answering questions asked by citizens. Being nice and polite and diplomatic isn't always my strong suit, but that was the price I had to pay to get back to work.

I met with Logan every day, but nothing happened. He was amazed I hadn't changed, but we talked about the attack, and my reactions to it. I guess even with all of the werewolf-y stuff happening to me, I also suffered reactions like a normal human, very similar to post-traumatic stress disorder. Logan was available when I was about to come out of my skin, at least figuratively. He helped me figure out what was a wolf thing and what was a traumatic reaction to the attack. I still didn't quite believe I'd go furry, but there was no sense in being unprepared. Anyway, talking about the attack did help.

On Monday, I went back to work. I hated to sit at that stupid desk. I hated to answer questions from people who wanted to get their cars out of impound, or wanted directions on where to get a copy of a police report. Worse were the people who showed up and wanted us to take a police report because someone else made a report about them. I was exhausted and cranky when I left police headquarters, named the Safety Building, at the end of the day. Even though my sleeping problem had tapered off, I still tired easily.

Justin was coming from a court appearance. He was still in uniform when he picked me up, and we went for dinner on Brown Street, near the University of Dayton. We walked into a coffee and sandwich shop, where the only customers were a group of people typing away on laptops in the back corner, and an older couple having dinner. I was grateful for the emptiness of the place. After a long day I wasn't able to deal with a large crowd.

I made a point of ordering a steak salad and a bowl of soup, to show Justin I was eating better and taking care of myself. He noticed, and made a satisfied grunt at me as I speared some lettuce on a fork and ate. It didn't taste right, but I was willing to compromise at least that much.

"So how was the first day back?"

"Fine, I guess. I don't know how anyone does that job on a regular basis. It's annoying to do the same thing all day, and the stories people tell are so stupid. 'Help, my crack-head son stole my car and geeked it out for drugs.' 'Yes, I know that his name is on the title.' 'I know I don't look anything like him.' 'No, I can't prove he's my son, but he owes me that car.' It's more like he owes his dealer for his crack. That's pretty sad."

"I take it you didn't release the car?"

"Well, let's see, the guy had no ID, no driver's license, no insurance, the dude who was driving it when it was impounded is the legal owner, and he's in jail at the moment. Um, no."

"You big meanie," He grinned. "Keeping that car away from the poor drug dealer who just wanted his crack debt repaid, you should be ashamed. Crack dealers have to eat, too."

"Yeah, poor crack dealers. It's such a cruel world for them."

He laughed. It was the first time I'd heard him really laugh since the attack. "God, Sam, I miss having you on the street. I'm dying of boredom out there. I miss having a smartass sitting beside me in the cruiser to keep me from taking myself seriously."

"I have a confession to make. I've been smarting off on purpose just to hear you laugh. You should laugh more often."

"I've been biting the inside of my cheek to keep from laughing. I'm never sure whether to encourage you or to keep my mouth shut."

"Damn. We should have thought of this sooner."

"No kidding."

"Not a bad way to end a day, though." I picked up my trash and threw it away, and we headed toward the door. He grabbed my hand as we left, and I glanced around to see if anyone noticed. After all, he was still in uniform. I had no wish to be number one on the gossip parade.

As we walked to his car, shots rang out. I was unarmed. I'd been in plainclothes all day, so I whipped out my cell phone as Justin unsnapped the holster on his belt and ran in the general direction of the shots. I wasn't far behind. My heart sang at the idea of action, and I had to remind myself that I wasn't armed or cleared for return to active duty. Then Logan's warnings reared their head, a little too late.

We got to the houses a block or so behind the restaurant, a mish-mash of run-down buildings, new businesses, and college apartments, and I heard another gunshot. I hung back, watching Justin, as he approached a moron waving a pistol on his front porch. I realized there was nothing I could do if Justin got hurt as the moron left the porch and wandered out into his yard, still brandishing his gun. I yelled into the cell phone at the dispatcher to send back up.

Justin pointed his service revolver at the moron and ordered him to drop his weapon and put his hands up. To both of our relief, he complied. Justin handcuffed him, and asked me to stand over the weapon as he called for backup. I felt helpless, and started to get angry. My skin began to itch. Oh, no, I thought. I can't do this here.

I remembered what Logan had told me. I fought to slow down the reaction of my body and the on-rush of adrenaline. I didn't hear anything Justin said. All I could do was stand with one foot on the moron's gun to immobilize it, and meditate on the ebb and flow of my own body. I have no idea how long I stood there, breathing slowly in my nose, and letting it out bit by bit through my mouth, barely registering anything else around me.

"Officer Hochenwalt? Hock? Um, we need to take the gun now. Are you okay?" I opened my eyes. I knew one of the officers who'd shown up to help. He and I were in the academy together. I was much calmer at this point than I should've been, but hadn't heard the other officer walk up behind me. That was scary. If that'd been another bad guy with a gun, I'd be dead.

I held up my hand to ask him to give me a minute and closed my eyes. I took a deep breath and let it out, feeling my body calm itself. I knew it wouldn't last long. I needed to get home, get rid of Justin, and get Logan's help, quickly, or my secret would be out.

"I'm okay, Officer Smith. Just a little shaky. I've done too much for the first day back."

"No problem. We're gonna book him for an unlawful discharge of a firearm, and Officer Noble's gonna take you home before he comes back to write up the report." He grinned. "Take it easy out there, Hock. We're pretty short-handed right now. We want you back chasing bad guys before the end of the summer."

I gave him a mock salute, and stumbled toward Justin's car. That, of course, had been the other reason we needed backup. He was in his own car rather than in a secure cruiser, and had no way to transport an arrest to the jail. I was unsteady on my feet, and Justin reached out to support me. Guilt washed over me when I realized I'd have to kick him out to call another man. I mean, if Justin was my boyfriend, and that was still a big if, it just felt wrong. I didn't really have a choice. At the moment, Justin couldn't help. There was no denying it. I'd be furry soon.

CHAPTER TWENTY THREE

I started shaking in the truck, and a cold sweat popped out on my forehead. Justin started asking me at every stoplight if I was okay, and all I could do was nod. I slowed my breathing, closed my eyes, and tried desperately to stay calm long enough to get home.

"Are you okay, Sam?"

I forced myself to respond. I was afraid if I couldn't talk, he'd run me straight to the emergency room, and I didn't think I could handle the delay. "I just need to go home. I think it was too much exertion on my first day back. I'll go home and lie down, and I'll be fine."

"You're sure?"

"Yeah, though I may call Logan Boyd before I crash. The gunshots really shook me up."

He sped up, which didn't help me stay calm. I knew he was trying to get me home in a hurry, but being anxious was rubbing off on me. Him not liking the idea of me calling Logan didn't help either. I could feel his anger and jealousy, as well as the effort it took to stay silent.

"You're sure you're okay?"

"Yeah, just get me home." I closed my eyes again, and concentrated. Maybe I needed to learn how to meditate. Yoga classes might not be a bad idea. Although if Logan told me to relax when I talked to him, I might just relax my fist into his face.

I kept my eyes closed for the drive to my house, but I felt my control slip as Justin pulled into my driveway. He turned off the ignition, and went around the truck to open the door for me. That would normally tick me off. I appreciate civility, but unless it's a special occasion, it just feels condescending. Today it was a good thing. I wasn't sure I could open the door on my own. My hands felt numb.

"Do you need me to help you inside?"

"No, I just need to go lie down. I'll be fine, and you have a report to file. They're gonna look for you to get back and call in that report." I got out of the car and hoped he wouldn't linger too long. I wasn't sure how much longer I had.

He cupped my face in his hands, and kissed my forehead tenderly. "I'll go call this in, and then I'll call to check on you."

"Seriously, Justin, I'm gonna go inside and call Logan, and then crash. I won't even hear the phone ring. We'll do something tomorrow night. I'll be fine. You said it yourself. I have to learn how to deal with this and not turn you into a walking comfort blanket. I want to be your girlfriend. I want to be myself again, so I have to do this on my own."

He looked unhappy, like he wanted to come in and hold me while I slept, like he'd done when I first came home from the hospital. I saw him soften a bit when I threw back his own words at him, and I knew it took a lot of effort for him to pull back and leave. "If you're sure, then I'll go. Please call if you need anything."

"I'll be fine, just go take care of that report. Let me know if I need to add a supp." I meant a supplementary report, an additional witness statement that would let the sergeant and the prosecutor know what part I'd played in the whole incident.

"I'll take care of it, and then talk to the sergeant. I'll let him know that you'll add it tomorrow if they need it."

"Thanks, Justin." I could feel my skin itch, like a million beetles crawling just under it. "I really need to go inside now, Justin." *Just go, Justin. Please.*

"Sam, I understand wanting to tough it out." He spit those words out, and I realized that my calling Logan was the real issue. He wanted to be the one to comfort me, not some other guy. "Please call if you need me. I appreciate the effort you're making, but it's okay to ask for help."

I didn't have time to prop up his ego. "I'll call if it's too much." *Go, Justin. Please. Now.*

"Okay," he stepped back, and kissed me again. I walked away, trying not to run.

I took great care to lock the door and latch the chain so Justin couldn't change his mind and follow me inside. My hands were trembling, but Logan answered on the first ring.

"Hello? Sam?"

"Yeah," My voice shook.

"It's happening, isn't it?"

"I think so. Oh, God, I don't think I can hold off much longer. I don't know what to do. Logan, help me!" I collapsed on the floor, the phone falling from my hands.

Dimly, I heard his voice through the phone where it fell on the floor, and I grabbed it. "I'm on my way. Stay on the phone. Take slow, even breaths, and sit down. Don't panic."

"I don't think I'm gonna make it," I whispered. Something about telling someone not to panic almost always ensures that they do. It's like saying, don't think of pink elephants. Once someone says that, it's all I can think of.

Logan kept trying to calm me down. I could hear horns honk at him over the phone as he sped toward me. That didn't help, but I could still hear his voice. "I want you to try something. If you've made it this long, you might be able to pull this off, but I want you to promise you won't get upset if you can't do it. If nothing else, the effort may take your mind off what's going on long enough for me to get there."

"Okay." I crawled back to the door. I looked outside to make sure Justin was gone, and unlocked it. I couldn't figure how I'd let him in if I lost control and couldn't get to the door. Justin was gone, so I left it unlocked.

"I want you to imagine pouring all that energy and anxiety into one hand. Relax that hand, and feel it come out through your fingertips. It's okay if your hand starts to change. Letting go that little bit may buy me a few minutes. I'm not far away."

"I'll try." I concentrated, and tried to visualize what he said. I could feel it in my hand. I felt the skin split at my fingertips, and claws poked out. "It hurts," I whimpered, and hated it. I was sick and tired of being weak and in pain.

"You've done well, Sam. I'm pulling onto your street right now. I'll be right there." He hung up abruptly.

I scooted back across the floor away from the door until my butt hit the wall, and pulled my knees up to my chest. Doyle appeared and started hissing and spitting at me in a corner. It didn't do much to keep me calm.

I tried to ignore him as I rocked myself back and forth and squeezed my eyes shut against the tears that leaked out. Logan burst through the door, slamming it behind him. I growled low in the back of my throat.

"Ease down, Sam, it's me. I'm here." He paused for just a minute, looking at my hand.

I followed his gaze and noticed that I no longer had a hand. I had a paw, with silver-gray fur that started midway between my elbow and my wrist. The fur was creeping up my arm, steady, but slow as molasses. "Make it stop hurting, Logan, please," I whispered.

His eyes opened wide as he took in the sight of me, with one paw, shivering and sweating and shaking in the corner. "Listen to me, Sam. You've put up one hell of a fight, and so we're gonna have to let it out slow and easy."

I nodded. He talked to me, and I let that awful tension out through my hand, then up my arm, and then my other arm and my legs before my body and head. The head hurt the worst. I felt my skull split and reform, and my mouth and nose expand into a muzzle as I cried out. I knew somehow that I could burst out of my skin and get it over with like ripping a band-aid off a wound, but I wanted to limit how much it would hurt. I wasn't sure what happened next. I followed Logan's voice through the entire ordeal, stopping to scream when the bones of my face reformed themselves. It felt like someone had taken an aluminum ball bat to my face and then welded it back together with hot tar.

Finally the process was complete. It stopped hurting, and without thinking, I scratched my neck. I almost fell over, and heard Logan laughing. That's when I realized I'd done it with my back leg. He patted the top of my head and scratched the same spot I was trying to reach. I wondered what I looked like, but even as I ran in circles trying to catch a glimpse, I noticed that I didn't see colors all that well.

I pushed up against Logan's hand, because the scratching felt glorious. I caught sight of Doyle zipping through the house, screeching in fear as he headed for the relative safety of my bedroom. Logan grinned, and I threw back my head and howled before he could stop me, an exultant cry of triumph ringing through my house, even over the tortured hiss of the cat.

Chapter Twenty Four

Logan shook his head at me, and I heard him say something about not howling while I was in the city. He didn't want to have to rescue me from animal control. I tried to laugh, but it came out as a series of barks. The mental image of it was too funny. I'd have to have my best friend rescue me from the pound. Nadia's internship could come in handier that I'd thought.

As I experimented with walking on four legs, Logan picked up my house keys and scooped up some clothes and old tennis shoes off my bedroom floor. He helped me untangle myself from the ruined mess of the clothes I'd been wearing. The shirt was split down the middle and the pants were shredded. I didn't remember causing the rips and tears I saw, but they were ruined. I understood now why the guy who'd changed at the barn earlier had stripped down. I was grateful Logan was thinking ahead to grab me clothes. Grabbing clothes must mean he'd help me change back to human form eventually. I wondered how long I'd have to wait, and how badly it would hurt.

He shut off all the lights, and ushered me out to his Mustang. When he opened the door, I clambered up on the front seat. I've never thought about how to sit on a human shaped seat when I walked on two legs, but walking on all fours required some adjustment. I turned in a circle until I found a comfortable way to sit.

I hoped no one saw us. I did have one nosy neighbor, and I hoped to hell she didn't call the cops at a strange man and a dog walking out of my house. Justin would flip out at the ruined clothes on the floor.

"Some people change into a wolf and they look rangy and lean, or they look sickly. I remember the first thing I wanted to know when I changed for the first time was what I looked like. I couldn't talk to ask the question, so I'll answer it for you, even if you haven't thought about it." Logan kept talking to me.

I cocked my head at him. I was interested in what I looked like. The only thing I could see was my paws, and I couldn't tell color real well.

"Your fur's a silver-gray all over. It looks like there are some black and white highlights here and there. It's actually really pretty. I don't think I've seen a wolf with quite that coloring before."

I wasn't sure how to thank him. It felt good to hear that I didn't look like a ravening monster. I had an urge to lick his face as a way to say thanks. I would've done so if I hadn't remembered he was driving. I settled for licking the back of his hand where it rested on the gearshift between the seats.

He laughed. "Yeah, I know, having someone talk to you sucks when you can't respond, especially when you're used to making smartass comments, doesn't it, Sam?"

I yipped in response and looked out the car window. Logan was headed for the barn where I'd met the other werewolves earlier. He'd mentioned going for runs at the barn when we were here before, and I hoped he was planning the same thing now.

We arrived at the barn and entered the same way we had before. As we went further underground, I could smell the drywall and the paint of the newest construction. I was distracted by Logan's own smell, a scent that seemed familiar, but stronger than I'd ever noticed before. I remembered the taste of the back of his hand, and licked it again to test it against the smell of him. His jaw dropped just as the lift stopped at the parking area.

"Sam, please don't do that. The first time wasn't a big deal, but beyond that, well. You have no idea what you're doing. I don't think you want to go there."

I cocked my head sideways at him, because I didn't understand, and didn't know how to ask. I hadn't meant anything sexual by it. Apparently he'd taken it that way. Oops.

He kept going. "Trust me on this. I'm your sponsor as well as your counselor. There are some rules of etiquette that I'm trying to observe, and you're making it difficult."

I could read a longing on his face that went deep, a sudden lust that had me feeling a response low in my own body. That wasn't right. I didn't want that with him. I wanted that with Justin. I whimpered softly, remembering the fight this afternoon.

"Sam, I'm getting out of the car right now, letting you out, and we're getting Max. I need help."

Puzzled, and not understanding what he was talking about, I leapt out of the car when he opened the door. As soon as my feet hit the concrete, I realized that I'd have had problems if I'd tried to open the car door myself. I hadn't minded him opening the door. Not having opposable thumbs changes the playing field when it comes to sexual equality.

Another man came towards me, with Max behind him and I growled. When they kept coming, I stepped in front of Logan and growled even louder. I didn't recognize the man with Max by sight or smell, but he was coming toward Logan a bit too fast for my taste.

Logan blanched, and took off toward a back room, Max following him. I figured it had to be something important for him to tear himself away from me so fast, or maybe I had made a giant faux pas. I felt lonely and frightened by the advance of the man I didn't know. I hoped Logan wasn't mad at me, and that someone would tell me what I'd done wrong.

"It's okay, little one. It'll be okay." He allowed me to smell the back of his hand, and I did so, cataloguing him as someone who was nice to me. I felt uneasy, but I knew where I was. I realized he was the man who changed in front of me when I'd been here the first time.

I took a deep breath. Logan wasn't going to abandon me to someone he didn't trust. After all, he'd thought to grab clothes for me, so that had to count for something.

Speaking of Logan, I wanted to know how to change back so I could ask a few questions. Like, why did we have to drive out here if I'd already changed? Why was it so important?

Finally, he came out of a back room where he'd been with Max. I sniffed the air, trying to become accustomed to the different smells. I caught the distinct smell of Logan, and then another scent that had to be Max. The look on Logan's face had me wondering what had been said behind closed doors, and if the man had been nice to me to keep me from investigating. I shook my head. It wasn't like me to get that distracted. I'd just have to find another way to get answers.

Logan looked shaken by his conversation with Max. I couldn't get a read on why, and I couldn't ask. I yipped at him and he came over. He nudged me over to a small door, and led me through a tunnel out into the late evening sun. I smelled summer grass and trees, and shook my fur, and then flopped over to roll in the mud. It was glorious.

He laughed, and while it wasn't as touchable and deep as Justin's, it was still a good laugh, and it sounded like he needed it. I caught myself panting happily at him, with my tongue hanging out, mud in a streak down the side of my front leg and muzzle.

"Hold on a minute, Sam, and I'll take you for a quick run to show you around the property. Most of us have our changes here, at least so others can't see what's going on. Where we're standing is sheltered from the road, blocked by the barn, and surrounded by a high fence. It's a good idea to look around before you change, but Max was just out here and checked it out. Our security guys said it was clear, so I'm going to go ahead and change."

He started to strip off his clothes, and I felt bashful. I mean, I'm dating Justin. I shouldn't look. I shouldn't want to look. If I'd been in human form, I'd be watching through my fingers.

I was busted. He cocked one eyebrow at me, and said, "It's okay, Sam. I'm not going to strip all the way down. I want you to have another chance to see the change as it happens, when you're not fighting it off like you had to do. It can be the most peaceful thing you've ever done, or the angriest and most painful. The key is to accept the change and relax into it."

He stripped down to his boxers and took off his shoes and socks, setting them on the ground beside his clothes, folded under a bush. I was grateful he stopped with the boxers, because a part of me didn't want him too. Yeah, I know, it sounds bad, but hey, just because I was with someone else didn't mean I couldn't enjoy window shopping, right?

He threw his arms straight out to his sides, and I could see his skin rippling over the planes of his chest and shoulders. I saw a cascade of fur that started at his chest and swallowed his entire body. I watched as his limbs changed and his body followed. He seemed at peace with it. I wanted to ask if it hurt, because it sure had when I'd done it earlier.

I hadn't realized it, but he'd slipped off the boxers when I'd shut my eyes. I hadn't even noticed, so wrapped up in watching his skin change that I didn't look. I'm still not sure how I missed that. Right in front of me, however, stood a lean black wolf. It had to be Logan.

We walked away from where his torn boxers lay in the mud, and took off at a run through the woods, chasing, playing and nipping at each other almost like a race where there was no finish line and no prize, a competition for the sake of the race itself.

CHAPTER TWENTY FIVE

L ogan followed Sam as she ran through the woods. Something was going to happen, and he didn't like being in the position of figuring out what was coming and how to stop it. He didn't know who was in more danger at the moment; Sam, or himself.

It's all a test, he thought, as he ran through the woods. Max was testing him, and Sam, and what they'd do. Logan figured he'd screwed up by not bringing Sam around Max more often. Her behavior when they'd arrived at the barn threw him badly. It wasn't the thought of being romantically involved with her. He thought he'd rather like that. The problem was her immediate deference to him as an alpha male in the car, and her own dominance display when she stepped in front of Max to protect Logan. Instead of going to her house all the time to counsel her, he should have brought her to the barn. No matter that it would have run the risk of Sam finding Stephen. And that was the excuse he'd given himself to keep away from Max.

Max hadn't been happy, although he'd professed understanding, and seemed pleased at her reaction to Logan. He'd dangled the same carrot in front of Logan again; more power within the pack in exchange for attempting Max's theories on breeding a born wolf. Not that Logan was opposed to the attempting with Sam, but he was no one's lab wolf. He was too afraid of the type of experimentation Max would require, and the level of involvement Max would want or demand. He had a sudden mental image of Max holding a flashlight above the bed and telling him what he was doing wrong while he tried to have sex with Sam. Oh, hell no. He'd follow his dad's example and kill himself before he allowed himself to be anyone's experiment. Of course, that thought made him wonder again at how far Max had pushed for his father to sink low enough to take his own life.

He followed Sam, letting her set the pace, watching her revel in the sensory overload he remembered from his own first run. Despite Max's plotting and deception with the rest of the pack, he had done one thing right. All the wolves had a place to call home. The woods, the grass, the mud, the wildflowers all coalesced into that heady soup that smelled like home. If Logan could find a way for the wolves to keep that feeling while getting rid of Max's power struggles and politicking, he'd be ecstatic.

He was disturbed from his mental category of worries by the far off scent of a menthol cigarette. He smelled unwashed men, far off, and realized Sam was headed right for them.

It was a security risk for strange men to be on their land. There had been one incident of strange werewolves seeking them out, just days ago. Max and George were the ones who found the wolves, trapped them, brought them back to the barn, and drugged them so they could dispose of them. Logan couldn't figure why Max had drawn the line at killing them himself. He'd felt the urge to fight them, to defend their territory, and knew Max had to feel it as well, but instead, Max had put together an elaborate plan to get them gone without bloodshed. He hoped Max was right that the two wolves would cooperate. He wasn't sure if he would have.

Last he'd heard the two interlopers were still guests of the dog warden. He wondered how long Max could spin it out before they were adopted out as pets or destroyed. When he'd asked, Max told him to mind his own business.

This time it was absolutely his business. He was the alpha wolf who'd caught the trespassers. He would be the one to take care of it. He could send a strong message to Sam, to the rest of the pack, and to Max that he was the rightful leader, instead of Max's regime of fear and paranoia. They'd be better off if he could just figure out how to pull it off.

Sam stopped and barked as he shot ahead of her, scenting the air to guess the distance between them and the men. He had no doubt they were men, and not wolves. He wondered if they realized the danger they were in. Max was known to order human trespassers killed, even if he drew the line at killing actual werewolves himself. In Max's own words, there weren't very many, and they were too valuable. It made Logan feel like a chest of gold coins rather than a sentient being.

Ah, there it was. That scent, baked beans and menthol cigarettes, men who hadn't bathed for a couple days, motor oil, and gun oil, tickled his nose and he stopped dead. The twigs suddenly felt brittle and unstable, and he felt them crack under his weight. He growled a warning at Sam to stop as he fell through the ground into a pit about thirty feet deep.

Logan didn't get a chance to catch himself. He'd been a wolf for fifteen years, but he still reached out with his forelegs to catch himself as a human would do with their hands, grabbing for any surface to break their fall. His paws hit solid, sheer dirt, with tree roots trimmed closely and not providing much of a handhold. Even if they had provided a handhold, his claws couldn't get a grasp to hang onto them and he fell to the ground, hearing a crack when his back leg buckled under him. He couldn't prevent a yelp of pain as his foot gave way.

Secondary to his pain was worry for Sam. She'd not been prepared for confronting humans that didn't know about werewolves when she was in wolf form. He cursed his lack of vocal chords. He couldn't tell her what to do without shifting, and couldn't risk hunters finding him after a shift, human, naked, and crippled. He'd have to stay in wolf form, which would take all his strength, and hope Sam was smart enough to go for help. He saw her worried face peering over the edge of the hole he'd fallen into, and realized that the walls of the pit were man-made, sheer, and smooth, as if someone had cut a perfectly square hole into the earth. Someone had planned this.

It had to be Max. And he couldn't do a thing about it. Max was the only one that could help him at the moment, and he wasn't sure his alpha would lift a finger.

He shut his eyes, and heard Sam's feet on the path running away. He felt the urge to change back into his human form, and fought it. The change itself would help heal his foot, but he'd never been able to rapidly change between forms. He hoped she had enough energy to hurry, and curled up in a corner, dragging his injured foot painfully behind him.

CHAPTER TWENTY SIX

I hate to run. It's something I do so I can catch bad guys. I hate running in circles around a track because it's boring. Running on asphalt hurts my knees and feet for some reason. I have a treadmill at home to stay in shape and watch movies at the same time. Nothing like watching Mel Gibson or Jackie Chan getting their asses handed to them to distract myself from the hell of running for exercise, and for training, because I needed it in my job.

This time it felt glorious. I could feel each new, or rather, changed, muscle in my legs and back stretch out and reach for the next bit of ground as I ran, almost heedless to where I was headed or my surroundings.

It was a beautiful summer evening. I could smell the wildflowers and the moss on the ground, and I reveled in it. Logan chased me, sometimes pulling ahead to point out the right direction, other times falling behind to allow me the freedom to run. My nose and my brain were full from the different scents, and my heart sang as I ran.

Suddenly, Logan stopped about fifty feet in front of me, and he sniffed the air. I heard a crashing sound, and a yelp, and he fell through the ground. Wait, that couldn't be right. Fell through the ground?

Yup, he sure had. I heard him whimper, and I inched my way over to him. I could hear the sounds of men coming toward us through the woods, and I caught the scent of freshly dug soil. Freshly dug? In the middle of a private wooded lot? It didn't make sense to me.

I took a ginger step forward and saw where Logan had fallen. There were long broken branches spread with grass over it. At the speed we'd been running, it was no wonder he hadn't seen it, but it was a trap. Just like in the movies, someone had dug a hole and covered it with branches to see what they could catch.

Logan wasn't moving much. I looked down, and saw him, still in wolf form. Even though he hadn't changed back, he was hurt. From my position, it looked like he'd broken his leg. I had no idea whether the fast healing he'd told me about would be a problem before someone could set that leg, but there was no doubt he needed out of that hole. I glanced at the edges, a perfect, almost smooth drop. There was no way he could climb out as a wolf. I couldn't begin to guess how I'd climb in to help, and if I did, I wasn't sure what I could do to help. I whimpered and jerked my head in the direction of the barn. At his nod, I turned toward help.

The men I'd heard in the woods were getting closer. I could smell as well as hear them, though I couldn't see them. If I'd met them as a human female, I'd be repulsed at how bad they smelled, but as a wolf, it was just a scent I could use to figure out how far away they were. I had no idea where the hole had come from, but if they found Logan, he wouldn't be able to get away. I had no gun. I had no badge. I was outside my jurisdiction, and I couldn't speak. I'd always taken my radio for granted. There was no backup unless I went all the way back to get it.

I found the scent of our trail and ran as if my life depended on it. Maybe Logan's life did. I had to get to Max. I hoped we hadn't crossed into someone else's property. That would be awkward to explain, and wouldn't look good on the newbie wolf joining the pack. If I did join, that is. I still wasn't sold on the whole idea, but I didn't yet know what my options were.

By the time I got back to the covered tunnel we'd left earlier, I was stuck. I had no idea how I was going to open that damn door. It was a regular door knob, and not something my wolf paws would be able to grasp and open. Out of breath and panicked, I noticed a security camera hidden near the door. It was time to get some attention.

I looked for an intercom with a call button, but I didn't see one. Even if there had been a call button, I had no idea how to change into a human to use it. It wasn't something I'd seen anyone do, so I didn't even know how to try. There was no doorbell. There were no windows. There wasn't even a doggie door. I'd think there'd be some way for us to slip into the building in wolf form, but I couldn't find it. Note to self; make suggestion for wolf shaped entranceway if I got Logan out of this mess.

I positioned myself in front of the camera and threw my shoulder against the heavy door. I figured a panicking wolf making a racket would bring some attention, in the form of someone who could help Logan, or at least show me how to change so I could tell them what I'd seen.

It only took three or four tries before Max came out with guys I'd seen watching the security camera screens. Six men poured into the woods behind us. Max recognized me, and knelt, concern and confusion on his face. I didn't like that the men behind him were armed since I didn't know them, but I wasn't in a position to complain. I had no idea what Logan was facing.

I felt blood ooze down my muzzle where the branches I'd crashed through left scratches on my mad dash back. My lungs hurt since I'd winded myself trying to get their attention. If it was possible to hyperventilate and pant at the same time, I was doing it. I whined in frustration. Even if I'd been human, I'd have been too out of breath to speak. I'm sure my eyes were rolled back with panic and exhaustion. I felt saliva dripping from my mouth as I gulped for air. Yuck.

"Damn it. Something's happened, and I don't think she knows how to change back yet. It's got to be Logan, we just sent him out with her on her first run. He wouldn't have left her alone if he wasn't hurt." He looked at me, and grasped my face in his hands, forcing me to look at him. "Sam, I know you're winded. You've done very well. I need you to take us back to where Logan is. Can you do it? Can you lead us to him?"

I tried to nod, still gulping air. Lassie never got winded like this. It wasn't fair, damn it.

"Let's go."

I yipped, and took off at a run, and they were able to keep up with me, even in human form. I was amazed at how fast they were, and made another mental note to ask Logan about it. That might make for interesting runs with the department when we did our yearly fitness tests.

We got there just as a group of men came out of the woods near the pit Logan had fallen into. We stopped before we got too close to them, and they didn't see us approach. I noticed that the men with Max spread into the woods and took positions that surrounded the men who'd found us. I heard the humans arguing over whether to shoot the wolf, and I growled softly.

Max caught up with me. He dropped his hand to my ear, and gave me a reassuring pat and scratch. "Good girl.

I've got it now. Don't worry. We'll get him. He'll be fine, I promise."

He stepped into the group of hunters dressed in a mish-mash of torn denim, plaid, camouflage, and dirty John Deere hats, calling out, "So, have you seen my dog?"

Their heads whipped around and took in Max and his visible backup, carrying military grade rifles, and wearing pistols on their belts. One of the hunters stepped forward and muttered, "No. What I have seen is a wild, rabid wolf, and I intend to shoot it before it can hurt anybody. We've seen wolves around, and we don't want them attacking livestock or tearing up fields."

Max was pissed. It was pure rage, and it came off him in waves. I let out a whimper at the ferocity of his emotion. That brought their attention to me, and then they looked back at Max.

"I breed and raise dogs. I see you've got this one's mate in that pit you've dug illegally on my land." Max stood, and I understood now how he was the pack leader. Some leaders just have that aura of leadership. Max didn't; he had a "you really don't want to fuck with me" aura. That works too.

"We didn't dig that pit. It was already here. And this property is part of the game reserve attached to the park, it's not private property. We've got hunting licenses, so there shouldn't be a problem." He pushed back the grease stained cap, and I saw the cigarette hanging from his lips. I wanted to shove it down his throat and rip the mullet from his head.

"First of all, gentlemen, let me tell you I've had my property surveyed to make sure of the boundaries, and you crossed a six foot high fence about two miles back that marks the edge of my property. Even if we were on game reserve property, it's illegal to hunt, even with a license, on government property. That dog's trained very well not to cross the property boundaries, so I have every reason to doubt what you say. Besides that, this dog belongs to me, so, in effect, regardless of whether you're trespassing; you're damaging my property. That's a valuable hunting and guard dog, as well as being highly valuable for breeding purposes. I'm sure you don't want to have to pay my damages if something happens to that dog."

Breeding purposes? His mate? I couldn't believe I was hearing this. It wasn't that it didn't make sense as a cover story, but Max said it like it was true. It made me wonder about other consequences of being a wolf. I'd have to find a woman in the pack to ask some very personal, but practical questions. Questions I'd feel uncomfortable asking Logan. I mean, a girl can't just ask a guy about how to carry tampons when she's in wolf form, can she? And what would it all mean for my relationship with Justin? Come to think of it, I hadn't seen any women in the pack at this point. I wondered why.

I growled at Max, and he shot me a warning look, so I turned that anger on the hunters. We'd talk later. I'm not here for breeding purposes, and if he thought otherwise, I'd have to disabuse him of that notion. I wasn't sure quite how I'd do that, but it wasn't up for negotiation.

"Damn you. This land is prime hunting land. There's no reason to keep it from the public. That's selfish." He actually pouted. "We have every right to be here."

I bared my teeth at him. This guy can't be this stupid. Only a moron surrounded by men who obviously outclassed him in weapons and gear would make such an asinine comment. Oh, wait. He couldn't see all of Max's men. Two of them had taken up positions a hundred yards or so away, and set up sniper angles. The other four were hidden by trees nearer to Max and me. With their human eyesight, the brave idiots couldn't see them. I don't care; it was still dumb.

Max called out to his non-sniper men who were still in the trees. I saw them edge out, guns aimed at the hunters. I could see that the rest of them were ready to leave. They dropped their own guns and raised their hands, then tried to tell their buddy to shut the hell up. He didn't want to, but they finally convinced him it was time to go.

"Actually, there's every reason to keep idiots like you off my land. My dogs are worth more than you. They're obviously under better control. Even if I didn't, I have the right as a property owner to deny permission to cross my lands to anyone for any reason unless you are a law enforcement agent with a duly executed warrant. I suggest you remove yourself from my property, and don't return. Not only are my men well trained to defend my property, but I'll call the police, and I'll file criminal charges for trespassing as well as a civil suit for damaging my dog. And that's if you don't get shot for sneaking onto my property armed and without permission."

It took a little more argument. I was happy to see Max invoking the power of the police to resolve the dispute, even in the center of our 'secret' hideaway. I wasn't sure if Max would actually call them, but the fact that he'd even brought it up made me feel better. The hunter who'd argued with Max kept trying to press his point, and his buddies dragged him away. They wandered back the way they came, and Max sent some of the men with them to point out the boundaries. In his words, they were to make sure that the hunters got the message to never do this again. His men nodded gravely, and walked them away.

Once they were out of sight, Max and another man climbed down into the hole to retrieve Logan, who wasn't as badly hurt as he'd looked. As they carried him back to the barn, I felt a sense of relief. Logan's injured paw hung from Max's arms. He opened his eyes and saw me, and if a wolf could smile, he was grinning wide enough for me to believe that he'd live.

Chapter Twenty Seven

Logan was okay, but he did need medical treatment. A young guy with a wild mop of blond hair, the same one who had checked my pulse when I was here the last time, whisked him away to treat his leg. I assumed the guy had some medical training. At least he talked like he did, though he looked too young to be a doctor. I heard the other wolves call him by name. Adam.

Someone else was going to have to talk me back into human form. I had no idea how to pull it off, and there was no way I could go home in this state. Doyle would have a fit, even assuming that I made it home as a wild wolf with no license or owner holding a leash. Max took it on himself to explain and walked me through it.

"Sam, you've got to relax. When you change into a wolf, you have to harness strong emotions, like anger or jealousy. You need to focus on something important to you as a human to help you want to change back. Sometimes it's really tempting to want to stay in wolf form, so we have to remind ourselves why we live a split life. Find something meaningful to you, something you'd miss if you didn't return to your human life, and make it your focus. We can always help you find a different focus down the road if you need to, but think of something that has a recent and emotional meaning," he patiently explained. "Sometimes fear or pain helps us become human again. Let's not go there, at least not your first time."

Gee thanks, I thought. Relax, or I gotta hurt you? Not great options.

I thought of Justin's laugh, and felt my own humanity, for lack of a better word to describe it, seep into my pores. After a few false starts, I got it. Max seemed surprised I'd pulled it off on the third try. "Well, that's pretty good. I think you're gonna surprise us all over time, Samantha."

As I'd suspected from watching Logan change earlier, it wasn't as painful to be able to go slowly and carefully, without a fight. I closed my eyes as I finished the change, not wanting to meet Max's as I became fully human and stood in front of him stark naked.

Any woman in her right mind is self-conscious to appear in front of someone naked for the first time. It's a little less intimidating when both parties are disrobing at once, or if the two of them are distracted by impending sex or foreplay. I had no such feelings for Max. He was old enough to be my dad. Yuck. And he'd been talking about me as breeding stock not twenty minutes ago. Double yuck. I wanted to cover myself, but I refused to cower in front of him. Hey, when all else fails, try appearing brave. If nothing else, it'll impress the person standing in front of you, even if the sight of your bare ass doesn't.

Max looked me square in the eyes rather than at my chest, which I appreciated. He said he'd go find out where

Logan had clothes for me. He pulled the door shut, and just before it closed all the way, he stuck his head back in. "I'd strongly suggest that you don't go wandering around in the halls until we get your clothes. Most of the pack members are men, and wouldn't be used to a woman your age walking around down here without clothes on."

"No problem. Trust me I don't plan on going far like this." Speaking felt odd, but I was grateful for the ability to communicate in ways I'd taken for granted in the past. I'd never take it for granted again. He'd also said that "most" of the pack members were men. That must mean that there were other women.

Before I could say anything, or ask about other women, he walked out, and I started looking at the room around me. I was in the room Logan had called the Lounge on my first trip to the barn. I didn't want to sit on any of the leather furniture without pants on, so I was stuck wandering until someone came back with my clothes. I started browsing books on the shelf.

I saw bestsellers, weapons manuals, and user's guides on security equipment, treatises on biology, genetics, chemistry, folklore, mythology, history, and religion. I thumbed through a couple of them, and a slip of paper fell out.

It was a childhood photo, and it looked a lot like Logan, but it was in black and white. It was clearly taken fifty years or so ago, making it very definitely not Logan himself. The child in the picture looked like he was about seven years old, with a dark brown crew cut and a gap toothed smile.

I flipped it over, and saw that whoever the child was had inscribed it to Bobby, his best friend. It was a sweet picture, of an obviously charming little boy, whose name was Mark, according to the childish scrawl at the bottom of the page. I smiled. I wondered if Mark or Bobby were a part of the pack. I hoped that freckle faced kid wasn't one of the men I'd seen in the hallway. I replaced the photo in the book, and kept on looking.

As I looked, I saw that the books had obviously been donated from different members or bought at secondhand shops. Different names were written on the flyleaf of each book. Some of them were dog-eared. Others had been highlighted, or notes written in ink in the margins. It looked as if different members of the pack had turned over their college textbooks to build a decent reference library, but none of them were interesting to me.

I couldn't help myself. I went back over to the leather bound book I'd seen when I was here before. Logan had said it was some kind of big deal, history or something, that none of them was allowed to see. I'd originally thought it was something old, but the binding on the book just didn't look aged. To my untrained eye, it looked like someone had bought a leather bound book ten or fifteen years ago and banged it up a bit to make it look older. I wondered if Dad would agree with me. Too bad I couldn't open the glass case and look at it closer. The case was locked shut, and I had no clue where the key would be.

Okay, someone could get here any minute with my clothes. It was a bit drafty here, and I crossed my arms over my chest. I was glad that no one had come in, but there really wasn't a lot of heat in the room. We were underground, after all. I started to wish that I was still in wolf form. At least that way I'd still have a fur coat.

I rubbed my upper shoulders, and kept moving around the room. There was one book I saw that looked interesting, and I plucked it off the shelf to take a look. It was a first edition, something Dad would've been over the moon about. It was a copy of Aldous Huxley's Brave New World. There was a bookplate inside the front cover, which would kill its resale value, but the bookplate was made out to Robert Andrews.

That wasn't a name I knew. I couldn't place it, but I probably wouldn't forget it. I wanted to tell the real owner of the book how much money he'd thrown down the toilet by putting his name in it, but at that point, there was a knock at the door. I shoved the book back onto the shelf and hurried over to the door. I stuck my head out, hiding my nakedness behind the doorframe. It was the friendly guy from earlier.

"Here are your clothes. I'm George, by the way."

I snatched them and mumbled a thank you. I realized Logan had grabbed a shirt and shorts and shoes, but no socks, and no bra. I guess he was in a hurry to get me out of there, but I grumbled. At least he'd remembered underpants. I'd have to keep a bag packed in the car for this sort of thing, with appropriate undergarments and socks.

I felt like a slut as I put on my clothes without a bra. Good girls just don't do that, or at least they don't do that if they possess boobs bigger than a B-cup. I'm a solid C, which meant going without a bra was an invitation to wobbly disaster and ogling embarrassment. Strange, I hadn't really felt that way when I was naked. It was just the lack of a bra that made me feel that way. The fact that the t-shirt was white didn't help.

I begged George to take me home. No amount of convincing could get me to stay and wait for Logan. Reluctantly, Max came in and allowed George to give me a ride. I kept my arms crossed over my chest for the entire trip.

He dropped me off a block away from my house, and explained with a mischievous grin that we didn't want too many different cars belonging to pack members to be seen at or near anyone's home. They were concerned about someone noticing strange traffic patterns. I was concerned about the entire neighborhood seeing me get out of a strange car wearing a white tee shirt without a bra. I didn't want my neighbors to think I'd turned into slut girl. That'd be more of a concern to them than strange cars. My next door neighbors are a couple of nosey old women who always want to give advice on what good girls should do. Their advice probably isn't far wrong for girls who were single and young fifty years or so ago, and they mean well, but it's still really annoying and embarrassing.

I gave him a nasty glare as I got out of his car. In the space of a day, I'd patched up a relationship, worried about my partner, faced down gunshots, changed into a wolf for the first time and back and then watched the closest thing I had to a friend in the pack hurt and scared by a bunch of redneck hunters, and he was worried about strange cars at my house? Sounded like a bad case of someone's priorities being out of whack.

A block of fuming later and I let myself inside, muttering about priorities in life. Doyle met me at the door, purring and glad to see me. I hadn't gotten that reaction from him in a long time. I smiled as he leapt into my arms. At least something in my life was getting better.

CHAPTER TWENTY EIGHT

I had to go back to work the next day, as if nothing was wrong. Halfway through the morning, which mainly consisted of filing vehicle impound releases in a battered steel filing cabinet, I got a call from Justin.

"Sam?"

"Hi."

"How are you?"

"I'm okay. How're you doing?"

"I'm fine." I heard something odd in his voice. He was upset about something, but I couldn't tell what.

I also couldn't ask him about it. Two officers came in to drop off incident packets, and any girlfriend-type questioning I wanted to do would have to wait for later or start the department rumor mill. Maybe I could be subtle. "I don't believe you."

"It doesn't really matter, Sam. Anyway, I'm not calling to talk about us. I'm calling to tell you that the forensics just came back on your attack. The assigned detective will likely come see you soon to formally notify you?"

"Notify me?" That caught my attention, and distracted me from his bad attitude.

"They have a suspect in custody."

I hadn't thought about the attack at all today, or in the past couple of days, and I gulped down a shudder when I thought about it all in light of what I now knew about the pack. I dropped the phone in shock, and then scrambled to catch it before it hit the counter.

"Sam?"

"I'm here. Do you know who it is?"

"You know I can't tell you that. I'm not supposed to know this much. The detective will tell you what he can, but they're really being careful on this one. No risk of tainting any testimony or identification. They're even doing a live ID line-up with all the witnesses to see what people can remember. No loopholes for defense attorneys."

He kept talking, but I had no idea what he was saying. My mind reeled as I tried to figure it out. Last night I'd been too busy taking it all in, with the final certainty of what I'd become and Logan's injury to think much about where I fit into the whole scheme of things.

There had been no mention of any other werewolves even existing outside of our pack. Even if there were other werewolves, there was no warning that they were in the area or that they were dangerous. I had to assume that if there were others, that I'd have been warned. If there were no other werewolves in the area than the pack itself, one of the members of the pack had to be the one who had attacked me.

I wondered if Max was aware of it, or if he'd ordered it. I didn't like the thought, but it would make a lot of sense, at least in my mind for someone who was so paranoid about security to recruit a person with law enforcement experience.

Wait a minute. That didn't make a whole lot of sense, either. Much as I thought of myself as a good police officer, I certainly wasn't an experienced one. If they really wanted someone to be a security expert, they would've chosen someone with more experience. Justin would have made a better target than me, since I'd been on the street less than a year. Much as I didn't like it, I was still a rookie. And Max did seem to have an experienced security force already at the barn, if the incident yesterday was any indication. So what was the motive?

"Sam, are you still there?" His concern came through the phone loud and clear. "Did you hear what I just said?"

I'd been so lost in thought; I'd forgotten I was still on the phone with Justin. "Yeah, I'm here. I'm sorry." I needed to concentrate more on his voice and what he was saying than the commentary in my own head. I wasn't going to come up with all the answers on my own.

"Detective Burns has been assigned to your case. Do you want me to go with you when you meet him?" Justin asked.

"I appreciate the thought, but I don't think it's a good idea. I think they'd figure us out. We need to keep a lid on this for a while."

He took a deep breath. "I didn't think about that. You're right. If I showed up, the department would figure out that we're together, and I don't want to make you the topic of the week at the station. And I guess I'm a potential witness, too, so they wouldn't want me there. Still, I'll go if you need me."

I didn't want him there. It was sad, but true, and I couldn't figure out how to explain it to him without telling him the truth. I wasn't ready to explain the fur yet, so I had to find another way to deal with it. Also, the civilian clerks working the desk with me were starting to pay a little too much attention to my conversation.

He sighed heavily. "Damn it, Sam. Are you gonna go alone?"

"If I can't handle it, I'll call Logan. He's been a big help, and he's not a witness. They probably won't say anything about him being there."

"Logan. Of course." He sounded disgusted.

"What?"

That same oddness was back in his voice. "Well, let's see, Sam. The woman I'm dating shoved me out of the house last night to call another man. I showed up later to see if you were okay, and found the clothes you were wearing on the ground. It looked like they'd been ripped off of you, and you were nowhere to be found, even though you'd told me that you just wanted to sleep. Your laundry was out of the basket and thrown all over the floor in your room. I know I told you to get into counseling, but I've been the one you leaned on up until now. And now you're ripping off your clothes, throwing stuff around the house like you're packing at the last minute for some rendezvous and disappearing just moments after you said you needed sleep? You gotta admit; it looks bad."

I closed my eyes and counted to ten. Yeah, I bet it had looked bad. "This isn't the right place for this conversation. I'm at work."

"You're right."

"You deserve an explanation, and I'd be happy to give it to you, but it'll have to be later."

"I understand." His voice was clipped and angry. I was pretty sure he didn't understand.

"Look, why don't we meet up at my place after work for dinner. It's nothing to worry about, I promise."

"Nothing happened between the two of you?"

"Nothing like that, I swear it."

"I trust you, Sam." Even though his voice said otherwise, he still said it. It meant a lot.

"Look, I'll take a quiet dinner with you after the interview, and a hug, over anything else you could imagine."

That brought a smile. I could hear it in his voice. "Done. Want me to pick something up? I can meet you with takeout if you want."

"Um, let's see. Chinese?"

"That works. What do you want?"

"Moo Shu Pork with extra plum sauce. Crab Rangoon."

"See you at your place at five thirty tonight. Call me if you need me earlier." I could hear it in his voice. He wanted me to call. He needed to see that I still needed him.

"I will. Thanks for the heads up."

"No problem."

He hung up, and I caught three clerks watching me expectantly. I told them that it was Mom on the phone and refused to elaborate. They teased me mercilessly about my "mystery boyfriend", but I didn't give anything away. If I couldn't fix this thing with Justin, there was no sense in giving them gossip material. On the other hand, there was nothing like the knowledge that a hot guy and a hot meal would be waiting for me at the end of the day. I could handle quite a bit with that to look forward to.

A few hours later, I recognized Detective Joseph Burns when he approached the window. I took a deep breath, and steeled myself to take whatever he said in a calm manner. Max had explained that I wouldn't need to change again for another couple of days at least, but it wouldn't be a bad idea to practice remaining calm. According to him, the trick was to spot stressful situations early and be proactive about managing stress. I was about to see if I could pull it off.

"Officer Hochenwalt, it's good to see you. You seem to be recovering well."

"A lot better than I thought I would, Detective." I grinned. Detective Burns was one of our top homicide/assault detectives and had a reputation for being hardworking, tenacious, and perceptive. I couldn't think of anyone I'd prefer to handle my case. Then I realized I now had something to hide. Heaven knows how I was going to explain it all to Justin tonight, much less to the detective in front of me.

"We have a suspect in custody for assaulting you."

Adrenaline shot up the back of my throat and I could taste it, sickening and sharp at the same time. As I took a deep breath, I realized that incarcerating a werewolf could be a huge problem for me as well as the rest of the pack. If that person was in jail he would eventually have to change. The secret would be out. What would that mean for me remaining on the force?

"Hock? You all right?" I didn't remember sitting down, but I was doing just that on the stool just inside the police information window.

"Yeah, I'm fine. I just didn't expect things to happen quite so fast."

"If you're up to it, we're setting up a lineup upstairs."

"You mean point him out while he's in the same room with me?" I took a deep breath. "Yeah, I'm okay to be there, but I'm not sure I saw enough to be able to identify someone. I'm going to ask a favor."

"Shoot."

"Can I call my trauma counselor? I'd like to have him here when I do this." If nothing else, maybe I'd get a minute to ask Logan what would happen if I identified a pack member as my attacker. I wanted whoever had done this to me to pay, but I wasn't completely stupid. I needed to be prepared for what would happen if I could point them out.

"No problem. I heard you were seeing Logan Boyd. There's no one better in my opinion. I spoke to him myself when I dealt with a shooting. Want me to call him for you?"

Several years ago, then Officer Burns had to shoot a suspect on PCP who charged his cruiser as he drove down the street on his way to an emergency call. I'd heard about it at the police academy and didn't understand why he did therapy. I understood why now. There was nothing like real life experience to teach the truth of someone else's words. Even without the fur problem I'd still have needed counseling of some kind. I agreed to let the detective call Logan. I couldn't very well ask what I needed to know with the other clerks listening in, so it wouldn't matter who called him.

"All right. I'll call and come back down to get you when everything's set up."

"Today? We're doing this right now?" I was incredulous. That was fast work.

"Yeah, right now. I've got the prosecutor upstairs, and we're transporting the prisoners over for the lineup as we speak.

I swallowed hard. "Okay, I'll be ready." I took a deep breath as he turned around and got back on the elevator. I knew I'd feel better once the man who'd done this to me was behind bars. The real question, though, was how the other wolves would take it. I hoped Logan could shed a bit more light on the situation before I had to make a decision.

Chapter Twenty Nine

Nadia answered her cell phone as she pulled out of her dad's driveway. "Hello?"

"Hello, Nadia. Have you talked to Sam?" It was Sam's mom, Kathy.

"Not for a day or so. She seems so much better lately."

"Yeah, she does, but I'm worried about her. Justin's not doing so well, and I'm wondering if they've had a fight. John's worried about him."

"Last I heard, they'd made up from their latest argument. It didn't sound like there was any trouble in paradise to me." Nadia smiled. She and Kathy had been trying to maneuver Sam and Justin together for months. She pulled onto the highway, headed for her job at the mall.

"Well, Justin called me last night, rather upset. He was looking for Sam, said he couldn't find her. I told him she was probably with you somewhere."

"No, ma'am, I haven't seen her. I haven't talked to her for two days. I know she went back to work yesterday, and I tried to call her when I left the animal shelter, but no one answered. I figured she was out with Justin, or exhausted, so I didn't call again."

"Well, apparently she wasn't with him." Kathy was worried, and Nadia could hear it plainly in her voice.

"Kathy, don't hang on too tight just because of what happened. Sam would hate that."

There was an awkward silence on the other end of the phone. "Nadia, I wouldn't want Sam to get upset, but I'm really worried about her. I know part of it's because of what happened, but there's just something here that's not quite right. Call it mother's intuition if you want, but something's wrong and I don't just mean a squabble between her and Justin. It's something bigger than that."

"Mrs. Hochenwalt, if there was something that big, don't you think Sam would have told me by now? Even if she asked me to keep it a secret, I'd know. I wouldn't betray her confidence, but if there was something to worry about, I'd tell you to go bug her about it. She hasn't said a word about anything other than arguments between her and Justin. I know she's on edge because of what happened, but she's talking to that Boyd guy."

"You think maybe it's the counseling that's causing her to act differently?"

Nadia knew that tone of voice she heard on the other end of the phone. It was the tone Sam hated. Nadia had played the go-between with Sam and her mom ever since Sam joined the police department. Ten minutes of calming Kathy down kept Sam from getting upset with her mom, and kept Kathy from driving herself nuts with worry. It was a compromise that Nadia was happy to fulfill, ever since her own mother died two years earlier. Kathy had been the mom that Nadia missed so desperately through her own mother's long fight with cancer, and she was happy to play mediator to repay the Hochenwalts' kindness during that time.

It also helped take her mind off the coming hours of convincing customers why they needed apple berry peach vanilla blossom body spray along with the matching lotion, and hand scrub. Nadia indulged herself every once in a while, but some things were just outrageous. Too bad she didn't work on commission. She'd started to dread driving to work because it drove her nuts, but she needed the job to help pay her expenses in the fall.

She smiled at Kathy's insecurity, knowing it came from genuine worry about her daughter. "Relax, Kathy. I'm sure it's just the counseling. Going over all of it can't be easy, but she'll come out of it better, and stronger in the end."

"You're right, Nadia. I'm sorry to bother you. I know you're busy this summer."

The two of them chatted about Nadia's job at the animal shelter for a few minutes, as Nadia headed toward the hours of drudgery. Nadia told her about the dogs she'd helped save and Kathy invited her over for dinner later that week.

"So, whose heart are you breaking this week?"

She laughed in response. "None. Ever since I dumped that guy who thought all veterinarians treated farm animals and asked why I wanted to spend my life with my hand inside a cow, I've been flying solo. Not that there's anything wrong with a large animal practice, but he was just weird. He kept talking about it, like he thought it was cool. He kept wanting to know what that felt like. I told him to go find out for himself. I think I'm just a magnet for weirdoes, so I'll take myself out of the running for a bit to see what else comes up."

Kathy laughed out loud, and repeated the conversation to Nathan in the background. Nadia could hear his laughter, and accepted the dinner invitation Kathy extended. She hung up the phone. Maybe now that the danger seemed to be over for Sam, she'd ask about cute cops, or even that counselor. Even Kathy said he was good-looking. It was time to go back to a normal life, instead of furtive phone calls between Kathy, Justin, and Nadia, worried about Sam.

She knew Sam would agree. She made up her mind to call Sam again when she got home from work, and make plans for a girl's night out. They'd all earned it, with all they'd been through, and she'd make sure to collect.

CHAPTER THIRTY

D etective Burns came back ninety minutes later. I'd just taken a bite of the sandwich I'd brought for lunch. I wasn't hungry, but I'd been lectured by Logan and Max about making sure to eat to maintain my metabolism and not get my blood sugar and adrenaline out of whack. Like everything else, keeping my blood sugar regulated was supposed to help control my shifts. I was sick to my stomach by the time he showed up, so I was happy to rewrap the sandwich and put in back in the refrigerator.

"Detective Burns, if you're working this case, then you know I was attacked from behind. I'm not sure I got a good look at anyone. I don't know how I'd pick them out of a line-up." *Please tell me I don't have to do this.*

"Yes, I saw your written statement. We're doing this because we want to make sure. And we'll do a voice line-up as well. You wrote in your statement that the person who attacked you spoke to you. We're doing everything we can think of on this one. If it turns out you can ID the guy, the case is stronger, and you know that."

"I know. I guess I'm just a little bit nervous."

"That's understandable, Hock. It's okay if you can't recognize anyone, but do your best. By the way, Mr. Boyd's waiting for you upstairs. He was already in the building for a meeting with one of our training lieutenants and the chief. You ready to get this over with?"

"Yeah, let's get it done." I transferred the phones to one of the clerks, and let them know where I was headed. I squared my shoulders and realized that he was treating me like another officer, a comrade rather than a victim. It helped.

Too many officers tiptoed around me now like they didn't know if they'd stop on my toes or make me cry. Officers tend to give others in stressful situations the stiff upper lip treatment when it hits a little too close to home, but I could see it in their eyes. They all wondered how they would handle it, or were afraid that it would happen to them. Some came up and wanted to talk about it, and how they were feeling about it. I was patient, although I had to suppress the urge to grab them by their lapels and scream into their faces, "Yeah, it could happen to you, but it did happen to me. Trust me it's worse than you could ever fucking imagine!" Yeah, I'm still dealing with post-attack anger.

I followed him to the detective section, the part of the building that housed the offices of most of the detectives for the Dayton Police Department. I've been in the room many times. I've escorted prisoners for questioning by the detectives and attended pre- and post-search warrant briefings, but it seemed to have taken on a different aura, for lack of a better word, when I walked in as a victim. Logan was standing near a small row of chairs that faced the old stage where they'd line up the prisoners.

Unlike what's on television and in the movies, we don't have the budget for the fancy interrogation rooms with the two way mirrors. We do photo lineups rather than live ID lineups because it's harder to find live bodies that look close enough to be a fair identification array than to find them in BMV photos and booking photo records. It was unusual to have a live ID lineup. It's also rare for an officer to be hurt as badly as I had been. They were going the extra mile.

When I say that, I don't mean that officers don't get hurt. Mostly, though, injuries to an officer are from being kicked by an angry crack whore, punched once or twice by a drunken wife beater, or they get a knee scraped when chasing a suspect over a chain link fence. It's much rarer that an officer would be hurt badly enough to go to the emergency room. A couple of times a month someone goes to the ER for stitches. It's only once a year or so that someone's hurt enough to be hospitalized overnight, and my injuries would've kept anyone else for at least a week, if not longer. It scared a few people, and I could see it in their faces after I came back.

Detective Burns directed me to a chair, and I sat down gingerly. I was grateful to have Logan there, but he gave me a hard look. I glared at him, since he hadn't said anything that helped me to understand why. He grabbed my hand and gave me the stink eye again. I was upset, but I took the look he gave me as a warning to calm down. I took a deep breath and closed my eyes and Logan patted my hand.

I opened them a moment later to find Jonathan Wingard walking into the room. A county prosecutor with a reputation for toughness, fairness, and thorough trial preparation, he'd been around for nearly twenty years. I hadn't had a case with him before, but I'd heard of him. He was no longer just an assistant, but was one of the supervisors in the office, and current word of mouth had him as one of the contenders for the top job should the head of the office ever decide to step down. He was well known in the police department for taking cases a lot of other prosecutors wouldn't touch with a ten foot pole, and he got convictions.

Logan got up and introduced himself to the prosecutor, and I noticed that he limped slightly. I realized that the fall he'd taken the night before would've put anyone else on crutches, but he'd be healed within a day or so. When they asked if he was okay, he explained the limp as a jogging injury, a mild sprain. That kind of rapid healing would take some getting used to.

While they finished setting up the room, I glanced around. I saw the wanted posters on their corkboard. There's always a corkboard with wanted posters in each main room in a police department. Some of them are brand new, and others were yellowed with age, their edges covered with new notices. I've stood in front of that corkboard wondering at the different faces when I've waited for other officers in the past.

As the others played the politics game, shaking hands around the room, I found myself too agitated to sit still. I stood up and walked over to the wanted posters. One of the older ones was so yellowed that the print was fading, and the photo quality wasn't great. The edges were curling up. The name read Robert Andrews, a name I'd seen somewhere before. He was listed as armed and dangerous, and was wanted for crimes ranging from rape to murder and assault with a deadly weapon. Since the poster was still up, I assumed he was still at large, but it was over fifteen years old. Who knew where he could be now?

Detective Burns cleared his throat loudly, getting everyone's attention, and the moment of truth was at hand. He called me back to the chairs to sit down. They darkened the room, and turned on the lights to the stage. Two officers led seven men onto the platform. I thought I recognized a few from previous arrests, and then I watched the last guy step onto the stage.

I knew him. It was Stephen Tipton, an asshole I'd arrested the day before I was attacked, a man whose wife and daughter were regular callers for violations of their protection order.

I remembered the night of the attack. My attacker whispered something along the lines of me now understanding. It all clicked into place. I knew he was the one who'd attacked me, but I couldn't point him out in that lineup. I hadn't even seen him that night, even though I'd been to his ex-wife's house just before he'd hurt me. I knew it was him, but identifying him would be a lie, since I hadn't seen him that night. And if he'd attacked me, he was the same as I was; a werewolf whose problems would be revealed if he ever spent significant time in lockup.

"Officer Hochenwalt, are you okay?" Detective Burns asked.

"I'll be fine. Let's get this over with." I continued to look over each and every one of them, trying desperately not to linger too long on Tipton.

"Do you recognize anyone?"

"Yes. I recognize several of them. I've arrested four people in this lineup in the past."

"Do you recognize any of them from the night you were attacked?"

I didn't dare look at Logan. His eyes bored holes into the back of my head. I knew now that he'd warned me not to say anything with the dirty looks he'd given me when I walked in. Tipton was a pack member. I could smell the fear coming off of Logan in waves. In fact, I wondered how no one else noticed it.

I wouldn't be able to explain my conclusions without spilling the beans to the detective, anyway. The only choice I had was to tell the truth. "No. The person who attacked me was behind me, and it was after dark. They grabbed the back of my head, and I couldn't turn to look at them. I know who four of them are from other incidents, and I can remember some details from their arrests, but I couldn't point a finger at any of them and say that one of them is the person who attacked me."

I felt Logan sigh in barely disguised relief beside me. That pissed me off. How dare he be so relieved? I knew who my attacker was now. We'd have to have a little chat about all this later.

Detective Burns asked me to detail the arrests I remembered. I had no problem remembering Tipton's, and was able to provide at least some details on the other three I'd recognized. One of them was the shoplifter with steaks in his pants that I'd arrested just before the attack. The other two were known for being drunk and disorderly in different bars in our district, but were more likely to argue over a football game while they were drunk than to lie in wait and pounce on someone.

Burns was disappointed that I couldn't point a finger at anyone. I asked him to turn them sideways, and asked to see them from the back, to be sure, but nothing struck me from that night. Regardless of how I felt about Tipton, I didn't want him to get off on a technicality. I had to be sure that I couldn't point the finger from something that night, and I wouldn't lie. I might have figured out it was him, but I'd be lying if I said I saw him attack me.

Detective Burns had each suspect read aloud a statement from that night. As each one of them spoke, I knew immediately that it was Tipton. Although his voice didn't sound quite the same today, I knew now why he'd sounded the way he did that night. I wondered what stage of the change he'd been in when he spoke to me. I knew he'd be unable to talk once he was in full wolf form, so he must have been in the midst of a change when he spoke. I identified his voice as "sounding like" the one I'd heard, but said that the voice I'd heard that night had been closer to a growl, and much deeper than his actual voice.

Logan squirmed in his chair when I said it. I could tell that he wanted me to shut the hell up. Even so, I was the victim here. I didn't do anything to deserve it. At least not that I knew of. I'd spent my days at work for the system. Why couldn't I use the system for myself now?

The officers led the men in the lineup down the steps and out of the room. The prosecutor seemed unhappy, and I could understand that. I mean, there were no other witnesses to the attack itself. The people who'd come out of the store after it happened, including Justin, hadn't seen anything but me on the ground bleeding. Of course, Justin had said something about forensics.

"Is there any other evidence you can tell me about?" I asked.

Mr. Wingard blinked hard. "Officer, you know we don't tell victims about all of our evidence. We don't want your memories to be affected by it." He clutched his file folder tightly, as if I'd been peeking inside.

"Yeah, I know that. I know you don't want to contaminate my testimony or bias my memory. Certainly you could tell me what evidence you're looking at, even if you can't tell me the results of the lab tests? I mean, I might be able to shed some light on why something might be somewhere or what something might mean. No matter how much defense attorneys want us to include 'everything of importance' in our reports and statements, it's really hard to know what's important until an investigation gets underway, isn't it?"

He smiled, and took another file from Detective Burns before he spoke. As he made notes, he said, "Once a cop, always a cop, eh? You know what, you're right. We do have forensics, but damned if we know what we're going to do about it. It's some of the strangest stuff we've ever seen. We have a print from your radio, and hair that doesn't belong to you. The problem is that I don't know where the hair came from. We haven't been able to identify a blood type, and it's looking like it might belong to a neighborhood dog, rather than your attacker. You landed on the asphalt parking lot, outside. Who knows what's walked around in that area before you were attacked? We've gotten preliminary results on the prints, and it does match a suspect, but there are some strange results, so we've sent it to the FBI lab to make sure we haven't made a mistake."

"Thank you, sir, for telling me." I turned to Detective Burns. "Can I go now?" I could hear a buzzing in my ears, and I knew I'd pushed myself about as far as I could handle for now. I was actually looking forward to going back to filing vehicle impound slips. I wouldn't have to think too hard about them.

"Yeah, you can. You're sure that you're okay?"

The buzzing in my ears only got louder. "I'll be fine. I only have a couple of hours left on shift, so I might as well finish it up, rather than go home and dwell on this." Not that I wouldn't dwell on it, but better to make the others think I could function normally. My brain could run at a million miles an hour but I could put on a brave face.

"Seriously, Sam, you should take the rest of the day off if they're willing to arrange it. Didn't we talk yesterday about stress management and how it could impact a crime victim in a stressful job?" Logan put a hand on my shoulder.

I'm not clueless. It was a warning. He was trying to get me out of there, and maybe that wasn't such a bad idea. "Okay. Fine. Hint taken. I'll take the rest of the day off. Not subtle at all there, Mr. Boyd. It's not like processing impound paperwork for hoopdies is stressful, but if you insist, I'll take off early."

Detective Burns nodded, but there was a look in his eyes as if he'd realized there was something else going on, though he had the smarts to keep his mouth shut. I knew he wanted to ask me more questions outside of Logan's hearing. I didn't want to answer them without more information.

I was irritated with Logan. I figured going home early would give me a chance to question him a bit. Oh, yeah, that would be a fun ride home.

CHAPTER THIRTY ONE

Instead of driving me home, Logan followed me to my place. I'd need my car in the morning anyway, so it just made sense. Because I'd left early, we were there a couple of hours before Justin was supposed to show up. Good thing, too, because I really didn't know how I'd explain Logan at my house when I'd told him I'd be at work. Justin's reaction earlier would make that awkward.

We'd barely gotten inside when I wheeled on Logan and started to scream. I felt like a real bitch doing it, no pun intended. "How dare you and Max and all of you. You keep telling me to stay in control of my temper and my emotions, and I have to face something like this with no warning. How dare you! He's a pack member, right? Of course he is, because if he wasn't, you guys would've warned me about others werewolves in the community. Was this some kind of plan? I deserve an explanation, and I want it now." I was livid. I felt my hands shake, and was surprised I hadn't lost control. Of course, I'd just changed last night. I was good for a while.

Logan sighed, and sat down heavily on my living room sofa. "You're right."

"The absolute fucking gall...I'm what?" I stared at him.

"You're right. You deserve an explanation. Max didn't want me to do this, but I can't wait for him to explain. I had no idea the police had Stephen in their sights."

"So it was Tipton."

"Yeah, it was."

My mind went blank. It took a second for the mental wheels to click back on. I now had the name of my attacker. He'd confirmed it. But it just didn't make any sense.

"Okay, that's not even close to an adequate explanation there, mister. I say he committed a crime, lock his ass up. Let's call the detective, and you can tell him how you know that." I headed for the phone, but he was right behind me and took it out of my hands. "Why do I get the feeling that there's more to it than that?"

"That's the understatement of the year. Max is bailing Stephen out right now, and taking him back to the barn, or another secure location until some of this settles down. If he's strung out again, he'll dry him out. I have no idea how long that will take."

"You mean Max is going to hide him."

"I meant that Max is going to sober him up before any other decisions are made. We need to find out why he did this, although I can probably guess."

"I don't fucking care why he did it. Look what he did to me. I'm the victim here, not him." My hands itched. I wanted to hit Logan. I balled up my fists and squared up to do it, but he was faster than me.

"You both are." He caught my fist before I could do anything.

"Bullshit."

"Honestly, it's true. You've heard Stephen was the victim of a violent attack?"

I didn't care. All I cared about was getting my hand free so I could try to hit him again.

"Well, regardless of what he's done since, can we at least agree that he didn't deserve what happened to him in the first place? He didn't deserve this either."

I had to agree. I couldn't think of anything that anyone could do that would earn them this. I nodded, and he released my hand. Much as I still wanted to hit him, I figured he had a point to make. He wasn't going to leave until he'd made it. The faster he made it, the faster I could kick him out. I could always hit him later.

"I don't approve of what happened. I was shocked. We'd started work on the barn, and it was clear to all of us that we had no idea how to plan what we were doing. We were digging tunnels and basements, with no idea how to work with the space we'd cleared. Max had grand ideas for the place, and we had no way to implement them. No one knew how to do it.

"All of a sudden we've got an architect who's just been attacked. He was perfect for what we needed, at least professionally. The only problem was Stephen, himself."

"You think?" I asked.

"Shut up, Sam. He didn't react well to what he'd become."

"How the fuck did you expect him to react? It's not exactly something a person volunteers for. I know I sure as hell didn't." I crossed my arms and sat down in my recliner.

"You're absolutely right. I'm sure that if he'd been given the choice, he never would've accepted. I have to give the man credit, although, he's done an amazing job on the barn."

"It's not like he had much of a choice."

"No, he didn't. However, things didn't go according to plan."

"You think, maybe?" All right, so my mouth was on overdrive.

"Stephen didn't handle becoming a werewolf well. No one's ever really happy about it, but we do try to protect and help each other. We don't actively recruit. No way do we want to inflict this on someone when we can't always handle it ourselves. We're trying to find out more about this condition. You saw that at the barn. There's always someone attacked that has nowhere else to go. We do a good job of policing our own. We're always trying to do better."

I had to admit, it was a noble cause, and I'm always a sucker for those. Learning more about us as wolves and working to protect the people in our territory appealed to me as a cop. I was appalled for Stephen Tipton, who sounded like he'd been a gift from heaven for the wolves, even though becoming a wolf was a gift from hell to himself. It was like being offered a job and being told that you aren't allowed to say no. I'd never heard of that outside of mob movies.

"Stephen did well at designing the barn, and showing us how to implement his strategies. We're still putting new ideas of his into place. Professionally, he's a genius. The rest of his life was another story. He couldn't handle the stress, and had a hard time controlling his changes. Unknown to the pack, he drank heavily. We didn't even realize alcohol was involved until we found out that he'd been arrested."

"Yeah, he was arrested for disorderly conduct and public intoxication a bunch of times. I think I've locked him up twice in the last month."

"Obviously we can't leave him in jail. We had no idea whether he'd be able to control himself, or whether he'd even care. Max went down and bailed him out, took him out to the barn, and kept him there until he was sober."

"Why do I get the feeling this isn't the end of the story?"

"Max had to explain that drinking like that wasn't a good idea, but drinking when he wasn't changing as often as he should was a recipe for disaster. Stephen told him to fuck off."

Try as I might, I was having trouble fighting off waves of sympathy for Tipton. Not an excuse. It was never an excuse, but maybe an explanation? In his position, I might've done the same thing. Oh, wait. I was in his position. The only thing really stopping me from doing the same was the fact that I wasn't really a heavy drinker. I mean, I might have a glass or two of wine with dinner. I've had a beer or two with pizza or hanging out with friends. That's it. I was always too concerned about what getting caught abusing alcohol could do to my career as a police officer. I smiled at the idea of Tipton telling Max to fuck off. Max must've gone ape-shit. Even I thought that was a bad idea. I wondered how long it took to put his teeth back in his head.

"Yeah, I see that grin. You'd have said the same thing, Sam, don't think otherwise. In any case, we thought we'd all convinced him that the alcohol wasn't going to fix the situation. We got him some referrals for new clients, trying to keep him busy, and his income went through the roof. He started seeing less and less of his wife and kid. The stress got to him again. He had to come to the barn and change on a daily basis. By the time he got off work, got here, changed, had a decent run, and then drove back, he never saw his family. We thought he understood the drinking thing, but he couldn't stop."

"That's his fault. He should've quit drinking." I felt bad even as I said it. I did feel sorry for him. I had to remind myself that this was the guy that had put me in the hospital. But then, if he hadn't, would Justin have told me how he felt? Not that our relationship was a bed of roses at the moment, but it was a good thing that had come out of the attack.

Logan didn't question me, he just kept talking. "He lost weight and didn't get enough sleep. He wasn't seeing his family enough, and using amphetamines to get going in the morning and alcohol to get to sleep at night. When that stopped working, he moved on to cocaine. He still wasn't getting home in time for dinner, and he's the world's biggest family man. You've seen his little girl. She loves her daddy, and she never saw him."

I did remember Rory Tipton. I remembered seeing her cry with her daddy in the backseat of the cruiser, and her tears took on a whole new meaning. She wasn't scared of a mean man coming to hurt her or her mom. She wanted to spend time with the father she loved, even though everyone told her not to. He'd inspired love in his little girl. That had to count for something.

I wanted Logan to stop. I didn't want to feel sorry for Tipton.

Logan leaned forward on the couch. "His wife cracked under the pressure. He told her the truth, and she couldn't handle it, either. He told us after he was arrested again for public intox that she knew everything, and was threatening to file for divorce."

"Somehow, this has to do with why he can't see his daughter, doesn't it?"

"Yeah, it does. His wife was so put off by the whole werewolf thing that she refused to believe it. He was high, they got into an argument, and he trashed the place. He changed right in front of her. Never laid a hand on her, but she claimed he was threatening her. When the cops got there, he'd torn the place up and took off before he could say anything in his own defense. By the time the situation settled down, she blackmailed him into paying alimony, agreeing to the divorce, and giving up all custody and visitation rights to the kid. Don't think for one minute that he did any of that willingly. Max had a hand in it as well, because she was threatening to blow the whistle on the entire pack."

"I wondered. His daughter didn't take it well, did she?" No wonder Rory was willing to exchange notes with her father despite the protection order. She wasn't scared of him at all. And that was why the police kept getting called for protection order violations...her mother kept catching notes getting slipped to the little girl. He'd never been accused of being violent on any call I'd been on, just that he'd broken the protection order, over and over again.

"I honestly don't think she even knows. They've done a pretty good job of keeping it all from her. It was one of the conditions Max insisted on. She's had no explanation for why they're keeping her daddy away from her."

"That explains why she keeps acting out." We'd had calls of Rory running away, and being unruly as well. And Rory never called about her dad making contact; it was only Mrs. Tipton who called the police on her ex-husband.

"Absolutely. The more immediate issue was damage control. The second issue was getting Stephen under control. We thought he was convinced to clean up, off the drugs and alcohol. Maybe we could've approached his wife about allowing some supervised visitation with his kid, but we weren't going to fight her to get custody when he refused to change unless he was forced to and popped pills like M&M's. He was a very real danger to her."

"So, what do we do about it?" Damn. I'd said 'we'. I was already identifying myself with the pack and its problems. I wasn't sure if that was a good thing, or not.

"I don't know what the answer to that question is, Sam. Does that little girl deserve an explanation? Yes. Is she old enough to understand the ramifications of our secret? I don't know. Her mother says no. How many lives do we destroy for one little girl's piece of mind? How many people could lose their jobs and families like Tipton if this became public knowledge?"

"That decision never should have to be made. That little girl is the real victim in all of this. She needs to know the truth."

"That's her mother's decision, and I'm not sure we've had much of a choice. We had Stephen dried out. We were even taking him to AA meetings, to help him as much as we could. It never failed, though. Something always happened to cause a setback in his recovery."

"Like what?"

"His daughter likes to send him letters about how much she misses him, and how much she hates her mom. If it's not the divorce proceedings, it's the protection order, the holidays, the sunrise, his little girl begging Daddy for help. How many excuses do alcoholics need to drink?"

"That's why he keeps going over to the house?"

"Yeah, he'll get a letter telling him that the ex is locking his daughter out of her room, or that she's refused to allow her out of the house, or a million other normal childhood and adolescent overreactions. He'll be okay until he gets that letter, and then he'll try to write a letter back to her, as we've asked him to do, instead of going over there, but he's learned that we won't send them. He'll get upset while he's writing it, and start drinking. Soon he's drunk enough to think it's a good idea to go check it out."

"Instead of calling us, the cops, or children's services, or even you guys to go look?"

"You got it. He doesn't think anyone who knows will help him, and those who don't know, won't understand."

That explained why my lectures had fallen on deaf ears, and why his ex-wife had acted like she had some reason to feel guilty. I felt sympathy for him. I felt bad for the little girl. And his pretty blond ex-wife was rightfully scared of him if his drug problems were that bad. Maybe he wasn't the only bad guy here, but he sure wasn't a good guy. I needed time to think about all this. I leaned my head back and stared up at the ceiling. I had a lot to consider before Justin showed up with Chinese food.

CHAPTER THIRTY TWO

Max glared at Stephen as he followed him out of the jail toward the parking garage. "Twenty thousand was your bail this time. It gets worse every time you get picked up."

Stephen hung his head. He knew he had the money to cover it himself, but he also knew that no one would let him out long enough to arrange it himself. "Thank you, Max. I mean it."

"What were you thinking? You knew why we wanted you to stay at the barn. Why would you leave while the police could be looking for you? After what you did, why even give them a chance to lay their hands on you? And do you know how much is at risk when there's a paper trail tying all of us together? My name on your bail receipts could be a problem down the road."

"I'm sorry, Max." And like any other alcoholic or drug addict, he truly was sorry. He felt terrible that he'd landed in this situation. A night in the county jail and facing that pretty young cop in that lineup wasn't worth the breath of fresh air and pack of smokes he'd snuck out to get. This time he really felt like he had kicked the drugs and the alcohol, but cigarettes were another matter. He figured he'd kick the stuff that was going to get him killed immediately first, and deal with the smoking later, but no one in the barn on a regular basis smoked besides him. Even Max had given up three years ago. No one had a pack for him to bum out of.

It had taken a lot of courage to sneak out of the barn. He'd hidden himself in Logan's backseat when he left the barn the night before, and slept in Logan's garage overnight. He knew Logan wouldn't kill him if he found him, and it was the best night's sleep he'd had in months. No drugs, no hangover, no fear of being killed in the morning. All of those things combined made him feel more rested than anything else he could have done. But then he'd gotten caught on his way back from the corner grocery.

They got into the car, and Max drove out of town and onto the highway to head back to the barn, when Stephen turned to him. "Max, I want you to know that I didn't mean for any of this to happen. I had more drugs in my system that I thought, and I was completely paranoid coming out of it. I was convinced that everyone at the barn was going to kill me, so I snuck out to get some cigarettes and a decent night's sleep."

Max sighed. "I know."

"How do you know?"

"Because you've been talking in your sleep, and Adam and Logan made sure I knew you were paranoid. They told me that posting guards on you would make it worse, and the best thing to do was to ride it out. I didn't think you'd try to escape, but then you were gone."

Stephen looked down at his hands in his lap. "And now you're going to punish me?"

Max looked at him. "No, Stephen. I'm not going to punish you."

"You're not?"

"You got very lucky today. Either little miss cop can't ID you, or Logan got to her to prevent pointing you out. You dodged a bullet here. It'll be real hard for them to make a case against you if no one can ID you. If they can't make a case against you, then there's no risk of you going to jail and our secret being exposed."

"And if they do make a case against me?"

Max pulled the car off the road, and pulled into a gas station. He pulled up to the pumps, turned to Stephen, and said, "Let's cross that bridge if we come to it. You really don't want that to happen, do you?"

It was exactly what Stephen feared. He knew Max would kill him rather than see him languish in jail, where he could be seen, if not caught on a security camera, changing into wolf. And as long as the cop could be convinced to protect his daughter, he'd much prefer being murdered than being locked up. At least his daughter would be spared the humiliation of thinking her father to be a criminal, even if he was one.

"No, I don't."

"Then pray that Logan can wrap all this up quickly. And that your little cop friend doesn't change her mind and finger you as her attacker."

"How are we going to keep her from doing that?" Stephen didn't want to ask the question, but knew, in his heart that something needed to be said.

"I think Logan's got it covered, but if we have to, we'll use more direct forms of persuasion. I'm sure there's motivation somewhere that we can find to convince her to lay off." Max sighed. "So what brand of cigarettes do you want?"

In other words, the pack would convince the cop with threats, pain, and humiliation. Stephen decided then and there that if he could stop Max, he'd do anything in his power to do so. It was time to talk to Logan, and see when he'd make his move.

"Camels, Max. Thanks."

Chapter Thirty Three

"We've taken a loving father away from his child, and his life is in a shambles. All because someone wanted a barn rehabbed and didn't know how to do it. Talk about wrong and stupid. Is it any wonder that we consistently bail him out and provide him a lawyer when he gets into trouble? And why I've spent so much time trying to counsel him on his addiction? Do you get now why he feels like he wasn't given a choice about his kid?" Logan's voice was strained, and I could tell he was upset, but other than the tone in his voice, there was no crack in his composure. Control, thy name is Logan.

"Why did he have to attack me, then? How did I get into the mix?"

"How many times have you arrested him?"

"I don't know. Several."

"There you go." He raised his hands to indicate that what he said was obvious.

It wasn't. "Sorry, I don't get it."

"You're Johnny-on-the-spot when he shows up, hammered, to protect his little girl. You're the one carting him off. He knows, intellectually, that he isn't allowed to be there. I'd bet you've wasted plenty of breath lecturing to him while he's high about leaving his ex-wife and his little girl alone."

I grunted noncommittally. He was right. I had lectured him, and more than once.

He took that as a yes and continued. "Stephen doesn't comprehend anything when he's drunk or high; he just sees a person taking him away from his kid. He can't explain to you what's really going on, because if he does, he risks being named a danger to the pack, and then his life is forfeit. It's not a fun position to be in. Every time he gets locked up, he sobers up, and then he realizes that he shouldn't do it. Then it all happens again."

"So the next officer that goes out there and hauls his butt in is in danger of him fixating on them?" Thoughts of Justin attacked and going through this raced through my brain. I realized there was a lot that I'd do to prevent that from happening.

"Yeah, that's a very real possibility. Depends on how high he is and the circumstances, but it could happen again."

"So, wait a minute. Are you telling me that he could be killed because of it? You guys gonna be judge, jury and executioner all on your own?"

"What choice do we have? We have a pretty explosive secret here. Is it worth your family, your job, or your own life? You want him in jail, but the rest of us would suffer for that."

I ran my hands over my face, trying to wipe it all away. "Why didn't you guys tell me? If not when I first showed up, then at least last night; why did I have to get smacked in the face with it today while I've got him standing right in front of me? Why did I have to figure out all this on my own? How do I decide whether or not to share all of this with a detective I know and trust as opposed to protecting you guys?"

"Believe me, Sam—we didn't know things would happen so fast. Otherwise we would've warned you and we'd have done something about it."

"Yeah, right. What would you've done? I think you guys were hoping and praying I was too dumb to figure it out, that I'd fall over with gratitude that you helped me with being a werewolf until I felt indebted to you. I mean, isn't that how things operate? Keep the truth from the new girl until she's in over her head?" I knew I'd gone too far, and that Logan wasn't the one responsible for all this. It was a classic case of blame the messenger, but at this point, I wasn't sure I cared. "Get out of my house, Logan. I don't want to talk with you right now."

"I'll go, because I know Justin's on his way over here. You shouldn't be alone."

"Yeah, he is. Wait a minute, how do you know that?" What the hell?

"You said you had dinner plans before we left the Safety Building. It doesn't take a rocket scientist to see what's going on between the two of you."

"Bullshit. I haven't mentioned Justin to you once."

"I work with a lot of cops, Sam. I hear the rumors, and the rumor mill is grinding faster than you think. People know, especially after the shooting incident just before you changed for the first time. Besides, the pack is having you watched."

"What the fuck is going on here?" I bellowed. "So not cool, Logan. I'm being watched, like I'm the dangerous one? What did I do to merit spies at my door?"

"You're a danger to Stephen, whom we've hurt in ways that we can never fix. Justin may be a target, because

Stephen may associate the two of you together with his problems. You're a risk to yourself, because of Stephen, and also because you have the power at the moment to destroy all of us. There are those in the pack, and they're in the minority, who feel you're too dangerous to allow you to live. Max has forbidden any action against you. However, there's no accounting for what one person may decide to do. For those reasons, we've been watching you. We believe that you should be allowed to make your own decision before the pack acts."

"You're saying that if I identify Stephen as my attacker that someone may come after me? Kill me? Or kill him?"

"I'm not sure which of you they'd move against, but that's exactly what I'm saying. The hope is that cooler heads prevail when it gets to that point. Time is your friend here."

I walked to the door. "Get out."

"Sam, I need to know what you're going to do."

I snarled at him. "I'll let you know when I know. For now, get the fuck out of my house. Don't call me, I'll call you."

He started to go, and then turned back. "No matter how bad your anger gets, you can hold off changing if you've been changing regularly. Don't fall into Stephen's trap. Don't drink heavily if you haven't changed for a while. For heaven's sake, avoid emotional upsets if you haven't changed in a while."

He walked out and I saw Justin's car pull into the driveway through the open door. Oh, shit, I thought, but all I could think was to make a strong point to Logan. I wouldn't put up with this from the pack. I wouldn't allow them to treat me as a casualty. Damn it, I had rights, too.

"Get the fuck out of my house!" My hands shook. I wanted to hit him, but I'd settle for him leaving.

Say what you might about sexy tempers, I look ugly when I get angry. I flush red, and sometimes it's hard to tell if I've been crying when I get really worked up. Logan stepped off the porch as Justin ran up and demanded to know what had happened. He took in my screaming red face and obvious distress, and shoved a bag of Chinese takeout into my hands. I didn't have much of a chance to react before he grabbed Logan and dragged him by the scruff of his neck to his car, which was parked on the street in front of my house.

Oh, crap. This couldn't be good. All I needed was the neighborhood biddies to call the cops on a fight in my front yard. That would take a little more explaining than I was prepared to do today.

I wanted to shout at Justin that Logan was just leaving. I didn't want to see the two of them get in a fight. Logan, as a werewolf, could fight him off without a problem, but I was struck dumb by the sight of Justin so angry and springing to my defense. I was shocked to find that I was turned on, even as I was worried about Logan losing control and attacking Justin.

But Logan had been a werewolf long enough and learned enough control to realize that Justin wasn't a real threat to him, and had the presence of mind to open the car door and duck inside to prevent Justin from slamming him into the side of the car. I heard Justin yell at him, and Logan stood there, just taking it. There was no getting through the anger Justin had built up, and no amount of calm Logan showed was abating it. Even my temper was cooling at the sight of Justin defending me. Maybe there was hope for us yet. Then again, maybe I should be concerned at how thoroughly he had lost his mind.

Justin kept yelling as Logan started his car, and I heard so many emotions in his tirade that I was wondering what he'd say when he came inside. Logan ignored him, gave me a little wave, and backed out of the driveway. The wave set Justin off, and he yelled again.

I was, however, feeling other emotions in the pit of my stomach, recognizing the feeling as something other than anger. I wondered at that point whether I would attack Justin when he returned to the house, and if so, exactly what kind of attack it would be.

CHAPTER THIRTY FOUR

Justin turned and came inside, breathing hard with a wild eyed look on his face, combined with a satisfied look. I like my independence. However, another inner part of me said that in protecting me, he'd earned the right to mate. For some reason, the whole him-Tarzan, me-Jane scenario worked at the moment. What the hell? That's not me.

Justin went to the window, ensuring that Logan drove off. I couldn't stop myself. I dropped the takeout on the floor and launched myself, grabbing him by the neck as I attacked his mouth. He grunted with the impact, but returned the kiss. He looked surprised, and he had every reason to be. I hadn't been interested in anything more physically intimate than a hug since coming home from the hospital.

Justin responded and I felt one arm snake around my waist. The other one slid up my back into my hair, as his lips trailed down off of my mouth to my neck.

I needed Justin like I needed air. It was a visceral reaction; a desperate need rather than just a desire. I whimpered as his teeth scraped my neck, and I felt him hit that one specific spot; the one just at the back of my neck, slightly behind my ear. It was like hitting an on switch for my libido, and my system exploded. I saw stars and moaned as I ran my hands into his hair.

He started to pull back at that reaction, opening his eyes. He looked at my face, and something in my expression had him diving right back into my arms. I felt his hand yanking my shirt out of the waistband of my pants, and that movement forced him back from my neck. I whimpered and reached for the buttons on his shirt, fumbling and ripping it open as he caught my earlobe in his teeth. He pulled away and yanked my shirt over my head. I caught a glimpse of his eyes. It was a possessive look. The glassy, unfocused need in his eyes sent another shockwave coursing through my system.

"Please, Justin. Don't stop." I whispered.

He growled at me, and I thrilled to hear the animal sound coming from his throat, even though I knew it to be a poor imitation of the real thing. As we hit the floor, he reached for me again, and I felt his hand reaching for the clasp on the back of my bra. I was grateful that I wore a nice one, even if it was boring white, rather than the ragged old comfortable ones I'd worn when I first came home from the hospital.

I needed his hands on me, his skin touching mine, anywhere and everywhere. He gave up on the fight with the back clasp and ripped my bra right down the front. The delicate lace shredded like tissue paper and he buried his face and hands in my breasts. I felt his hands on the outside edges, just under each arm, as he lifted them up to his mouth, and I cried out for him.

My desperation seemed to slow him, much to my dismay, and he lifted his face from my cleavage to study me, as if planning his attack. He touched one nipple with his tongue, and my whole body bucked and arched. I had never had such a strong physical reaction in my whole life. I felt my body clench, and my eyes rolled back in my head as I yelled. "Please, oh please, I can't stop, oh God, Justin!"

I ended on a moan, and, in amazement, he lifted his eyes to me. I reached for him, and ripped his shirt the rest of the way open, shirt buttons flying everywhere.

I felt him settle his weight on top of me, and I locked my ankles around his waist as he settled himself between my legs. I could feel the hard bulge of him pressing against me, and I cried out again when I felt the pressure of him separated by our clothing. I reached for his zipper, but he stopped me, pinning my hands above my head. I wanted to beg him, but he silenced me with a bruising kiss.

He began moving against me, speeding up as he heard the hitch in my breath, and another moan cross my lips. I fisted my hands in his hair, hoping that such an action would prolong the delicious feeling of anticipation worming its way down each limb to the very tips of my fingers. Instead of prolonging those feelings, he sped up and pulled his mouth away from mine. When he looked at me again, I could see the whites of his eyes as he went wild.

Justin's rhythm began to suffer as I felt him move faster and faster against me, and he groaned. It brought tears to my eyes and blinded me temporarily to everything except the comfortable weight of his body as we both tried desperately to catch our breath.

After several minutes of lying there and hearing our hearts race, we opened our eyes. I had little to no feeling in my lower body, and I felt Justin struggling to remove his weight from me before he'd completely recovered his strength. If I could've moved, I'd have held him tight against me, savoring the feel of him comfortably trapping me to the floor.

When I could finally move, I realized that I heard a noise, like someone slurping up soup. I looked at Justin. It wasn't coming from him.

We turned our heads in unison to find Doyle's marmalade tabby cat butt sticking out of the upended bag of takeout Chinese, tail dancing as he slurped noodles and sauce to his little heart's content, and I laughed. Justin shook his head and grinned.

"Hey, um, Justin?" I had to clear my throat a couple of times, and my voice sounded raspy even to me.

"Yeah?" He was pretty groggy as well.

"I think our dinner's been claimed."

The cat, startled by our sudden interest in him, panicked, one sesame noodle hanging from his mouth, and ran for cover, while we laughed together, holding each other. "Interested in ordering a pizza, instead?" he asked, chuckling softly and nuzzling my ear.

I grinned. I couldn't think of anything better.

CHAPTER THIRTY FIVE

Justin's cell phone rang, and it broke the spell of togetherness surrounding them. He got up from the floor, helped Sam to stand again, and held her close in his arms. Thank you, he thought. She's coming back to me. He ignored the phone tucked into his pocket so he could hug Sam again, and kiss the top of her head. As much as he'd wanted to strip off both of their clothing and let things go where they would, he hadn't had any form of protection with him, and he was very aware of exactly who was right outside her door. He just didn't feel right about it.

He could smell the shampoo she'd used that morning and wondered whether that Boyd guy had gotten close enough to smell her shampoo. That was irrational, but he didn't trust the guy. Something just didn't feel right to him.

Boyd was a good therapist. He'd checked the guy out thoroughly, and there hadn't been a whiff of anything inappropriate or out of line in the guy's background. The department liked him, and several cops had recommended him. It didn't matter. Nothing could get past the feeling in his gut that this guy was competition, or the sinking feeling that Sam was in danger. Every sense he had screamed that there was a threat out there against her.

He couldn't push Sam too hard. She was still fragile from the attack. She was showing signs of resuming her normal quirky, snarky self, and he welcomed it. He knew part of the reason she was better was because of the counseling, but how much did she need to see the guy? She didn't need counseling every day, did she?

She smiled at him and it took his breath away. He still couldn't believe that she was here with him, that he'd had his hands on her. Something was bound to go wrong. It was the story of his life. He gave himself a mental shake. His cell phone was burning a hole in his pocket as he wondered what was going on outside.

He dropped a kiss on her forehead and excused himself to go to the bathroom. He used the facilities, washed up, and then looked at his cell to see who had called. When he saw the number on the caller ID, he dialed immediately, camouflaging the sound of his conversation by running water in the sink.

"Hi Dad, what's up?" He opened the door a crack to watch Sam. He hoped he was just paranoid, but he couldn't help it. She'd been hurt once, and he couldn't let it happen again.

"I just thought I'd let you know that the men we saw earlier made another pass by Sam's house about ten minutes ago. Nathan and I are sitting outside in my van. They didn't stop, but they sure slowed down when they went by."

And that was the person outside that had made him too uncomfortable to take advantage of Sam; her father was sitting in his own father's vehicle, just yards from her front door, and Sam had no idea they were there. He winced, as if he was a teenager, having broken curfew, knowing that they were right outside. "Dad, I'm here now. I'm getting dinner with her, so if you guys want to take a break, I'll be right here." He leaned out the door to see if Sam was listening, but she seemed to be busy looking for take-out menus to replace their purloined dinner.

"That's not a bad idea, Justin. If you're going to be there a while, then we're going to call it a night. Nathan and I don't want to tip off Kathy that there's something to be worried about, and one of my old buddies from the department has volunteered to be here in an hour or so to watch out for her for the rest of the night. Do you remember George?"

"Yeah, Dad. You guys were partners at one time, weren't you?"

"Yeah, we were. He works as a bailiff for one of the judges downtown now. Good man in a tight spot. He's got a day off tomorrow, and volunteered to give us a break so we could get some decent sleep."

Justin grimaced. He felt bad at asking his dad for help, but he couldn't watch Sam all the time. He didn't really worry about her when she was at work, but he couldn't work his own shift and make his court appearances and watch out for her all the time.

His dad hadn't questioned him. Justin was glad. He wasn't sure how to explain his concern. He just had a feeling in his gut that Sam was in danger. At least his dad understood the importance of a cop listening to his instincts. "Are you sure you should be mixing Nathan up in this, Dad? He's not a cop. I don't want him to get hurt trying to protect Sam."

"Yeah, but it's his daughter. He has a right to help. Don't worry, Justin. He's not gonna bust your chops for leaving the curtains open."

Damn it. He heard Nathan in the background asking what he meant by curtains, and breathed a sigh of relief. The last thing he needed to worry about was Sam's dad thinking he was taking advantage of his little girl. The thought of her dad watching what they'd just done, even though they'd both been, well, mostly dressed, was worse than standing waist deep in ice water. That effectively killed his libido for the night, if not the rest of the year. "Not funny, Dad."

John hooted with laughter. "I'm just fooling with you. I didn't see anything but you throwing that counselor out on his ear."

"Thanks for the heart attack."

"Hey, if us acting like fools out here keeps you from screwing this up, I'm okay with it. She's good for you. I don't think she's in danger, but I do agree that there's something weird going on. You sure she hasn't said anything? No one's made any threats to her, or anything like that?"

"Nothing she's said, but I still think there's something going on. She's scared of something. They had her try to pick someone out of a line-up today, and she couldn't do it. Says she couldn't see the person. That's likely true, but she's still pretty upset." He watched through the crack in the door as Sam came out of the kitchen with a handful of pizza coupons and menus, petting Doyle, who had emerged from his hiding spot for a second or two of attention before shooting off into another hiding place. "Gotta go, Dad. And thanks."

"Don't mention it, but keep pushing. Let me know if there's something said to her, and we'll get a few more of my friends out here to keep an eye on her. It'd be just like old times."

"I bet." He hung up the phone, and pictured John and his old friends sitting outside in their cars, drinking cold coffee and having the time of their lives, reliving the good old days on surveillance. They'd have a ball, and Sam would be safe enough for him to go to work. Just knowing they were watching made him feel better.

Now if he could just find out why every instinct he possessed told him there was something wrong, he'd sleep better.

Chapter Thirty Six

After we'd recovered our strength and got up from the floor, Justin headed for the bathroom and I went into the kitchen to get the pizza menus. When he returned, we decided on an extra large extra meat double cheese pizza, and he called in the order. While we waited on the delivery guy, Justin decided he wanted to talk. I'd have been happy to curl up on the couch and take a nap. It had been a long day.

"So, Sam, did you hear from the detective? I heard Burns was assigned."

"Yeah, they had me come in for a line-up." I walked into the living room with sodas for each of us, worried about how this conversation would go. It seemed no matter how good things seemed to be between us, there was always an argument on the horizon, and I didn't want to talk about the attack when we were getting along so well.

He gave me a funny look, narrowing his eyes at me. "What happened?"

"Well, I recognized some of the people in the lineup from previous arrests, but I had to tell them I didn't recognize them from that night. I didn't see anyone's face and didn't see anything that stood out. The guy who did this to me grabbed the back of my head. I couldn't have looked at him if I wanted to. I did hear him say something just before I passed out, but I wasn't able to recognize a voice for sure."

"None of them were close?" He sat down on the couch, and I sat next to him, trying to figure out a way to change the topic. Nothing came to mind.

"Not close enough for me to be exact. But, you know what? Saying something cold in a room where you might be implicated in a violent crime is probably going to sound different than when you're worked up and committing a violent act." *Please, Justin. Stop talking.* My brain couldn't seem to come up with another topic. I was willing to talk about anything but this, but I was drawing an utter blank.

"That's true. Did they tell you anything about the forensics?"

"Just a little. They didn't want to bias my testimony by telling me too much, but they said something about fingerprints and hair, how they matched someone but there were irregularities, so they sent them to the FBI for more specialized testing." *Where was that damn cat?* I looked around, hoping Doyle would come out, but he was nowhere to be found. My change-of-topic on four legs was probably sleeping off the Chinese food underneath my bed. I just hoped he didn't get sick from it. Cleaning up cat vomit was not my idea of a relaxing evening.

"That's a good sign, isn't it?"

"I don't know, Justin. I really don't." My previous rage having been spent, the events of the last few days had me worn out. Even as I wondered if I could kick him out to sleep, or better yet, find a way to curl up and sleep with my head on his shoulder, I felt bad.

I could see him getting frustrated, and reached out, hugging him around the waist. He'd been a rock for me when I was first home, and now I needed him to allow me to process all the information that I'd been given.

He started to hug me, but he stopped himself. Instead, he leaned back and ran his hands over his face. "Sam, I need to know if you're hiding anything from me."

"What?" I moved away from him on the couch, and crossed my arms.

"It just seems like you're not telling me everything. I'm trying hard not to make a big deal about it, but I'm losing my mind. We care for each other. No question there's chemistry. We just proved that. But let's think about this. Our first date turned into a screaming match. Okay, fine; you started counseling. Things have gotten somewhat better.

"Our second date we end up chasing a suspect and you were unarmed, running straight into the fray. I thought my heart was going to explode seeing you like that. No sooner do I get you out of there and home, you're kicking me out of the house saying you'll call Logan Boyd. Okay, he's your counselor. No problem. I understand that situation would be upsetting even without everything that you've been through lately."

I kept my mouth shut. He had no idea just what the situation was, and I couldn't tell him.

He didn't wait for a response. "You told me you were going to come home to crash. I went back and filed my report, and spoke to the sarge. He wasn't happy that you were involved in the shooting, but agreed there wasn't much we could've done, other than respond. I finished up everything at the station, got the overtime approved, and headed home. I decided to stop by here and check on you. I still had my key and I figured I'd come in, see if you were all right, check on Doyle, then sleep on the couch to make sure you didn't need anything."

I closed my eyes. This wasn't going to be pretty. I could only imagine what was going through his head at the time and it wasn't good.

"You weren't here. The clothes you'd worn that day were ripped to shreds on the floor. Your purse was still here, but your keys were missing. I wanted to call the police and make a missing person's report, but Dad called my cell phone just as I was about to dial 911. He came by and looked at the house, and we fed Doyle. There were no signs of forced entry, and no signs of a struggle other than your ripped clothes, so we called your folks and Nadia and then Boyd's phone, since we figured he might be the last to talk with you." He stood up and started pacing.

"Justin, I'm sorry I worried you."

"Boyd's answering service said he was meeting a client, so we figured that was you. I still wanted to call the cops, but Dad convinced me to wait. You hadn't been missing more than an hour or so. For all we knew you'd ripped up your own clothes and left, but your car was still here. Dad was convinced that you'd gone somewhere with Boyd."

The idea of me being alone with Logan was clearly upsetting him. His jaw tightened when he said Logan's name. I tried to think of some way to convince him that he had nothing to worry about, but if our earlier wrestling match on the floor hadn't done the job to reassure him, I wasn't sure what else I could do. I watched him as he vented his frustrations, pacing and gesturing with his arms as he ranted.

He continued. "I was worried you'd be upset about us in the house without permission, so Dad and I locked up and waited in the car down the street until we saw you walk back up."

Great. He saw me walk up to the house in a white t-shirt, with no bra on. That wouldn't do much to convince anyone that I wasn't stepping out on him. "Justin. It's not what you think."

He put up one hand. "Let me finish this. We saw you go into the house on your own, so I figured you'd been off seeing him somewhere else. I started to get mad, because I wondered if there was more there with him than I thought, but then I saw two people watching your house."

My gaze flew up to meet his at that statement. Not what I'd expected him to say. "Someone was watching the house?" It had to be pack members. Logan warned me they were watching, but I figured that started today, after Stephen was arrested, not yesterday as I was in the throes of my first change. I wondered how long they'd been watching. Hopefully they weren't out there looking in my windows a few minutes ago. Then again, what had they seen? I hadn't noticed anything, and sure hadn't talked to anyone in the neighborhood in several days. Some cop I am. I'm not even paying attention to my surroundings at home. I should be ashamed of myself. "Did you talk to them?"

"No, I didn't. By the time we figured it out and got out of the car to approach them, they split. Dad's retired, and I was off duty. We hadn't seen them do more than stand on a public sidewalk and watch your house, so we didn't report it. I didn't recognize either of them. We stayed out there all night to make sure they didn't come back."

"Oh, Justin, I'm sorry you felt the need to do that." I tried to be dismissive of the problem, but he must've read something on my face. It wasn't hard to guess what he'd seen.

I was scared. Had they gotten inside as well? What had they gone through? Was there anything different or missing? Doyle. They could have hurt my cat. I reassured myself that he'd seemed fine when he'd gorged on Chinese food earlier. I felt violated at the thought of some strange person in my house. I swallowed back the urge to cry, because I couldn't explain it, but I was too slow. He saw it.

He knelt in front of where I sat on the couch and took my by the shoulders. "Damn it, Sam. I know there's something going on. Why won't you tell me? You'll spend half the night running around with Logan, and then come back here the next day and freak out at him. There are strange people watching your house. Then you all but attack me sexually, not that I'm complaining, but then you won't tell me what's going on. You've got to let me in. I know the attack wasn't something you expected. I know that life with you is never going to be dull, but I'd at least
like to know where I stand in all of it."

I hoped he'd take me in his arms at that moment, but he stood up and backed away. That hurt. "Justin. I don't know what to say."

"I just don't know what to do anymore. I'm falling in love with you, Sam, but I cannot keep doing this. I keep thinking it'll get better, and you'll start being yourself again, or at least being yourself for longer stretches of time. It's not happening, and I don't know what to do."

Oh God. Was he leaving me? I felt tears prick the inside of my eyelids. I would not cry in front of him. I would not be one of those clinging, needy women that I saw all the time at work. "Justin, you're right," I whispered.

"What did you say?"

"I said that you're right. My emotions have been all over the place. I just don't feel safe in my own skin anymore."

"Aw, Sam, why didn't you tell me?"

Damn. I really was going to cry. Two big fat tears slipped down my cheeks. "Because I felt, still feel, sometimes, like I have to handle this myself. I can't count on anyone else because I'll be let down. And I can't afford that right now. I can't let things get any worse."

CHAPTER THIRTY SEVEN

"What're you saying, Sam?" Justin glared at me. I knew he was pissed. Maybe that wasn't the best way to handle it, but it was already out there. He stopped pacing, grabbed me by the shoulders and hauled me off the couch.

I was horrified at what I'd said, but it was true. I blamed him for wanting to stop that night, and for not protecting me. I blamed Logan and Max because if they'd handled Stephen Tipton, I wouldn't have been hurt. I blamed my family for letting me become a cop. I blamed Tipton, obviously, for not dealing with life like a normal person, instead of turning to drugs and alcohol. I blamed everyone and everything, for every reason I could come up with. As the tears rolled down my face, I whispered some of that, knowing that I really shouldn't. Knowing it would shove him away from me. It wasn't fair to him, but he wanted in. He wanted to hear what I was going through, and I needed someone other than Logan to hear it right now. "You heard me. I can't count on anyone but myself or I'll get hurt again."

He let go of me, and stepped back. I felt my heart rip in two, knowing he'd leave me for thinking those things, much less saying them out loud. I caught myself crying hysterically, and hugging myself for the comfort I couldn't let myself take from him. I vented the anger and distrust of everything around me after the attack. He let me cry, and sat down in a chair, stunned.

It didn't take long before he reached for me. It looked like he wanted to hug me, to comfort me, but I couldn't handle it. I didn't deserve it. I shot across the room to escape his arms, where only moments before I'd felt loved and safe. I scrambled like a crab on my hands and knees off the couch to get away from him. I moved faster than I should've, but Justin was oblivious to my too-fast reflexes. He closed his eyes.

"Sam, you're killing me. I couldn't protect you that night, not as your partner, not as your friend, and not as the guy who was and is in love with you." He came over to where I hunched in the window seat in my living room, and he knelt in front of me. By this time, I hiccupped from crying, and my nose was running. Yeah, that's attractive. He cupped my chin in his hand and I couldn't quite meet his eyes, but he held my chin in place until I looked up.

He waited patiently until I met his eyes, and I saw the pain and hurt in his as he spoke. "How do I protect you? I failed once before. You are a strong, independent woman, and, God, I love that about you. How do I give in to my need to keep you safe all the time and not stifle one of the biggest things I love about you?"

I couldn't talk. My heart was in my throat. How could I reconcile my world crashing around me and Justin telling me he loved me at the time?

He paused for a moment for that to sink in, and then continued when I didn't respond. "There's a big part of me that wants to find the person who did this to you and beat him into a bloody pulp. I'm so angry myself that this happened to you that I want....." He trailed off and stalked out the door. When he got outside, he turned in a blind spin, balling up a fist and smashing it into the brick exterior of my house. I guess we all have our limits, and he'd hit his.

It scared me, but his desire to protect me felt both good and bad at the same time. He punched the wall over and over. I saw the blood drip off his knuckle, mirroring the tears leaking out of the corner of his eye when he turned away, breathing hard.

"Justin..." I tried to reach for his hand, to see how bad it was, but he backed away.

He looked down, as if he'd just realized he was injured. "Sam, I'm sorry. I don't know what the answer is. I know you're dealing with a lot. Maybe we're moving too fast when you have so much to deal with. I'm willing to give you the space you need, if that's what you want. You're not gonna lose me, but damn it, Sam, please remember it's my heart you hold in your hands. Be careful with it." He looked down at his bruised and bloody knuckles, as if just realizing he'd hurt himself, and spun away, stalking off toward his car.

I stood there, staring in disbelief and shock, tears drying on my face at the shock of the dependably solid Justin driven by frustration to violence. The pizza delivery guy pulled in as I started to go after Justin. It was too late. He'd already pulled out of the driveway. I paid for the pizza and went back inside, with Doyle curling around my legs. I took the pizza into the kitchen and set it on the table before I picked up Doyle, and cuddled him to me as I cried.

He let me hold him for about five minutes, which was longer than normal, and purred, a deep vibrating rumble, strong as a diesel engine. He had a tummy full of Chinese, and attention that he hadn't gotten in a long while. Who could blame him? After a while, he wanted down. I set him down on and he curled up in a ball beside my foot. Holding him had helped, but it wasn't enough. I opened the pizza box, and forced myself to eat a slice while

I examined my options. It tasted like cardboard.

What do you do when you have to face your attacker in court, you're facing bodily harm or death if you identify him, your boyfriend has shown a violent side you never expected even if he didn't hurt or threaten you, and you've learned that you're being watched in your own home? Why, you call someone you trust. In my case, I snagged my cell phone out of the pocket of my jeans and hit the one number always on my speed dial right after my parents. Certainly the best person to call when your love life was collapsing was your best friend. It was time to call in the cavalry, in the form of Nadia.

CHAPTER THIRTY EIGHT

Logan sat in the back of the conference room at the barn, listening to three different wolves argue about how to handle the situation with Sam. Stephen sat in the corner, a cloth gag in his mouth. Max had already decreed Stephen didn't get a say in the proceedings.

Stephen's eyes darted around in terror. He needn't be so frightened at what would happen. If Max wanted him taken care of, there wouldn't have been a meeting about it. He'd already be dead.

Instead, Logan was getting a good view of why Max had these meetings. He knew Max had already made a decision and had a plan of action. He'd overheard Max talking to some of his right hand thugs. They really weren't good for anything else but Max's dirty work. Some of them might have been good guys originally, but they were now solidly Max's men. He'd long since stopped wondering at what hold Max had over them. Any move against Max would involve a move against them. If he could find a way to neutralize them, he'd have a clear shot at getting Max knocked out of power.

These meetings served to let Max know how the pack would react to a decision, but Logan knew that Max had already decided what to do. It was a way of manipulating the pack into what Max wanted, rather than giving them any kind of voice in the proceedings. It was a way of licking Max's boots if one could figure out what his plan was and throw one's voice in support of it. Logan didn't play that game, but others did.

Max was gauging reaction. Logan knew that if the pack voted against Max's wishes, that he'd find some way to have one of goons do what he wanted anyway, and keep it quiet. If he had the support he wanted, he could take open action. The final result would still be the same.

Two men, Max's goons, argued to set up a hit on Sam. Logan's blood ran cold on that thought. Whether he ever got a chance to ask her out or not, he certainly didn't want to see her hurt, and she was smart enough to be an asset to a real pack leader. Another man argued for patience since she'd failed to point out Stephen in the line up.

"Why should we take the chance? We should eliminate the threat now, before she has the chance to do it. If we wait until she does, it'll be too late." Goon Number 1 said.

"We're not murderers! What if someone said that about you when you were attacked, Jenson? Should we kill all new wolves to protect the old ones? That's not right either." Logan recognized Adam's voice, raised in the back of the room. He grimaced. He'd asked Adam repeatedly not to get involved in pack politics. Adam was too valuable to risk, since he was the only medical doctor in the pack.

"She's a loose cannon. And why this sack of shit is still alive, I don't know." The other goon gestured at Stephen, trembling in his seat.

The arguments went on and on and no one agreed. Logan caught sight of Max, and the self-satisfied look of arrogance on his face terrified him. He looked at the group of men arguing for Sam's death, and realized the bastard was using the situation to solidify his position as pack leader. Putting a stop to the argument would place him squarely in opposition to Max's leadership. Adam had just made himself a target. Logan making any comment or taking any side would declare himself, and he wasn't ready for that yet. Most of his supporters weren't here, the ones who'd been the voice of reason in similar meetings in the past.

Max knew. Max was waiting for his response.

He needed to act quickly. He caught George's eye and tried to signal him to keep his mouth shut and spread the word. He snagged his pager off his belt, and pantomimed getting an urgent page, waving it at Max to excuse himself. He left the room, but instead of stopping in the Lounge to use his phone, he ran for his car, leaving George to cover his exit.

Sam needed a warning. She was in danger. He wished he had the number for her friend, Justin Noble. Logan didn't have the training for combat or weapons that the two cops did. He was afraid he'd have to fight in wolf form to be effective and wasn't sure that was a good idea. He was supposed to be a mild-mannered counselor. He couldn't call the police. They'd ask for an explanation. Maybe Noble would as well, but he'd seen the man spring to Sam's defense. He knew her partner would protect her first and ask questions later.

The only thing to do was drive as fast as he could to Sam's house. She might still be mad at him, but she was caught in a power play even she didn't understand. He pulled out of the dirt road in front of the barn and drove cautiously away, hoping none of Max's sentries heard him leave.

He breathed a sigh of relief when he got past Yellow Springs. It was late at night and the road was deserted, so he floored the gas. The Mustang roared to life, eating up the miles on Dayton-Yellow Springs Road as the speedometer edged over ninety miles an hour. He figured he had a head start on anyone sneaking out to pre-empt the pack meeting and earn brownie points from Max for solving a tricky situation.

And then he saw it. A police cruiser was right behind him, its lights illuminating the dark country sky like a slot machine that had just paid off. He was busted. He slowed down as quickly as he could and pulled over just as the cruiser's siren bleated once in his ear.

His heart took off at a sprint, and he swallowed hard against the panic that threatened to expose his wolf. He closed his eyes as he waited for the officer to approach the driver's side of his car, carefully leaving his hands at ten and two on the steering wheel, right where the officer would see them. It didn't pay to argue with a cop. The faster the guy wrote him his ticket, the faster he could get moving again toward Sam.

"Good evening, sir. Do you know how fast you were going?"

Logan blinked hard and took a deep breath."I do, officer. I'm sorry. My name is Logan Boyd. I'm a trauma counselor and I just got beeped by one of my patients."

"Do you have some ID?" the officer shone his flashlight in Logan's eyes. He hoped he'd controlled them enough to look normal.

"Sure do, officer." He handed over his driver's license, insurance card, vehicle registration, and his business card, praying that this cop would recognize his name. Maybe he'd get a break.

The officer walked away to run his name and plate number through the computer. Logan sat in the car, perfectly still as he watched a dark van pass him. I hope that's not a pack van, he thought. Sam's really in danger if someone's already on the way while the meeting is underway. Max could deny any involvement if it's taken care of before the meeting is over.

It took just minutes for the officer to write his speeding ticket, but it felt like hours, as Logan worried over what could be happening to Sam. He just hoped he wouldn't be too late.

CHAPTER THIRTY NINE

All I could think as I dialed the phone was, please be home.

"Hello?"

I was in luck. "Nadia. Thank God you're there."

"Sam? What's wrong? Are you okay? Where's Justin?"

"I screwed up." I said it quietly, as if whispering it made it better than it was. "Do you have plans tonight? Can you come over?"

She must have heard the tears I'd managed to hold back. It was clear in my voice that I was upset, and she knew me better than most. She immediately agreed to come over, promising to be here within twenty minutes. I felt bad asking her, but when I hung up the phone, I couldn't hold it in. I was crying again, feeling it come from the pit of my stomach. It had been years since I cried like this, slumped over the kitchen table.

I finally stood up and went into the bathroom to wash my face and hold a cold washcloth to my swollen eyes. There weren't any tears left, or at least I didn't think so. Doyle came out and rubbed against my legs before he scooted off to watch the birds through the picture window in my bedroom. I'd been abandoned for big-screen Cat TV. He could spend hours watching the birds in the backyards, acting as if he was watching some kind of big game hunting entertainment, twitching and meowing as if he had a chance to catch them. It made me smile even as I wrung out the washcloth.

True to her word, Nadia didn't delay getting to my house. She carried in a heavy burden of chocolate and wine. God love her, it was our long standing tradition to comfort each other like this. We'd done it with breakups and boys, nasty professors, fights with our folks, and general insecurity. The wine thing was still a relatively new addition, but it worked, or at least it had in the past. I didn't have the heart to tell her that chocolate just didn't appeal to me, but then I noticed that she had blocks of cheese to go with the wine, and beef jerky sticks. Apparently someone had filled her in on my crazy meat obsession.

She put down the bags and dug out some cheesy girly movies and sappy music as well as a giant box of tissues. I'd neglected my friend badly. We used to meet once a week for coffee or drinks, and we hadn't done it since before the attack. Something clicked back into place and I felt more myself than I had in a long time. Just seeing her concerned face helped me feel better.

She sat down next to me on the couch and put her arms around my shoulders. "So what's wrong, Sam? What's the problem?"

"Would you believe that so much has happened I don't know where to start?"

"Sam-sam, you can tell me anything, you know that." She brushed my hair back from my eyes, and I saw that my silence with her lately had hurt her feelings. I was carrying too big of a secret to keep to myself. I needed to tell someone, and at the list of people I trusted, Nadia was at the very top.

"I didn't believe it at first, Noddy. You're not going to want to believe it."

"We can tell each other anything, can't we? Will you promise to hear me out completely before you say anything?"

"Of course. But hold that thought. If it's that serious, we need wine first. Red or white therapy?" She waved the wine bottles at me.

I smiled as she bustled into the kitchen. Sounded like she's planned to come over and get me drunk to see if I'd spill my guts about what was wrong. I couldn't help thinking about Stephen Tipton, and swore I wouldn't get too drunk. "White, please. And mix it with some Sprite or something if you could."

Good friend that she was, she did exactly as I asked. Of course she brought out a giant tumbler full to the brim instead of one of my good wine glasses. That would teach me to specify the size of my drink along with the contents in the future.

I'd procrastinated enough. I needed to bounce my wild speculations off of someone, and Nadia was the most level-headed person I knew. "I don't think I ever got around to thanking you for stage-managing things at the hospital."

She tried the innocent look. "I don't know what you mean."

"Bullshit. You arranged things so Justin would take a chance."

"You'll never prove it. And I plead the fifth." She smiled, and took a sip out of her own glass, folding her long legs underneath her and preparing for a long talk. "So how goes it with Officer Yummy?"

"Terrible. And I'm the one who screwed it up."

That got her attention. "Why? You're in love with him. I know you are."

"It's not about how much I love him." I popped a cheese cube in my mouth and chewed thoughtfully, washing it down before I attempted to explain. "I know who attacked me. I just can't prove it."

Her jaw dropped. "Okay," she said. "You're going to have to explain. How do you know that? And what does that have to do with you screwing up your relationship with Justin?"

"I was bitten and attacked by a guy I've arrested in the past. I'm not going to tell you his name, because I think that's dangerous information to have right now." I stopped and took another small sip of wine. "The guy who attacked me was the survivor of a violent attack himself, and it destroyed his life. They never caught the guy who ripped him up, and apparently he got it even worse than I did. I've actually caught myself feeling sorry for him, and that's way out of character for me."

"No kidding." She put down the Oreo she'd been about to bite into and sank back into the cushions of the couch. "That doesn't sound like you at all, making excuses for someone who's committed a violent crime."

"It's not an excuse. It's maybe an explanation, and I can see why it was so hard for him to deal with. There's more to it. Yes, I'm having a hard time processing that I was attacked. I keep reliving it in my dreams, and I have a hard time not thinking about it during the day."

"Oh, Sam, why didn't you tell me? Has anything kept it out?"

"Not that I've found." I popped another cheese cube into my mouth and washed it down with more wine. "Justin realized it, too. He's the one who pushed me so hard into seeing Logan for counseling. He was right. I really needed to start dealing with it. Logan was great, at least at first.

Then he told me something I never thought I'd hear outside of a cheesy horror movie."

"Logan? The cute guy that visited you at the hospital? Now I'm dying to hear this." She scooted forward, and took a sip of her own drink. "Your mom told me about him."

I hoped she'd poured alcohol in her own drink, because I had a feeling she would need it before the night was over. I took a deep breath, and let it out in a single burst of words, almost afraid I'd chicken out if I didn't say it quickly. "I was bitten by a werewolf."

She gave me a funny look, like she thought I was playing a joke. "Sam? You're serious?

I looked her square in the eye. "As a heart attack."

"Does that mean...?"

"Yeah, it means I'm a werewolf now, too. You can't tell anyone."

"Are you sure?" She stared at me. I guess I'd had a bit more time to get used to the idea than I was giving her. She shook her head, muttering something under her breath about the hallucinogenic properties of painkillers. I could see her declaring me crazy in her head.

"Nadia, I haven't taken painkillers since the day after I came home from the hospital. This is the first alcohol I've had since before the attack."

"Post-traumatic stress disorder?"

"I do have that. That's what I'm in counseling with Logan to deal with, but I'm not psychotic. I'm not seeing visions, and I'm not hallucinating. I'm not crazy, or at least not any crazier than normal. I understand your reaction. I felt the same way at first."

"How'd you get convinced of this?" She crossed her arms in front of herself.

I could tell she would take some convincing, but I wasn't ready to change in front of someone yet. "I've turned into a wolf."

She stage-whispered, "You don't think you're one right now, do you?"

I grinned. "No. You'd know if I was. Wolves don't have vocal cords that can handle human speech, and they don't have opposable thumbs. I'd have a hard time talking and holding my wine glass." Among other things, I silently added.

She snorted. "All right, so you got me there. When did this happen?"

"A couple of days ago."

"Where?"

"A place outside of town, in the country."

"Were you alone?" She leaned forward, putting her hand on my elbow. Even if she didn't believe me, she wanted to support me. That meant a lot.

"No, there are others. They've been helping me to learn about it, and what I have to do to control it."

"What do you mean, control it?"

"It means that I have to change often, like once or twice a week to keep it under control. It's affected by emotions, and I'm shoveling enough emotional baggage right now to stock my own luggage store. If I don't change regularly, it'll be hard enough for me to go anywhere, much less keep working if I've got to be afraid I'm gonna spontaneously sprout fur."

"I sure hope you're kidding."

"I wish I was."

"Okay, assuming what you're telling me is real, when do you have to change again?"

"Probably tomorrow, at least to make sure it's not an issue later, at work, or somewhere equally problematic."

"Problematic? I think that might be the understatement of the year."

I could see a desire to see such a thing with her own eyes warring with her impulse to show me I was more than just a scientific curiosity. I knew she wouldn't treat me like a lab rat, but it was interesting to watch the conflict cross her face. After a minute or two, I let her off the hook. "Yes, Nadia, if you're around when I change the next time, you can watch it."

That settled, she moved in on the next issue. "Does Justin know?"

"No, he doesn't, and I'm not going to tell him yet. That's too much to drop on someone when we haven't even figured out how to make all this work. And right now I've got bigger problems."

"What do you mean, Sam? I thought the problem with Justin was the bigger problem."

"I'm caught in the crossfire of a screw up in the local pack. If I identify the guy who did this to me in court, the secret's out. He'd have to change in jail and you just can't hide it."

"So you're gonna let this guy get away with it? Sorry, I don't mean to tell you what to do, but that's just not like you." Her eyes went wide. "I don't buy it."

"You're right, Nadia, but if it comes out, how long will they let me be a police officer? How long before the media gets hold of it? How long before we're locked up for public safety? How long before someone wants to run medical experiments on us? How many families will disintegrate out of fear? Can I be responsible for that, knowing I'll suffer right along with them?"

Nadia always was quick on the uptake. "And who's to say there won't be another cop attacked if you don't stop him?"

I nodded. "You've grasped the exact problem. It could even be Justin on the receiving end of it. Besides, I didn't even see the guy at the time. I've put together all this from what everyone else has said. The only way they can link it up with a pack member is because they might have a fingerprint match."

Nadia slowly sipped her wine, and I watched her process everything. I wondered what her next question would be, and hoped I could answer it, not just to convince her. There were some things I still needed convincing of myself.

CHAPTER FORTY

"Fingerprints? How are you going to get around those, assuming that's what you want to do? It might be out of your hands."

I was surprised that Nadia's first question was so practical. I thought she'd ask more about being a werewolf rather than the immediate concern, but I was glad she understood my dilemma so neatly. "There's some kind of irregularity about them. I don't know the details, other than the crime lab wasn't sure what to do about them. I'm more worried about what could happen in the meantime."

"What do you mean? There's more?"

"Yeah, there is. Logan let slip that some of the other wolves are watching my house and I could be in serious danger if I decided to identify the guy in court. He even said that there have been others in the pack who expressed a desire to have me killed to prevent me from being able to do it. Yet, as you said, the fingerprints could take it out of my hands. Now, add that I can't report the fact that I'm being threatened over the outcome of the case, and the fact that the whole thing made the news, and you see the recipe for disaster."

"Could this get any more complicated?" She bit the edge of her fingernail as she said this, a nervous habit I thought she'd stopped a long time ago.

"Well, add that I screwed up with Justin, and you see why I've been a bit off lately. I should have called you earlier, Nadia. I didn't mean to cut you out of my life; I just didn't know what to do." I looked down at the floor.

She grabbed me in a hug and didn't let go. I realized then just how much I'd been holding my breath throughout the entire conversation. I was concerned she wouldn't want to be my friend anymore, that she would find it too dangerous or complicated, or that she would see me as a freak. I should've known better. She opened her arms and accepted me, fur and all.

"So, Sam, what happened with Justin?"

I spilled the whole story to her, about everything that had gone wrong. Every little fight, every little misunderstanding, leading up to the recent explosion. We analyzed it to death, and she never judged me, never made me feel like a failure. I felt bad about waiting so long. I should have known she'd support me no matter what. Some friend I am, if I doubted her that much.

"I'm going to say one more thing, and then we're going to try to get you to forget your problems for a couple of hours and enjoy the fact that you're alive, you survived, and that it's possible to have hope. Justin would be more understanding if he knew the whole truth. You guys are friends and partners as well as caring deeply for each other. I think he understands you might be in danger. Tell him, at least part of it. He might feel more included and that might help you and him to connect better and cement your relationship."

I leaned back and sipped my wine, mulling over the thought. "You know, you're right. I guess I better start hammering out exactly what I'm going to tell him, and how. I still think the whole werewolf thing is a bit much to tell him, but the stuff about being threatened and the stress of the attack is on the list of things he absolutely needs to know. There's just one other issue. How much can I feel free to talk to Logan? He's my counselor, approved by the department, so I can't really go to another counselor. I couldn't explain why I had to switch. Yet he's a member of the pack that's talking about killing me."

She grabbed another Oreo, and munched for a minute in silence. "I think you have to keep seeing him. I would, however, start limiting anything about your decision as to the court case. I wouldn't invite him to come with you if you meet with the police or the prosecutor again, although I don't think you can exclude him from the court hearings. Don't tell him anything he could report back, but you do need to keep talking to him. The man is a specialist in trauma counseling, and you've certainly been through trauma. It would be foolish to stop."

"I agree." And maybe that was enough answer for tonight. I needed a break from all the heavy emotional lifting of the day. I gulped the rest of my drink as she watched.

"So, are we solving the world's problems tonight, or is it time for some mindless entertainment, wine, junk food, and tearjerkers? I mean, I came prepared, so we better get busy or I've wasted sixty bucks." She grinned.

I couldn't help it. It didn't matter that she didn't really believe me. It mattered that she supported me, and whatever I might decide. I could tell that it wasn't real to her yet, but she was standing beside me whether I was furry or crazy. I'd take it, and hope Justin did the same.

"So, are we looking for sappy girly movies or big explosions?" She waved a handful of DVDs in my face to let me pick. I knew which one she'd pick, and it didn't seem a hard choice.

"Believe it or not, I'm thinking a sappy girl movie might be just the thing, but only if there's a happy ending."

"I've got just the thing."

"Romance sounds good. I feel like there's hope for Justin and me, so bring it on. And pour me another glass." I waved the empty tumbler at her. Talking had been thirsty work.

We settled down to watch Love Actually. I'm not one for sappy movies, but I'd been through the ringer. Sometimes finding a way to get the emotions out for someone else helps me handle them myself later. I'd never admit it, though. And Nadia enjoyed them better than the shoot-'em-up movies I preferred. I could always blame her.

We finished off two bottles of wine, a package of Oreos, pepperoni and jerky sticks, cheese, and roll of crackers before I finally felt full, half nauseous from the sugar and chocolate. I was definitely drunk. She must have poured heavier than I thought she had. I made Nadia promise that if I got out of control and started to shift that she'd lock me in the house and step outside to call Logan for help. I'm not sure that the message came out coherent, but I think she understood me. She seemed sober, and I realized I'd had most of the wine. I passed out with Doyle kneading my back with his front paws. As heavy as he was, and even with his neglected claws catching on my quilt, I didn't care. Cheap wine and junk food with a friend, analytical problem solving and love from my kitty to finish off a pretty stressful day of emotional ups and downs; not a bad way to end an evening.

CHAPTER FORTY ONE

N adia tucked Samantha into bed and waited for her to drift off before she went into the kitchen and poured herself a cup of coffee. She was concerned enough about Sam that she didn't want to leave her alone and drunk in the middle of the emotional upheaval of the last few weeks, but she was also concerned about Sam's claim of being a werewolf. She'd never known Sam to be crazy or a liar, but she had a hard time wrapping her head around it.

But what if it was true? If it was, then she was spending the night in the house of a brand new, drunk, werewolf. That couldn't be good. Sam needed normalcy, and she'd brought it, but she wondered what the cost would be. Justin had mentioned that he was afraid for Sam's safety, so Nadia couldn't just chalk it up to just a stress reaction from the attack. Sam wasn't paranoid if someone really was out to get her.

Nadia had a hard time believing Sam's story. She wanted to believe, for the sake of their friendship. Sam had been there for her during her mom's death, through her dad's breakdown, and had come through as a friend when she left her last boyfriend. It had been Sam, who'd held her hand when she pressed charges against him for hitting her for the first, last, and only time, and stayed with her through every step of the process. She owed Sam her loyalty and trust.

There was only one thing to do about it then. She poured herself a cup of coffee, adding cream and sugar, and turned Sam's recliner toward the big picture window in the living room that faced the street. She opened the curtain, and sat in the dark, sipping her coffee and watching the street with her cell phone in her hand, ready to call for help if anything strange appeared while she mulled over the revelations of the evening.

As she analyzed the conversation, she saw a shadow pass in front of the driveway off to her right, heading for the west side of the house. She was out of the chair like a shot, running for Sam's gun cabinet. She was confident with guns. Sam had insisted she learn in case of an emergency after the abusive boyfriend fiasco. If what Sam told her was true, then not only would she believe her, but this definitely would qualify as an emergency.

She checked the gun carefully, and jacked a round into the chamber in case she had to fire in a hurry, remembering all the hours on the gun range with Sam. She hugged the wall from the kitchen into the laundry room toward the noise. When she reached the utility room window, she took cover behind the edge of the heavy curtain and peered around the edge. She could still hear Sam snoring softly, oblivious to the potential danger in her shrubbery.

Hiding in the bushes was a man with blond hair, fitting the description Sam had given her of Logan Boyd. He was just under the window, on the west side of the house. It didn't look like he was doing anything but standing there, hidden in the bushes, watching the street. There was no indication that he was trying to get in. She hadn't heard the window rattle, or any of the doors tested, and the window over his head was securely locked. He didn't seem to be doing anything but watching.

She followed his gaze through the window to the street, and saw a nondescript gray van parked on the curb, just down the road and across the street, facing the house. It was a good lookout point, giving the occupants a clear view of the front door and driveway. She cursed softly under her breath, and eased the window open. "Don't move."

"Sam?" The man in the bushes whispered, starting to turn. She aimed the barrel of the gun at him, just in case.

"Are you Logan Boyd?"

"Who are you?" he asked.

"I'm a close friend of Samantha's, more than I can say for sure for you. You need to show your ID right now if you're Mr. Boyd. I do have a gun, and it's pointed right at your head." She poked him in the back of the head with the barrel of the gun to emphasize her point.

"I am Mr. Boyd, and I do have my ID. If you'll allow me to get it out of my wallet and hand it to you without shooting me, I will happily prove it."

"Fine." *Oops*, she thought. *Not sure how I meant for him to do that without moving.* "Nice and slow, Mr. Boyd."

Nadia took his wallet from his hand and used the light from a passing car to read the license inside the flap of the wallet. She saw the name Logan Boyd, a couple of credit cards in his name, and a few snapshots matching the photograph on the license. If it was a forgery, it was a good one. She handed it back and withdrew the gun.

"Thanks." Logan slipped the wallet back into his pocket. "What now?"

"Slip around to the back door. Don't let anyone see you. I'll meet you at the kitchen patio, and we'll see if we can't figure out what's going on here." She shut and locked the window before he could say anything else, and was gratified to see him slowly slink into the shadows toward the patio.

She headed straight for the kitchen. Nadia saw him approach the patio, and kept the gun in her hand. She took one look back into the house, toward Sam's darkened bedroom. She was still passed out face down on the bed. Doyle came out to investigate just as Logan rapped on the glass sliding door.

"Mr. Boyd, give me one good reason to trust you." She showed him the gun again.

"You must be Ms. Jeffries. I wondered if Sam told you the truth. Look, I'm not here to hurt her. I've been trying to protect her, and I came here tonight to warn her. Is she here?"

"Why would I tell you that? And how do you know my name?"

"I know your name because Sam told me your name. She felt bad that she hadn't told you the truth. She's dating a cop named Justin. The feline terror at your feet is Doyle. Let me in and I'll give you as many details as you require verifying what I'm telling you, but talking like this isn't safe for you, for her, or for me."

Nadia shrugged. He'd gotten enough details right to convince her to give him the benefit of the doubt, and she reserved the right to keep the gun. Something about him seemed trustworthy. No wonder Sam was conflicted about whether or not to trust him. "All right, but I'm keeping the gun out."

"Fine." He moved aside to allow her to open the door.

She let him inside, and he sat down at the kitchen table, not making an effort to get past her. "What are you doing here, Mr. Boyd?"

"Do I need to ask what she's told you?"

"That depends on why you care." She was feeling ridiculous holding the gun, but didn't feel right putting it back down. He was inside now, and within arm's reach.

"Where is Sam?"

"Asleep."

"You're kidding, right?" He cocked one eyebrow at her, looking surprised.

"I'm not sure what she tells you in those counseling sessions, but she seems to be getting worse instead of better."

He sighed. "That's not unusual in cases like hers, Ms. Jeffries. It's not unusual for a trauma survivor to hold it together through the initial tragedy and into the physical recovery process and then exhibit post traumatic shock when they start trying to resume a normal life."

"How many cases like hers have you counseled, Mr. Boyd?" Nadia knew she was treading a fine line, but she and Sam just didn't know enough about the situation to make wise decisions. She found it hard to keep an angry, sarcastic bite out of her voice.

Logan's eyes glittered in warning, as he grabbed her by the shoulders, heedless of the gun in her hands. She whimpered. "What exactly are you trying to tell me, Ms. Jeffries? It seems obvious Sam's told you a bit about her situation and the dilemma she's facing. You must have some idea of the danger she's in, or you wouldn't be patrolling her house with her gun while she sleeps." He loosened his hold on her arms as she whimpered. "But the real question here is whether you realize that by finally telling you the truth, she's also put you in danger."

Nadia's eyes grew wide. "I'm in danger?"

"Think about it. Think about what she's told you. Anyone watching her house is going to believe she's told you everything she knows, even if she hasn't. They don't know anything about you, and have no reason to trust you. If something happens to Sam, you have nothing to hold you back from spilling a very dark secret. You are now as much of a threat to them as she is."

"Don't you mean a threat to you?" She snapped back, jerking out of his grip.

"So she told you everything, then." He sighed. "I guess I should've expected it."

"Yeah, because that's what friends do. They take care of each other, they trust each other, and look out for each other. So I have to ask you, Mr. Boyd, if you're here to help her, to spy on her, or to hurt her. Are you a friend, or not?"

He appeared shocked by Nadia's question. He blinked hard and swallowed, then rubbed his hands over his face and looked her square in the eye. "Truth is, I'm here to help her, and I've likely made myself a target doing it. I have no plans to physically hurt her, and I'd like to find a way to avoid anyone trying to hurt her. She doesn't deserve this. How's she holding up?"

She took in his earnest face, and realized this was the best source of information on the threat against her friend. "Not good. Her emotions are all over the charts. She's purposely starting arguments. Not that she doesn't like to debate things, but these are knock-down, drag-out, emotional upheaval type arguments. She's holding on by a thread, and I don't know how long that'll hold, since it's affecting her personal life, too. I understand stress management is huge for you guys. All this pressure isn't helping."

He raised his hand to stop her. "How's she sleeping through all this?"

"A lot of liquor, a bunch of chocolate, and the shoulder of a friend to cry on will put your mind at ease when nothing else works. In her case, all she needed was the liquor and the friend."

CHAPTER FORTY TWO

I woke up the next morning to the drumbeat of hammers inside my head and a mouthful of cotton. I'm never drinking again.

I figured Nadia had sacked out on the living room couch or in the spare bedroom. She'd been up later than I was, so I was surprised to hear conversation and laughter coming from the kitchen. I stepped into the room, and cringed when I realized they'd thrown open the blinds on the sliding glass door, letting in the harsh morning sun. Once the pain in my eyes dulled, I realized Nadia was talking and laughing with Logan, of all people. When did he get here?

"Morning, sleepyhead," Nadia sang out as I grumped past them to the coffee pot. I ignored her long enough to realize there was only a half cup of coffee left in the pot. I took what was left and started brewing another pot. My stash of specialty coffee was almost gone. Apparently the giggly twins in front of me had been on a caffeine raid all night. That alone should be a hanging offense.

"Did you stay up all night? And drink all my good coffee?"

"Yup," Nadia said, "and it's a good thing we did."

"What's that supposed to mean? And when did he get here?" I asked, pointing to Logan, who seemed a little too perky for this early in the morning. Why the hell was he here?

"There was a meeting last night, Sam. Max has forbidden them from killing you, but they were talking about coming here last night. I tried to get over here to warn you, but you'd passed out before I got here. So we kept watch all night. And, Sam, I did warn you about drinking, didn't I? Nothing happened, thank God."

"I didn't plan on drinking much, Logan, and since our last trip to the barn was just a couple of days ago, I should be okay, right?" I asked. Then, as he nodded, another thought occurred to me. How did Nadia know who Logan was? "What did you do when he showed up, Nadia?" I sat down at the kitchen table, willing the coffeepot to brew faster.

"You once showed me where you stash your extra handgun. I remembered, and after you told me everything last night, I figured you needed the sleep. I only had the one glass of wine, so I stayed up to watch out for you. You needed the break from all the worry, so I worried for you." She smiled, and it was hard not to smile back.

"Why do I not like where this is going?" I rested my head on the table. This couldn't be good. Maybe getting drunk last night wasn't such a good idea. In fact, it hadn't been my idea. How much alcohol had she put in my glass?

"Logan was hiding in the bushes under the utility room window. I pointed the gun at him, and he showed me his ID. We realized we both just wanted to protect you, so we've been sitting here talking all night."

"Great. So you've solved all my problems, and found a way to grant world peace?"

"We're good, but we're not that good." Logan grinned. "You're the one with the experience in the criminal justice system, so we can't help you navigate that. We have a plan to keep you from being alone for more than a few minutes at a time until you get to that point."

"Oh goody, my own personal bodyguards. Have you guys forgotten that I'm a cop, and have at least a passing knowledge of self-defense?"

"How would you have protected yourself last night? You were so upset that you were head blind. Even if Nadia hadn't gotten you hammered, you wouldn't have heard them until they were right on top of you. They certainly wouldn't take turns. They'd have all jumped at once. As it is, I'm not sure why they haven't acted yet." Logan added.

"Nice group of friends, buddy. Not making me want to help them."

"Okay, Sam. You've only met, what, about four pack members? I think you need to meet some of the others, in a different setting. You need to meet some that aren't just out to kill you, who are good people, as well as good wolves. I've called a few of those people, those that I trust, and they're going to watch your house. Once you've had enough coffee to feel awake, we're gonna go meet them for breakfast."

I wanted to be mad they'd planned the day for me. It was, however, my day off, since I almost never worked a Monday through Friday week, and I'd gone back just a couple of days prior to my regular day off. I did want to meet other werewolves. I wasn't sure that it would sway my decision on what to do about Tipton. I desperately wanted him to spend the rest of his life behind bars, but it couldn't hurt to know more about the people who would be affected by whatever I decided. They deserved my attention before I made up my mind. It might not have been my idea of a day off work, but I was interested.

"So if we're going to meet these guys, where are we headed? Do I have time for another cup of coffee, some Advil and a shower?"

"Yeah, you have time." He smiled at me and sipped his coffee.

I poured myself another cup of coffee and looked closely at Logan and Nadia. As much as I didn't know whether to trust Logan about the wolfy stuff, he seemed like a decent guy, and good looking to boot. Nadia deserved a nice guy. I had the sudden thought that if Logan proved to be trustworthy, I might have to consider setting them up.

I shook my head. I wasn't sure setting up my best friend with a werewolf was a good idea, no matter how nice he was. She didn't need mixed up in all that. I shook off the idea that I'd already mixed her up in it just by telling her my secret. There was no sense getting her in any deeper than she already was.

I ran through the shower, and dressed quickly. I threw a ball cap onto my still-wet hair, and chose some older clothing. I figured old crappy clothes wouldn't matter if I shredded them. I did feel a little bad that I was dressed like a sloppy teenager when I was meeting other pack members, but I could feel the wolf just under my skin. It wouldn't take much to force a change today; of course, it could just be stress, nerves, and paranoia making me feel that way. Maybe drinking really hadn't been a good idea last night.

I threw together a small duffle bag with extra clothes, underwear, a bra, socks, and shoes. No way did I want to do the slut-girl walk of shame back into the house later with no bra and a white t-shirt again. I walked back into the kitchen to Logan asking if I was ready to leave.

I followed Logan out to his car, which he'd parked on the street around the corner. I waited until we got inside to ask where we were headed.

"Just around the corner."

I started laughing and couldn't stop. He wanted breakfast. The breakfast place just around the corner was open, and I couldn't think of a better place for a werewolf summit meeting.

Bunny's Hasty Tasty Pancake House, here we come.

CHAPTER FORTY THREE

Logan drove us to Bunny's. It's a local restaurant with home-cooked meals as its main attraction, especially breakfast. On a weekend morning, it's popular, and today was no exception. The early birds were thinning out but some were coming in for an early lunch. I was surprised when we joined three others already at a table.

Why was I surprised? They just didn't look like my own mental picture of how werewolves in human form were supposed to look. Not that I knew what a werewolf was supposed to look like, but whatever they were supposed to look like, this wasn't it.

The one woman at the table was about my mother's age, but even in casual weekend clothing, she looked like she belonged in an upscale office, wearing a suit. I really felt bad in my cut off jeans. She had a polish to her that made me feel like a scruffy orphan, with her classy makeup and perfect hair. There were two men, one in scrubs, like he worked in a hospital, though he looked my age or younger. Sure enough, he wore a badge from Miami Valley Hospital, the one I'd been taken to when I was attacked. His badge announced him as Dr. Winters.

The other man was the one who had changed for me my first time at the barn, the one who'd driven me home after my first change. I couldn't remember his name, but something about him just screamed retired law enforcement. I wondered why I hadn't noticed it the last time I saw him, but I guess I'd had other things on my mind at the time. He was in his early fifties, just shy of six feet tall, and sporting a buzz cut.

I sat down, and the waitress, a middle-aged woman with a loose gray bun, approached and asked for our orders. I noticed that, even though none of them ordered the same thing, there was something in common among all of us. No one ordered a salad or a vegetarian lunch. I smiled as I ordered my own omelet with a side of bacon and extra sausage. Guess we had some similarities after all.

After the waitress left, the guy in the buzz cut reminded me that his name was George, and asked how I was doing.

"I guess as well as can be expected. It's not like there's any going back, is there? So we might as well see what we do from here." I shrugged.

He frowned at me. "That seems a bit defeatist."

"I haven't had enough coffee for perky and positive."

The whole table laughed. George smiled at me. "No question you're a cop. Something about law enforcement seems to attract those with a smart ass attitude though I'm not sure they put that in the recruiting brochures. It just seems to be a side effect."

"And you?" I couldn't help grinning at him. He was right.

"I was with the county sheriff's department for twenty five years. Retired a couple years ago, and I work with Judge McCall's court as a bailiff."

The waitress brought us our coffee, and I grabbed for mine like a life preserver thrown to a drowning man. The woman sitting with us at the table gave me a warm smile. I wanted to like her instantly. Maybe it was just that my brain was finally kicking over with the influx of caffeine, but she just reminded me of Mom. And that was a very comforting reminder to me at the moment.

And just like Mom, she took charge. "We're all here now. Logan, you wanted us to talk with Sam about our situation, and how we all came to this?"

"Yeah, Judith, I do. By the way, Sam, this is Judith Renault. She works as an executive assistant in a law firm downtown. You've met George now, and this is Adam Winters. Adam is a resident at Miami Valley's emergency room."

"Were you there when I was brought in?" I wanted to know if he had a hand in my treatment. If he had, I wanted to thank him. I was surprised he was a doctor, though. He must be older than he looked.

"I wasn't on duty until the next morning. When I went on rounds, I read the case notes and realized what must've happened. I'm the one who contacted Logan. Since you were stable, it seemed more his field than mine."

"Well, thank you," I said. "He has been a big help, even if I still feel like I don't know what's going on."

Logan grimaced. "That's why I brought you here, Sam. To help explain all the things I couldn't explain on my own, things you need to hear from other people."

"Is this another case of I need to see it to believe it?"

"Maybe. I just figured you needed to hear it from more than just me."

Our food arrived just then. Conversation stopped as the waitress served us. I didn't wait for the others to get their food, because I wasn't sure I would have much of an appetite once the others told me all their little secrets. It took little effort to demolish my breakfast in minutes. I would have ordered a second plate, but no one else did, so I leaned back in my chair.

Once the others had finished their food, and the waitress filled the coffee cups again and left, Logan asked me for my impressions of Max.

"I don't know what to think of him. On one hand, he seems like he wants to help others, and the barn is impressive. On the other hand, there's something about him I just don't trust. I don't know what it is, but something about him wants me to turn around and run the other way. He's kind of scary," I paused, considering my words. "Something about him just rubs me the wrong way, I guess. I can't put a finger on why."

Logan sighed heavily. "It's good that you recognize there's something about him that's just not right. Some of the information we're going to share with you has been pieced together from all kinds of different sources. I'm sure we've missed something. I don't know exactly where it all starts, but I can bring you up to date on where we're at."

"How do you tell a story if you don't know where it starts?" Okay, I was being nitpicky, but I wanted to know it all. I was tired of secrets. I was sick of being afraid.

"We weren't here for the beginning, so we've had to figure it all out from random comments, odd hints, old records and some guesswork." Judith commented.

"Is this even going to live up to the buildup you're giving it?" I tried teasing, but they were serious. No one laughed.

Logan looked around the restaurant. The crowd was thinning out, and the hustle and bustle around us was down to a soft hum. Judith suggested that we adjourn elsewhere. It made sense to me. If they were that secretive, it would be easier for someone to overhear something they shouldn't in a quiet restaurant.

Chapter Forty Four

Stephen heard voices and an electronic tune as he walked toward the conference room at the barn. He stopped, his arms full of blueprints for more improvements to the facility, and listened intently. Maybe Max would let something drop that he could use to warn the cop. He was still surprised he'd been allowed to live through the night after being tied up and gagged and made to listen to the others debate cold-blooded murder.

Max's voice was hard and angry. "Where's she at now?"

There was a short pause, and Stephen poked his head around the corner to see Max holding his cell phone to his ear. Two other wolves sat at the table next to him, stirring sugar into their coffee mugs, and waited silently for Max to finish his conversation.

"He did *what*? Where are they now? And you say her little friend's at her house all by herself? We're on our way."

Oh, no, thought Stephen. Max has decided to take matters into his own hands. After whipping the others into a state of panic the night before, Stephen knew Max could set things up to take care of matters on his own and then blame the cop for threatening to expose them. He knew he had to do something, so he flattened himself against the wall outside of the conference room, waiting for Max to let his plans slip. It didn't take long.

"Come on, you two. We're going to go buy ourselves a bit of insurance, and get rid of some frustrations. It looks like we've got a mutiny on our hands. The boy is gathering his allies at Adam's parents' house. Looks like they're gonna move against us." Max stood up, his metal folding chair making a scraping noise against the concrete floor. Stephen sucked in his breath, not daring to make a sound.

One of the men sitting at the table asked the stupid question. "What are you talking about, insurance?"

Max sighed, and then, fast as a snake, punched the idiot in the eye. "We're gonna go get Samantha's friend and bring her here. If the pup won't listen for her own sake, we'll start going after her friends and family until we find one she'll protect. It's the best insurance I can think of. Little miss goody two shoes will only last so long against other people getting hurt. Wonder if her little friend's cute. That doesn't work; we'll go find us that officer she's sweet on. Noble was the guy's name, wasn't it?"

Another voice spoke up. "Yeah, it's Justin Noble."

Stephen's jaw dropped.

More people were getting hurt because of his stupidity. He needed to do something. But what could he do? There was no phone line he could call out on. Max had confiscated his own cell phone a long time ago so he couldn't call his dealer and order drugs. He wondered how he'd get a message out. He snuck quietly away from the conference room back into the hallway as Max and his goons headed the opposite way toward the cars.

He passed another pack member in the hallway. "Quiet night, tonight."

The guy nodded, grunted, and kept walking.

Stephen kept walking in the other direction, and headed for the barracks rooms. Another young pack mate was sound asleep on one of the bunks, facedown. Stephen wondered for just a minute if he could convince the guy to help him, and then he saw it.

The guy had taken his wallet and cell phone out of his pants and left them on the floor beside the bunk. Stephen saw his life line and shifted the blueprints in his arms onto the empty bunk beside him.

Inch by precious inch, Stephen eased himself across the room, lit only by a slender finger of light coming in from the hallway. The phone was just inches from the sleeping man's hand as it dangled off the edge of the bed, almost touching the floor. He left the lights off to keep shadows from falling across the man's face and waking him up. Stephen sank to his hands and knees on the linoleum floor to scoot over and avoid the possibility of his tennis shoes squeaking as he walked. His breath echoed in his head against the silent stillness of the room.

Halfway across the room, he heard the pack member he'd passed in the hallway walking back toward him. It had to be the same man; Stephen could hear him humming as he walked down the hall. Footsteps came closer and closer in the hallway, and he saw a shadow outside the door. He froze in place, unable to hide without alerting the sleeping wolf in front of him. Just as the door started to open, he heard another voice calling down the hall.

"Yo, Dave, you forgot to turn off the coffee pot."

The man outside the door cursed under his breath, and the shadow outside the door walked away. Stephen took a deep breath of relief, and one arm shot out to grab the phone. He slid it into his pocket, and eased his way back across the room before standing up and claiming his blueprints. His heart thudded in his chest as he left the room.

Where to make the call? Not in the barracks, that's for sure. He slipped into the Lounge, and dialed the number for Logan's cell phone. He got a message saying that the customer was out of range. He cursed and dialed Adam's number. No answer from Adam's cell. He tried George. Voice mail picked up. He left a quick message that he needed to talk to Logan or Samantha, and that someone was about to get hurt.

What to do now? He didn't have any other numbers he could call but one.

It was time to make that call.

He dialed the number for the Dayton Police and got an operator.

"911, what's your emergency."

"Ma'am, I have an emergency message for one of your officers, and I don't know how to reach him or if he's on duty. Can I leave the message with you and someone can get in touch with him?"

"Sir, is this a police matter?"

"I'm trying to prevent it from becoming one, ma'am."

"What's your name, sir?"

"I can't give that to you. But please contact either Justin Noble or Samantha Hochenwalt and tell them that someone has threatened Officer Hochenwalt. I'm afraid they might be after Officer Noble as well."

"Neither one of those officers are on duty at the moment. Do you mean that someone's trying to hurt them?"

"Yes. Three men, probably in a dark blue late 80s model van or a black Ford extended cab truck, plates out of Greene county, are looking for Officer Hochenwalt, to hurt her, maybe kill her. They mentioned trying to find Officer Noble and hurting him as well. This has to do with Officer Hochenwalt's attack."

"Sir, how do you know about that?"

"It's not important. Just find them. And warn them. And tell them not to go home."

He hung up the phone as the operator protested, and then he hid the phone in the cushions of the leather sofa, where it could be explained away as having fallen out of the owner's pocket, and muffled in case the operator tried to call back. Then he left the room. There wasn't much else he could do but wait and hope his message got to them in time.

CHAPTER FORTY FIVE

We paid our bills, and headed to our cars. Adam suggested we head to his parents' place. Logan and Judith nodded, but I had questions.

"Why are we going to your parents' house?" I asked.

"After I became, well, you know, I asked my parents if I could use the basement. They know the truth about what I am, and they've been very supportive. My dad and I spent weekends that summer converting the basement room into a place where I could go to safely change if I didn't have enough time to get out to the barn between shifts at the hospital. I didn't even want to work at the hospital until I had a place I could run to in a hurry. I work in the emergency room, sometimes 72 hours straight. There's a limit on how long you can hold off. We installed a lock on the door so that only someone with a key can get in, and it unlocks on either side with the key. We also put a lock on the inside of the door that I can't unlock if I've changed, and if it's engaged, it can't be unlocked from the outside. It was my way of making sure I'd get through the change without being interrupted, and know I couldn't hurt anyone else." Adam shrugged.

He seemed so laid back about it. I'd certainly never thought about those kinds of precautions, but of course I lived alone. Then again, what if Justin came in as I was changing? Maybe I needed to put together something like that in my own basement. "Is it really necessary to be that secure? It sounds a little paranoid."

"Well, I guess I was a little paranoid when I first became a wolf. I didn't trust my family not to be completely terrified of me and think of me as a monster. I didn't trust myself not to hurt them. By letting me be paranoid, they showed me how much they loved and supported me. It took a while for me to realize that the room was unnecessary. But then we started having problems in the pack, and it became a good place to talk about what was going on without worrying about others overhearing us. The only people who know about that room are standing right here with us, except for Mom and Dad." He smiled. "It's safe."

Logan nodded. "He's right, Sam. And we need to get off the street to have this conversation." I followed him to his car and we drove off.

Adam's parents lived in a well kept brick house in the Oregon District. I'd always loved the historical houses in the Oregon District, with their distinctive air of tradition and culture. I saw a weeping willow in the park across the street and it made me smile. There had been a tree similar to it in my grandmother's front yard when I was a kid, and it brought back good memories. I remembered hiding behind the big branches playing hide and seek with my grandfather before he died. I always hid in the same place, but he'd always made a game of it. It was good to remember something so innocent right now.

Adam pulled into a driveway and parked inside a garage with Judith and George in his car. That left Logan and I to park about a block away, just around the corner. I thought we were lucky to get a parking spot so close. Parking in the Oregon District can be a tight squeeze.

We approached the house and Adam's dad answered the door. He let us in without a word, and gave Adam a bit hug. He had a worried look on his face when he saw all five of us. "Adam, is everything all right?"

"Yeah, Dad, we just need to talk private business. I couldn't think of anywhere I trusted more."

His dad's face softened at his son's vote of confidence. "Let me know if there's anything we can do to help. You guys want anything to eat or drink?"

"No, Dad, we just had breakfast."

I could see his dad wanted to do more to help, but didn't know what to offer. I smiled at him, and followed Adam down to the basement. I could see my parents being that supportive. I really needed to think about telling them. They'd be completely in my corner.

Once we got downstairs, I couldn't help myself. "Adam, how old were you when you were attacked?"

"I was a very painful eighteen," he said, as he unlocked the heavy door. "I had skipped a couple years in school, and was done with college, already started in medical school. I didn't really have any friends. I didn't do much on weekends except watch horror movies. That didn't help when I realized what I'd become."

"Jeez, I bet it didn't. Don't feel bad. It's what I thought about, too."

He smiled. "I'm glad I'm not the only one."

Logan cleared his throat as we entered. He looked at Judith, who nodded, and I wondered who was really in charge of this meeting. Adam just looked uncomfortable and George excused himself to get out a couple of folding chairs.

It was time to get down to business. As they all sat there looking at each other to start, I opened my big mouth. "Okay, I don't care who tells me your big deep dark secret, but someone please tell me what's going on. The suspense is getting old." I crossed my arms.

Three heartbeats of awkward silence later, Judith shot me a hard glare. "You have no idea how hard it is for us to trust you. Patience is a virtue, Sam." I'd misjudged her. For all the polish on the outside, she was a woman who got things done. I'd just seen her as a contemporary of my mom, instead of a power in her own right.

I couldn't help it. I grinned at her. "If you're looking for someone with a boatload of patience, you've asked the wrong woman. You can trust me. You wouldn't have brought me here if you couldn't, but patience is only a virtue of mine when I don't have to wait for it."

A sharp bark of laughter came out of Judith's throat. "Okay, smart-ass. We've brought you here, as you said, so we've obviously decided to trust you." There was no question who was really calling the shots here. It wasn't Adam. Logan might have thought he was, but even he had looked to Judith. George hadn't said a word. I hadn't expected it. A part of me was happy to see it. Seeing a woman in this situation, rather than a man, isn't always about female empowerment. Sometimes it's just about comfort and familiarity.

CHAPTER FORTY SIX

Judith turned to Adam. "The best place to start is probably with what happened to you."

I looked around the room, waiting for him to start. It seemed like some sort of weird twelve step program for recovering werewolves, with the bare concrete walls, and all of us sitting in metal folding chairs. I fought a giggle. I was saved from embarrassing myself with my internal monologue when Logan got up and walked away. I watched him leave, wondering what was wrong.

I didn't get a chance to ask. Adam started talking instead.

"About a week after I was attacked, I came home from the hospital to recover. The doorbell rang after my folks left for work, and my little sister was at school. I was home by myself, so I answered the door. I figured it was a neighbor, or one of Mom's friends coming to check on me. I just wanted to be left the hell alone, and people weren't taking the hint."

I knew the feeling. I nodded.

He got up and paced around the room while he spoke. "It was Max, and Logan, at the door. They asked me about strange symptoms, things I'd wondered about, but hadn't asked anyone about yet. I told them to get lost."

"Max must have loved that." I laughed.

"He got persistent, and I got mouthy. I was eighteen and stupid." He stopped and looked at me, grinning at the memory. "I remember telling them that if I had weird symptoms, I certainly knew how to handle it. I was almost a doctor, after all, so they could kiss my ass and get the hell out of my house. To Logan's credit, I think he was horrified at what happened next."

Logan made a choked sound. "I was, Adam. I never expected you to be stupid. You were supposed to be this gifted kid, but you stood there and told him, let's see if I can quote you, to 'get penetrated with a cattle prod.' I'd have laughed at it if Max hadn't lost his temper." He turned to me, and I could see that he no longer found it funny. "Max has a temper, but I've never seen him lose it quite that bad."

The moment of levity was over. Adam's shoulders slumped. "I know you didn't plan it, Logan. I know you pulled him off me. We've had this discussion. We're okay. That doesn't mean it's fun to remember, but Sam needs the whole story, right?"

"Yes, I do. I appreciate you telling me this, Adam." I laid a hand on his shoulder to encourage him.

He resumed his tale. "Max got up in my face, and told me to respect my elders. The funny thing was that I'd been telling adults what to do and where they were wrong for years. I didn't feel like a kid any more. He slapped me in the face, and then he hit me, really hit me. He punched me right in the face, over and over again. I started begging and crying for help, for him to stop. I'd had a hairline skull fracture from the initial attack. One good solid hit to the right spot on my head, and I could have been killed. I was terrified."

Logan interjected. "Max was going too far. He'd told me about Adam's attack, and wanted me to go with him to find out whether Adam would become one of us, and wanted me to go with him to meet our newest wolf. That's how he said it. I'd never gone with him to meet new wolves before. I knew he wanted me to start taking over that job for the pack, so I let him talk me into it. I thought he gave people a choice. I didn't know what happened to people who refused to join our pack, but once I saw what he'd done, I realized why. No one ever had. I hauled Max off of him and told him to take a hike so I could talk some sense into Adam."

Adam interjected, "After Max left, Logan helped me clean up a bit. I had a puffy lip, and ended up with a black eye. Logan helped me ice down my face enough that I could convince my folks that it was just bruising coming up late after the initial attack, and we talked for a long time. Logan changed in front of me, and I saw what I would be facing."

"Adam's attack came at a time when I'd noticed other things, strange things, happening within the pack. Little things said by pack members made me think there was a plan to bring in someone new, almost like a recruiting drive. I never actually heard what the plan was, and no one ever came out and said, 'hey let's make a bunch of new wolves.' Instead I would hear one or another talking about a young kid with a medical degree or a secretary to a prominent lawyer or a court bailiff and the next thing I knew we had a new pack member fitting that description. It doesn't take a trained investigator to realize people were being targeted for membership. The question was who was behind it, and why." Logan stood up and walked away from us. He stuffed his hands into his pockets and his shoulders slumped.

For some reason, I was surprised to see Logan so upset. I'd just never seen him react to anything. He hadn't reacted to my screaming fits, hadn't been upset by Justin's temper tantrum. He hadn't seemed shaken when they pulled him out of the hole in the ground after our run-in with the hunters. "Logan, I'm not sure I understand. Are you saying that someone is handpicking members of the pack for their skills? How could any one of us do this to anyone else? Especially knowing what this is like?"

George stood up and walked over to Logan, putting his arm around his shoulders. "They'd do it for power, Sam. Why do people do anything these days? Someone is building the pack piece by piece to build up an enormous amount of power and influence in this area. Our pack doesn't really cross a lot of socio-economic barriers. Most of us are highly educated or have well established professional reputations, or are completely dedicated to Max. He demands loyalty. And after someone finally accepts there is nowhere else to turn, they end up working for the pack itself."

"And that job is why they were recruited in the first place," I guessed.

"Smart girl," said George. "Exactly right. Adam was given the job of setting up a first aid station for us at the barn, and to keep an eye out for new recruits at the hospital. Max demands that Adam give him a copy of his on-call schedule, so he knows when Adam is there to cover up any symptoms in the medical charts. Judith works for a prominent attorney downtown, and knows all her boss's little secrets. Don't worry, Judith, even I don't know what they are. I just know they exist, and that's part of how Max gets low cost and prestigious legal counsel for pack matters without having to declare ourselves a business entity or finding his name on a file."

"Don't tell me, George, you're there to get Judge McCall's ear if someone gets into trouble, or to nudge him in favor of us if there's a ruling we're concerned about."

"You got it, Sam. Judge McCall is the presiding judge for the common pleas court. His hands touch just about every case that comes through there in some way or another. Evidently this has been going on for years. We just don't know where it began."

Logan cleared his throat forcefully. "Yes, George, we do. Or rather, I do." He paused. "I just put the last pieces together in my head."

The others all looked at him, questions written all over their faces.

He started to explain. "It all began with two childhood friends. One went off the big city to seek his fortune, and the other stayed local to raise a family. Eventually the city boy returned home and requested the help of his friend. The help was given, and the city boy bit the hand that helped him, so to speak." Logan stared off in the distance. I wondered what he was looking at.

Judith broke the silence that followed his announcement. "How do you know this?"

"I've known for years that the pack started this way. I just didn't tie it all together as one person's ambition until just now. It all fits. It's not an accident. It was planned from the beginning to be like this. I understand now why I was beaten way back then. They wanted to prevent me from saying anything."

"Who beat you, Logan?" I asked, completely bewildered.

"My father was Max's closest childhood friend. My father was the first person attacked; the first new member of the Dayton pack. Max had moved away years ago, and came back to hide from some sort of trouble. Dad was a real estate agent, and Max used him. Dad knew how to transfer property without registering it under a specific name that could be traced in public records, and Max needed a very low profile. Max repaid that favor by attacking him and making him a werewolf to ensure his silence."

My jaw dropped.

Chapter Forty Seven

Justin fidgeted sitting the front seat of his truck. He'd watched Sam leave the house with that Boyd guy early this morning, and followed her to Bunny's, where the two of them had met up with three other people, including his dad's friend George. It was an odd coincidence. He didn't believe in odd coincidences. There was no such thing.

Something was going on, and Sam was in danger. She had no idea what she was getting herself into, and the dark van that had remained outside her house all night was just another indication of how bad it was getting. And how was George involved?

John had told him to go home and get some sleep, but he just couldn't leave her. Every nerve in his body was strung tight, every instinct he had screamed that something was wrong. He'd gone home after their last fight just long enough to toss and turn fitfully in bed for an hour, and realized that he'd pushed her too far. She was pushing him away, because he was demanding too much of her this early in a relationship. When he saw the van outside her house, he felt like a fool. She might feel the way she'd said, but he'd be damned if he walked away when she needed all the protection he could give.

He shook his head. God, he sounded like a stalker when he thought that way. Nothing could make that train of thought sound better. He'd almost gone home eight hours ago, but his cell phone rang with a warning from dispatch that someone was trying to warn him of danger against himself and Sam. He'd loaded as many caffeinated sodas as he could into the front of his truck and parked himself in front of her house watching for trouble.

He'd seen Nadia walking around inside the house, and hoped Sam had at least confided in her friend. Even if Sam couldn't talk to him, and boy did that thought hurt, he hoped she was talking to someone other than this Boyd guy. He was trouble. Justin just couldn't put a finger on why he felt that way, but he couldn't shake the feeling that something was up with him.

He'd watched the house all night, fending off calls from his dad. John called on an hourly basis to check on him, worried that he was losing his mind and blowing things out of proportion. He'd reminded his foster father repeatedly that he was a cop as well as Sam's boyfriend, and he didn't intend to ignore his instincts. John had finally given up, and resigned himself to the hourly check in phone calls.

He hadn't had anything to eat since lunch the day before, the day he'd stormed out of Sam's house before the pizza showed up. His stomach growled as they left Bunny's, and Justin followed at a discrete distance as Sam got into the car with Boyd and followed the others to a house in the Oregon District. He saw which house they went in, and parked so he could watch the house. He could see if someone pulled out of the driveway, but he couldn't find a better vantage point without giving them a chance to get out of his sight. He opened another can of Mountain Dew as watched them go inside, wincing as the carbonation hit his already raw stomach. Sooner or later, he had to put in real food, or all the soda was going to eat a hole in his stomach lining.

Justin had called Nadia when dispatch had alerted him of the anonymous tip. He hoped she'd already left, since there was no answer at the house. Since she didn't answer her cell either, he prayed she'd gone home to sleep off the late night she'd spent with Sam the night before.

His cell phone buzzed in his jeans pocket, and he dug it out, annoyed at the distraction. "Hi, Dad," he answered.

"Son, have you gotten any sleep yet?"

"Don't start."

"Justin, if you don't get some sleep soon, you're gonna have to call in sick. You can't drive around in a cruiser if you don't get some sleep. I can come out and keep watch for you if you want, but you're gonna get hurt if you try to go to work without sleep."

"Dad, I'm not at her house any more. I followed her."

A long sigh sounded in his ear. "You're taking this too far, and if she catches you following her around town, she's going to lose her temper. You're risking a lot for your instincts. She'll be pissed at you. You're gonna ruin this if you keep it up, Justin."

"She already is pissed at me, but I'm telling you, there's something else going on here. I keep wondering if she was trying to warn me off. Hold on, Dad. There's someone pulling up to the house she's in. It looks a lot like the van I saw the other night outside her house. I gotta go."

He dropped the phone, and started the motor on the truck, easing up at the curb. His truck blocked a fire hydrant, but he could see the front door better. Those two men meant business. He'd wait and see if they were there for Sam, he decided, as he checked his service pistol and disengaged the safety. If they were there to hurt her, he'd make sure they hurt as well.

CHAPTER FORTY EIGHT

Judith was the first to speak, although all of us were staring at Logan, slack-jawed in surprise. "Logan, what happened?"

"My father went along with Max for the first few years, and then he figured it out. He kept a journal. I was just a kid at the time. Dad decided he didn't want any more to do with it, but he couldn't tell Max that. He was afraid of what Max might do to us. After a while, the stress caught up to him. I was about fourteen at the time, and I have a mother and two sisters. I came home from school alone on a day that Mom had plans to take the girls out shopping, and found Dad. He'd killed himself, and left me a note with a key to a safe deposit box and strict instructions never to tell Mom or the girls about it.

"I finally went to the bank to see what was inside. Dad left all the records detailing his land transfers for Max, and his journal. I asked the bank manager, the father of a friend of mine, if there was a way for me to keep the contents safe without carrying a safe deposit box key, since I had a tendency to lose things. In fact, I still do. He helped me set up a transfer to another box that I could access after showing my ID and knowing a combination. I haven't looked at it since.

"That small stupid question about transferring the contents probably saved my life. Max and two of his thugs were waiting for me outside the bank. They threatened me, and told me that they would kill Mom and my sisters if I didn't tell them where Dad's records were, and give them the key to his box. I told them I didn't know what they were talking about, and they beat the hell out of me. In the midst of it, someone bit me. I knew what that meant, since I'd read Dad's journal."

I was horrified. Fourteen? That was much too young to be thrust in the middle of this nightmare. We were all silent for a while, letting it sink in. I stood up and walked away, toward the windows at the top of the basement wall.

"Logan, I've got to ask. Was Stephen Tipton a part of some recruiting plan?"

Adam spoke up first. "Yes, he was. He was a heavy hitter in architectural circles, but he preferred Dayton because his family was happy here. He made a lot of money, but he could have made a hell of a lot more. He said he'd have given up work completely, but he wanted his wife and daughter to have a good life, with everything he could give them. He's the biggest family man I think I've ever seen."

I remembered the photo I'd seen at the Tipton house. The photo lent credence to the idea that they had once been a loving, tight-knit family.

He continued. "Max thinks in terms of permanent loyalty. To Max, that means control. He had to explain about us to get what he wanted in the design for the barn, so he ensured Tipton's silence by tying his future up in ours."

Judith interrupted. "It doesn't seem fair that we're talking about this. There are other issues in the pack. This isn't the only problem."

"This is the biggest one," Logan growled at her. She bared her teeth at him, and I thought they were going to fight. After a tense moment, she shrugged, waving a hand, as if to tell him to go ahead.

George picked up the story again. "Max has been building us to the point that we have fingers in just about everything. The problem with all that careful planning is that it doesn't take into account human nature."

"Yeah, I've heard about Tipton's problems." I nodded. I understood why they were banding together.

Just then, I heard an intercom buzz. Adam leapt into the air, and ran to the unit on the wall. His dad's voice boomed out of the intercom, "There's a man outside in a red pickup truck that's been watching the house, and there's a dark van that just pulled into the driveway. Someone's coming to the door, Adam. You guys need to decide whether you want to show yourselves."

"Thanks, Dad. I need you to stall them." Adam turned to us. "That dark van sounds like Max, but I don't know anyone with a red pickup truck. Anyone know who that might be?"

I looked around the room with a sinking feeling in the pit of my stomach. The others shook their heads, and I knew exactly who the driver was. Damn it. I flushed red with embarrassment. Slowly, they all looked at me.

"It's my boyfriend. It's Justin."

They all stared at me in horror.

CHAPTER FORTY NINE

Judith immediately turned to me, and snapped, "What does he know about us?"

"Nothing."

"Then why's he out there?"

"I don't know. He mentioned something about someone sitting outside my house before. The only thing I can imagine is that he's following me to protect me. I haven't told him, but he's a cop, like me. He's not stupid. He's got to know there's something going on."

Logan jumped up. "If Max catches us down here, I'm sure it won't go well. His punishments for anyone he even thinks might be plotting against are pretty severe. We need to get out of here without being seen."

Adam looked me over carefully. "Can we trust Justin?"

I looked at them, all wondering if they really were willing to put their live on the line based on my judgment. I realized they really had no choice. "I trust him with my life every night. He's my partner and my training officer, as well as my boyfriend. It sounds like he might be our only option for a clean getaway. Adam, is there a way out of this basement without going back upstairs?"

"Yeah, a back door leading out into the yard. We can cut across back yards and find our way back over to the street where he's parked."

Judith nodded, and Adam hit the switch on the intercom to provide his dad with a cover story. The rest of us put away the chairs and George grabbed a can of citrus air freshener. When I gave him a dumb look, he explained that citrus smells could confuse a werewolf as to the number of people who had been in the basement, in case someone got caught as we ran.

Adam led us silently out the basement door, and I could hear Max questioning his dad about Adam's whereabouts. The man was doing a pretty good job of snowing Max, but I caught him looking sideways toward where we hid around the corner. I wondered if he'd caught our scent, and we flattened ourselves against the foundation of the house, hiding from Max's gaze.

Judith motioned for George and I to go ahead and get to the truck, and we slunk along the backs of the houses toward Justin's truck. George dove into the bed of the pickup, lying flat on his back, and I jumped into the cab, crouching on the floor.

Justin looked at me, his eyebrows cocked so high in surprise that they almost reached his hairline. "I don't have time to explain," I blurted, "but to say we're in danger. I need you to get us the hell out of here as soon as the others get in the bed of the truck." I heard George rap on the glass on the back of the cab, and saw Judith and Adam huddled in the back, trying to lie low in the bed of the truck. "Just go, Justin, please!"

He threw it into gear, taking off quickly and careening around the corner. As he drove past the house, I saw Max smack Adam's dad and run for the van. They peeled out and took off after us.

Crap.

Both Justin and I had taken courses in driving at the police academy, and he'd certainly had practice at chasing suspects safely, but I don't think either of us had ever been in a situation where we were running from someone. It was scary to think what might happen if we were caught by Max, who certainly didn't care about being safe while he chased us. Logan hadn't explained the scary punishments that could happen, but they couldn't be good. My imagination was on overdrive. So was Justin's lead foot.

I asked Justin for his cell phone. He gave me a questioning look, and asked, "I hope you and the people hiding in the back of the truck aren't in trouble with the law."

I gave him a dirty look. "Justin, you have got to know me better than that. The cell phone, Justin, please. I need to see if Nadia's okay. She's at my house, and I think these people are looking for me to hurt me."

He tossed me the phone as he sped up onto the highway and I saw that my home number was the first number on his speed dial. For some reason, that made me smile before I hit the button to call my house. The phone rang and rang. And rang again. I got no answer but my answering machine, and I began yelling directions to Nadia to pick up the phone.

Someone did pick up, but it wasn't Nadia. It was a voice I didn't recognize. "You must be little Samantha. Your friend here hasn't been a very good host. You should teach her to be respectful of her betters, and she won't get hurt next time."

"You son of a bitch, what did you do to her?"

"Ah, my mother wasn't a canine, but I certainly am. And your friend is oh so tempting. Brave, obviously, and trying to be very protective of you. You better do what you're told or your friend here won't stand a chance. Then again, I'm not real sure I want you to do as you're told. She's a pretty delectable little piece of meat."

I heard Nadia moan in the background, and I growled, deep in my throat. "Leave her alone, you sick fuck. It's me you want. Come and get me and leave her alone."

"Oh no, she's my ticket to making you behave. I'm leaving your house with her right now. Oh, and that little snack you keep in the house? Delicious."

"Snack?"

"Never thought I'd meet a werewolf with a pet cat. It's too funny for words."

"What did you do to my cat?" I shrieked.

Justin jerked the car into the next lane, and I was thrown against the inside of truck cab. I hoped the others were hanging on tight in the back.

"Come home and find out. After you do, I want you to call this number." He spit a phone number out and I spied an ink pen rolling around on the floor. I wrote the number on an old receipt I found in the glove box. He stayed on the line just long enough for me to repeat it back.

"I got the number," I said. "Leave her alone and I'll meet you."

"You'll do it anyway." He hung up.

Justin started to ask a question, but tears stung the inside of my eyelids. That was all it took for a wash of pure rage to run through my body from head to toe, threatening to bring out my wolf. I could feel the fur pushing under my skin to be let out, and I couldn't do it. I couldn't let it go. There was too much that could go wrong. I couldn't do it with Justin driving like a maniac to get away from the Max. I could see the questions in his eyes, and wondered what my own looked like at the moment. I curled up on the floorboards, rocking and whining and fighting the change.

I heard a noise, and Justin slowed down. I lifted my head to ask what was going on, but I couldn't speak. Logan had slid the back window open and said, "Oh, shit."

Justin whipped his head around. "The van isn't behind us anymore." He took an immediate right without signaling, and then made an illegal u-turn, and there was no one behind us. He wasn't looking at me, but in his rearview mirror.

Logan was looking straight at me. "We need to get to Sam's house right now."

"Are you sure it's safe?" Judith muttered. I saw her sit up in the back of the truck. She looked a bit green, hanging onto the side of the truck for dear life.

Logan turned to her. "We don't have a choice. Sam, how are you feeling?"

I rolled my eyes as best I could. Typical response from a counselor, I thought, and growled. *Oh, no. I'm really in trouble.*

Justin floored it again, flinging Judith backwards. I heard her curse, and then Justin asked, "Do we need to call her mom? She's a nurse."

Adam piped up. "It's under control. I'm a doctor."

"Oh." Justin went silent again, driving wildly to my house as I shivered and shook on the floor of the truck. I would have made some pithy remark, but my body chose that moment to seize rigid as a board, almost like a strychnine poisoning victim, and I groaned. I'd waited too long. Adam was reaching for me through the window, and Justin hit the gas hard, driving onto the shoulder to move faster around the traffic. Judith and George hung onto the sides of the truck and each other as I fought again to control my body and prevent the change. Justin threw the truck violently into my driveway. I hadn't noticed Adam's medical bag before, but saw him snag it out of the truck as George grabbed me by the waist and hauled me inside.

It was almost too late.

Chapter Fifty

It hurt just as much this time as it did last time, but at least Adam was there to help out with some pain medication at the end. Lesson learned. No waiting to change later if the urge appears to do it now. It's a lesson I don't think I'll ever forget.

Between the pain and the medication, I don't remember much of the next hour and a half. I finally came back to myself in human form, lying in my own bed as the late afternoon sun filtered in around the blinds. Justin sat beside my bed in a folding chair, and he held my hand. I felt like every inch of my body had been bruised and abused, and just moving hurt. I heard a soft meow, and my heart leaped as I saw Doyle jump into Justin's lap and lean over to lick my hand.

Justin saw me open my eyes, and brushed my hair back from my forehead just as Adam came in and took my pulse. He brought out a stethoscope and I jerked back from the cold metal as it touched my chest just below my collarbone. Justin got out of his way, holding Doyle in one arm while Adam examined me.

"Is he okay, Justin?" I rasped, my throat still sore from the shift.

"He's fine. Adam took a look at him after you settled down. He's a bit bruised and sore, but otherwise, none the worse for wear. I found him spitting mad inside your guest bathroom. You might have to replace the inside of the door. He scratched some deep gouges in the door trying to get out."

I smiled. "He knows he's not allowed in there. He probably thought he'd get in trouble." I reached out for him, and he purred as he butted his head against my hand. And then I remembered that all was not well in the world. "What time is it? Get me a phone."

"It's about four-thirty in the afternoon, Sam."

"Damn it. Get me a phone or Nadia's in real danger. I have to call before four thirty."

Justin handed me his cell and Adam started packing up his medical equipment. I took the phone and dialed in the number as I lay on my side in the bed. It was about as upright as I was going to get for the moment. My head throbbed as the phone rang.

"You're almost late, Samantha," I heard Max's voice on the other end of the phone.

"Couldn't be helped. I want to talk with Nadia."

"She's a bit busy right now. I've got a few boys here who are really fascinated with her. They haven't touched her at this point, but I don't know. Another couple of hours and I might not be able to hold them off her. They sure do want to have fun with her."

"Max, if you kill her, I'm not going to do whatever it is that you want me to do."

"Sure you will." He chuckled.

"Are you so sure about that?"

"Yeah, I am. You have other people in this world you care about as well. You don't care so much about yourself, but you're pretty damn loyal to your friends and your family. You just have to learn who the right people are to be friends with."

"What are you saying, Max? Say it straight out." My voice got hard. He was threatening Nadia. He was threatening Justin. He was threatening my goddamned family. No fucking way was I going to stand for that.

"When and where, Max?"

"The barn, at eight o'clock tonight, and I'll give you my word that Nadia won't be touched until then. After that it's up to you." He hung up with a click.

"Motherfucking bastard piece of shit," I said, under my breath. It didn't matter how many obscenities I came up with, I couldn't come up with a combination that truly encapsulated how I felt. I lay back on the bed, and realized at that I was naked under the covers, with three men in the room. I'll deal with that in just a minute, I thought.

Logan hung his head. "And so it starts."

"You mean this is how he roped in all you guys?"

"Yeah," he said. "He only goes after people that have something to lose, or those who owe him something they could never repay."

All right, I thought. It was time to make it backfire on him. "Logan, I need to know a few things, because I may have an idea. Justin, do you have your gun and your Kevlar with you? Judith, are there others that might join us? George? Adam, am I okay to go out tonight?"

Adam looked at me, hope in his eyes. "You sound like you have a plan."

"I have the beginnings of one. It should all come together depending on how many people and how much firepower we can get together."

Justin stood up. "I've got my gear, but I can get more, Sam. Dad's got a collection of guns, and I'm sure he'd help get Nadia back if I ask him."

I was glad he was willing to help, despite whatever doubts he might have. "How much ammunition can we get our hands on?"

He nodded at me. "I'll go find out." He left the room to call.

I waited until he was gone and the door shut behind him. "Adam, did I change?"

"Yes, you did." He didn't look me in the eye.

"Did Justin see it?"

"Yes, he did, Sam." Logan stepped forward. "He was shocked, but he's handling it well. I didn't know you hadn't told him, or I'd have had Adam stop the change."

I was shocked. That was even possible? "How would you do that?"

"I can do it on a short term basis with a massive amount of drugs. The side effects aren't always pretty, but it can be done. I wouldn't have wanted to spill this secret to him without your approval, but I thought he knew, and I didn't want you to deal with the side effects of the drugs with everything else going on right now. Pain killers were about all I thought you could handle."

"I wish I'd told him. I should have trusted him. I'll talk to him once we're past this. I've just got to worry about Nadia first. Adam, he needed to know. I didn't have the guts to tell him myself. And you're right. I don't have time to be bogged down with drug effects." I pulled myself to a sitting position, grabbing the covers to hold them in front of me. I didn't need to add flashing my allies to the list of embarrassing things happening today. "I take it that shifting back and forth so quickly is why I feel like I went ten rounds with Mohammed Ali?"

Adam laughed. "Yeah, it is. Shifting back and forth so fast is really abusing your muscles. Give it an hour or so, though, and you'll be fine. You okay to dress yourself, or do you need help?"

"I'm fine."

"I'll give you a few minutes to yourself then." He ushered everyone out of the room, and then followed them.

I waited until the door shut, and then started rummaging for clothing. Clothing makes everything better, and planning an invasion needed to get easier in a hurry. I'd never planned anything like this before.

I found a pair of jeans and a t-shirt, and fastened on a shoulder holster I'd had custom made to fit when I graduated from the police academy. I'd get my belt holster from my uniform as well. I knew I had two guns in the house and a decent switchblade. Just before I padded back into the living room in my stocking feet, I scooped up Doyle, my little guard cat, and hugged him against my chest with his head on my shoulder.

Hearing him purr gave me hope for Nadia's safe return, and brought tears to my eyes. Losing Doyle would upset me, but losing my friend would break my heart. Losing my family, well...I just didn't want to think about that. It wasn't going to happen while I had breath left in my body.

CHAPTER FIFTY ONE

Logan paced outside the room until Justin came out. He wasn't quite sure how to handle the situation. Sam had kept her word, and their secret, from the man she was dating. Justin would likely have questions, and he wanted to be available to answer them, but there wasn't much else he could do. He wasn't even sure Justin would ask him those questions.

"Officer," he said, flagging Justin's attention. He didn't want to be too informal at this point. He knew the guy was crazy jealous of him, God knew why. He hadn't put one foot wrong with Sam. Justin couldn't possibly know that Logan would like to date her himself, especially since he'd just figured out that he was interested beyond any grand plans of Max's when he'd watched her shift this time.

Justin whirled on him, pain and anger in his eyes.

"Look, it wasn't my place to tell you." Logan started.

"You're right. It wasn't. It was hers. She didn't trust me. That's fine. I'll help her as much as I can to get Nadia back. She'll need all the help she can get. We can't call in the cops on this, so we're on our own. I'm going to go call in. I can burn some personal time, and the department won't be any the wiser." He stalked off. "She and I will have to talk later."

Well, that went better than it could have, he thought. Logan shook his head and saw George standing off to one side of the living room.

"Boy's hurting."

"Sure is. I don't know what to say to him. I haven't had much experience in counseling significant others on accepting their partners."

George laughed. "Well, maybe we should start. We're social creatures, Logan. Whether we're wolves or human, it's in our nature to seek out a mate. And I still think Max is wrong. It isn't possible to keep something like this an absolute secret. We need to be able to have lives, and not live in secrecy all the time. I know all the arguments against it. I know all the risks. I still think it's wrong."

Logan shook his head. "It's hard to know sometimes what's right and wrong when you're trying to protect others."

"And Sam's going to learn that. I know Justin. I've known him since he was a kid. He's always had trust issues, so they're gonna have to work that out themselves, but he's a good guy. If he can get past his own self-doubt, he can handle this. And he'd be a good man to have at our back tonight. He's a good cop."

"I've never doubted that. But he is a man, not a wolf. He doesn't think like we do. That could be a liability."

"It could also be an asset."

The conversation stopped as Justin re-entered the room, stuffing his cell phone back into his pocket. "Dad's on his way with some extra firepower, and then he's going to go sit with Sam's parents. George, I must say, I didn't recognize you in the back of the truck. Are you a...?"

"Wolf, son, and yes, I am." George gave him a warm smile. "I've been one for about five years now."

Justin's jaw tightened. Logan wondered if the man would ever unwind. They had dealt him quite a blow with the sudden news about Sam, but his jaw had to hurt from the stiff way he held himself. It made Logan's jaw hurt just thinking about it.

"Justin, I know you don't like me, but we need to talk about some realities if you go in with us. Most of the wolves that will stand with Max will be highly trained with guns, fighting, and personal defense. You don't want to get within arm's reach of them. If one of them hesitates, shoot them. Don't let them shift on you. If they shift and bite you, you will be incapacitated. Don't let them get close enough for that to be an issue."

"Right." Justin pulled out his service pistol and ejected the clip to make sure it was full. He pulled empty clips from his back pockets and a box of ammunition from a duffel bag he'd carried into the house when he came back from making his phone calls, and began loading the empty clips.

"Do you have any questions?" Logan asked, amazed that there hadn't been any screaming or yelling or arguing.

"Can any of you besides George handle a firearm? Do you have any other ideas for weapons?" Justin didn't look up from what he was doing, his voice flat but firm over the clicking noise of the ammunition as it was loaded.

Logan was shocked. He'd fired a shotgun before, but he'd never fired a pistol. All his plans, all his hopes to end Max's reign peacefully were dying. Even when Nadia was taken, he'd hoped to negotiate her release. He didn't want to go in violently. Other pack members would die, and that was part of his reason for waiting as long as he had, for being subtle and diplomatic, for trying so hard to place himself in a position to mitigate Max's rampages. It had taken too long, and it had failed, he thought. Maybe it was time to step up to the plate. He informed Justin of his experience with a shotgun.

"Dad's bringing a shotgun. Excuse me. I'm going to go outside and wait for him." Justin laid down his loaded clips and leftover ammunition and walked out the front door.

Yikes. Logan didn't know what to think, so he looked over to George. "Is this really the right way to handle this?"

George unzipped the fanny pack that had been hidden underneath his sweater and drew out a gun. "I think it's the only way we have left."

As much as he wanted George to be wrong, he knew it was the only avenue open to them. He just hoped they could pull it off.

CHAPTER FIFTY TWO

As I walked out into the living room, I saw Justin standing outside on my front porch. I stepped out to join him.

"Dad's on his way, with as much of his gun collection as he can fit into his car. He's not going with us, though. I told him you'd gotten a threat from someone you'd arrested, so he's going to go sit with your parents and watch out for them."

"Thank you." I was relieved. I couldn't be in two places at once, and I couldn't worry about them while I fought for Nadia. I looked at him, standing so tall in front of me, and realized at that moment that he trusted me with not only his life, but the life of what little family he had. It made me feel ashamed that I hadn't trusted him. "Justin, are you okay with this?"

"I wish you'd told me all this yourself, Sam. I didn't like finding out this way. I don't know how I feel about all this, or what it means for us, but I do know that this explains a lot about your behavior lately. I'm willing to do whatever we have to do to see Nadia safe, and to see any threat to your family eliminated. Then we'll figure out what happens between us."

I swallowed. That certainly wasn't a ringing endorsement for a happy ending. "Justin, you're endangering yourself and your dad to save me and my family. This means more to me than you'll ever know. I truly am sorry." I wanted to hug him, but I wasn't sure how he'd take it. We were back to being awkward to each other again, and it made me want to cry.

That veneer of calm cracked. "Sam, don't you get it? You've made me a part of your family, just as you did with Nadia years ago, whether we're together or not. I don't have much of a family, but you've given me one. I have no other family except Dad. He feels the same way. Regardless of whether we're together or not, I will do whatever we have to, to keep your folks safe. Nadia is the one who gave me the courage to tell you how I felt. She deserves all the help we can give her. When all this is over, we'll sit down and figure it all out, but until then we need to deal with what's in front of us." He walked away, toward the driveway as John pulled in, and he and his father carried boxes of ammunition and gun cases into my living room.

John nodded at me, but didn't speak. I didn't know how much detail Justin had given him, but I couldn't speak. I tried to thank him, but I couldn't get the words out.

Okay, now I really did want to cry. I wasn't sure whether it was out of gratitude for Justin's protective attitude toward my family, his determination to help my best friend, or the cold shoulder to me, so I hastily rubbed my eyes and started loading up. I walked over to the closet where my gun safe sat, and retrieved my two guns, my knife, and a box of ammunition.

Judith, George, Adam and Logan had watched the entire exchange between us in silence from the window, but they sprang into action the minute I popped the clip on my service pistol and started loading bullets. Judith pulled out a short, but slim pocket knife, George began to load his own gun, and Adam dug through his medical bag and muttered something about supplies.

We moved in an intricate ballet of preparations. I tossed George my extra bullets as he loaded his backup clip. Judith and Adam disappeared into my bathroom with Justin returned. Justin took off his belt and attached his service holster, and stuffed his handcuffs in his back pocket. Judith and Adam returned with armloads of items I'd never thought of as weapons. Logan stretched, popping his neck and shoulders like a boxer about to step into a ring.

It struck me as ridiculous, but no one laughed. It was too deadly serious to be funny.

My sense of ridiculousness returned. It was a veritable buffet of weaponry and equipment laid out on my rustic wooden coffee table. We had walkie-talkies, bullets, shotguns, handguns galore, mace, three extending ASP batons, knives, brass knuckles, and....hairspray? I turned and looked at Judith with a question on my face, and she handed me a lighter.

Jesus, was she really willing to go that far? "Um, Judith, are we shooting things or setting them on fire?"

"Whatever works, Sam. Whatever will work to pull this off."

I nodded. She was right. I'd do anything to get Nadia out of danger and save my family. I went into the bathroom and rummaged under the sink for a couple of smaller, travel sized bottles of hairspray. I always buy them before I go on a trip somewhere, but I never use them. I was ready to sacrifice them for the greater good.

Justin and I had our gun belts from work, and I had my shoulder holster. George had his fanny pack. Judith, Adam and Logan declined firearms.

"I need to be where I can patch you guys up, not causing damage," Adam said, still rummaging in his medical bag. He brought out an economy sized pack of diabetic needles. "Besides, I've got an idea for a weapon that I've never shared with Max, though I would be surprised if he hadn't thought about it."

Justin raised an eyebrow.

"Well," Adam continued. "Logan and Judith are refusing firearms. I can only assume they feel more comfortable with the idea of violence if they shift, but neither of them is as well trained in fighting as Max's thugs. He picked them out with the idea of violence. They have martial arts training and weapons training, and experience in general mayhem. Making them werewolves doesn't make them easier to defeat."

"What's your point, Adam?" Judith asked. I don't think she liked the implication that she wasn't strong enough to deal with them, even if it was the truth. I didn't question it. I was too busy cleaning and loading one of the shotguns.

"What if I could keep them from changing? They'll still be a handful to fight, but it levels the playing field."

Six heads swiveled in his direction, and all other noise and activity ceased immediately. Logan was the one to break the silence. "How do you propose to pull that one off?"

"Well, it won't be easy. These guys will start with guns first before they go to hand to hand fighting. I've seen them do it. So we have to dodge bullets long enough to get in close range with them, or hit them with our own bullets and drug them to keep them from shifting. Changing speeds up the healing, so it will help to keep them in human form long enough for us to gain the upper hand."

I didn't like how this sounded. "You say Max doesn't know about this? What is it?"

"I never let on that I was researching it." Adam pulled out an ampoule of a clear but viscous liquid. "This is a medication that will prevent the change."

"What is it?" I assumed that he was talking about the drugs he'd mentioned using on me earlier if he'd decided to stop the change.

"Thorazine mixed with an opiate painkiller. It's an early anti-psychotic medication that also induces muscle spasm and convulsion. The two together can help prevent or slow down someone attempting to shift. Of course, too much of it could result in coma or death."

Oh, my God. No wonder they didn't want to use it. No way could I live under the influence of that much heavy medication, much less be lucid enough to make sense.

There was, however, another concern. I wouldn't be able to stand it if Justin went with us and became one of us, even by accident. "So, we've got someone with us that isn't a wolf. How do we keep him from getting infected and still dose others with this stuff?"

Adam shrugged. "As long as they haven't shifted yet, they can't infect someone else. It takes a transfer of bodily fluid to effect the change, not just a bite. The goal is to prevent the transfer by preventing the change."

I nodded, and looked at Justin. He was very pointedly not looking at me, but instead locking eyes with George. George nodded at him, and he nodded back. I swallowed the huge lump in my throat and finished strapping myself into my Kevlar vest, slid my knife into my pants pocket opposite of my waist holster, and strapped on a fanny pack to hold extra ammunition. I completed the ensemble with a small travel sized hairspray and a lighter in my back pockets. I guess we were loaded for werewolf.

CHAPTER FIFTY THREE

We piled into two vehicles, Logan's car and Justin's truck, bristling with weapons and ammunition. Each of us carried six syringes of Adam's secret weapon. I was in Justin's truck, sitting in the middle with George joining us in the cab. I wanted so badly for Justin to take my hand, but I couldn't ask. All I could do was focus on Nadia.

I realized we were in violation of about a gazillion weapons laws in the state of Ohio. We were armed in a motor vehicle, with loaded weapons ready at hand, some of them illegal and some a flagrant violation of federal weapons bans. I didn't care. If my carrying a weapon illegally would keep Nadia safe, I was okay with it.

We pulled into the driveway leading up to the barn, but it was quiet. The drivers parked the cars in the woods, about two hundred feet from the barn. We were hidden by the trees, and night was beginning to fall as we stepping outside the vehicles. I looked up at the sky, and saw the fading light from the setting sun, but it was a quiet night in the country. I even heard crickets. It was a shame that we were here to cause so much damage in such a quiet, peaceful, setting.

George took point, with Justin and I following close behind, looking for signs of life in the barn. When we reached the back door I'd once thrown myself against to get attention, I stopped just outside of camera range and motioned for the others to follow us quietly. As they caught up to us, I leaned over and asked Logan about the door. "Is it locked?"

"We didn't want anyone worrying about a key after they change, or wondering where they dropped it. You just need the security code for the keypad."

"I assume you know the code."

"Of course I do."

George nodded as well. "Everyone in the pack knows the code. Max won't write it down, so if someone forgot it, they had to wait for someone at the security cameras to see them."

"Why did it take so long for someone to see me when you were in that pit, Logan?"

He sighed. "There isn't someone at the desk watching the screens all the time. There's no alarm unless the door opens without the correct code being punched in. You know, Max is so convinced that this is a secure facility that I never thought about it. George and Judith should be able to get inside without an issue and then report back to us."

I wasn't sure I liked this plan. If Max realized they were with me at Adam's house and that we were all in league together, there was no telling whether they'd be able to get word back to us. If that happened, we'd have two more hostages to rescue instead of just one. "What if we sent someone in with them?"

"And risk someone seeing them on camera? I understand, Sam, but this is the easiest way to get in without raising suspicion. Logan, is there a way to signal the outside, with a light switch or something?" Justin had finally joined the conversation.

Judith shook her head. "We can call out with a cell phone. Why make it complicated?"

There was a brief flurry of activity as we all exchanged cell numbers. There were only two walkie-talkies, and we weren't sure how far they would reach underground. I chuckled to myself. We'd planned for weapons, but not how to get inside or how to communicate. It was the Keystone Kops raiding the werewolves. How stupid could we get?

I got a dirty look from the others, and I stuck my tongue out in return. I saw a faint smile on Justin's face when I did it, so it was worth it. George and Judith headed inside as the rest of us huddled behind a bush outside of the door, just beyond camera range. I shared my observation with the others in a hushed tone. Logan was the only one who didn't laugh. The others joined in the chuckle, and it relaxed the tension that sang through all of us as we waited.

Logan's cell phone beeped a few minutes later with a text message that the coast was clear. Logan led the way and entered the code into the touchpad I'd seen before, and we were inside. We crept slowly along the hallway, Logan in front, me behind him, and Justin bringing up the rear.

Logan ran into someone he knew along the hallway of the first corridor we entered. I motioned to the others to flatten ourselves against the wall around the corner. I heard snatches of the conversation but didn't get a look at who it was.

"Hey, Logan, I'm surprised to see you here tonight."

"Why's that, Rob? You know I don't have a social life." Logan laughed. To me it sounded like he was trying too hard, but the other guy seemed to buy it.

"Max was pretty pissed when he left here tonight. Do you know what's going on?"

"I know some of it. You probably don't want to know. In fact, it would be a good idea if you left. You know how Max is when he's pissed off. You don't want him to take it out on you like he's done with some of the others."

"You're right. I sure don't. You sure you don't need any help?"

"I appreciate it, but really it's better if you just remove yourself from the situation. If this goes badly, you don't want to be mixed up in it. You don't need to worry about the political ramifications. Just turn off the security cameras."

"I'll take off. I get it. Best of luck to you, then, Logan. I mean that." He left.

A few steps later, Logan greeted another man, whose name I didn't hear, again encouraging him to leave. I heard a slapping noise, and a grunt. I peered around the corner to see the two bear-hugging and slapping each other on the back. I shook my head. Only men would show that they cared by smacking the crap out of each other. I pulled my head back before they parted.

Footsteps led away from where we hugged the wall around the corner. I stuck my head out again and saw Logan standing alone, and the other man walking away down the next corridor heading to the exit. He motioned for us to follow, and so we did.

We continued our stealthy progress through the barn past the security cameras. The security booth was empty. I got chills down my spine when I saw that. Something just didn't seem right to me. If they were holding a prisoner here, shouldn't someone be standing guard to thwart a rescue attempt?

We kept walking into the conference area, and it was almost empty. One man stood at the conference table poring over some blueprints. I recognized him immediately. His average brown hair and average wire-rimmed glasses were the same as the photograph I'd seen in his ex-wife's living room the night before I was attacked.

It was Stephen Tipton.

Chapter Fifty Four

Nadia opened her eyes and groaned. She didn't think she'd ever felt this much pain before.

When the men had shown up at Sam's house, she hadn't wanted to open the door, but they told her that Sam was hurt and asking for her. She should've known it was a ruse, but she'd been so worried since Sam left that she couldn't help herself. She'd gotten a fist to the mouth for her trouble. By the time she'd realized what was going on, there were three of them inside. One of them grabbed her legs as she tried to kick her way free, and the other two grabbed her arms. She'd fought and scratched at them but they were too strong.

Doyle, bless his heart, had tried to come to her rescue. He'd been hissing at the door when the doorbell rang, and when they hit her, he pounced. Ten pounds of ticked off orange fur wasn't much against three hulking brutes, but she'd smiled when she saw the scratches on their faces after she'd been tossed in the back of the van. She hoped he was okay.

She tried to shift her weight off her side; sure she'd have a hell of a bruise in the morning. Her feet were tied together, her hands secured behind her back, and there was a blindfold over her eyes. She licked her sore lip and tasted blood.

The floor lurched under her and she realized she was still in a vehicle, probably the van they'd tossed her into before she hit her head. She lay quietly as they spoke.

"Max ain't gonna be happy she's so beat up," one of them said.

"He said bring her. We didn't hurt her any more than we had to. She fought like a devil." Another one responded.

Nadia felt a small warm knot of pride for having fought so hard. It helped her keep her mind of her ribs and her face. They continued to talk. A third voice said, "No one bit her. That was Max's one rule. We could do anything it took except bite her, rape her, or kill her to get her here. He don't care if she's bruised. He'd care if her friend had no reason to protect her. That's all that's important. Besides, he wants the little bitch to know what will happen to her loved ones if she don't cooperate. A few bruises could only help that."

"You moron," the first voice said. "She's an insurance policy, not a bargaining chip. 'Sides, do you want Max mad at you? I sure don't."

So it was true. They'd talked specifically about not being allowed to bite her. So that must mean they were werewolves. Sam had been bitten when she was attacked. She'd claimed that was what had made her into a wolf. So they didn't want her bitten? Hopefully that meant they wanted her alive as well. She breathed a sigh of relief, and then felt bad. She didn't blame Sam for what she was now, but that didn't mean she wanted to join her friend in the woods.

She wondered who Max was. He must be the guy Sam was afraid would come hurt her. Instead he'd sent goons to kidnap and hurt Nadia. She was glad it was her, and not Nathan or Kathy Hochenwalt, or Justin, or his dad. She wasn't sure who else could have been on the list, but she was happy that the others were safe, at least for now.

She turned her mind back to what she could do to help Sam. She'd do just about anything to protect Sam's family. She felt something sharp on the floor beneath her and began working quietly on the rope around her wrists.

Fifteen minutes later, she almost had her hands free. One more minute and she'd have to see about her feet, but she didn't get that far. The van stopped and the doors opened behind her. She heard an older man's voice, a new voice, cursing at her three chauffeurs.

"You morons, she's almost gotten herself untied. How could you let her lie near a set of bolt cutters? Could you be any dumber?"

The other three didn't say anything. She didn't see what they were doing since she still had a blindfold over her eyes. Strong hands grabbed her arms and she tried to pull away. Nadia was able to evade them in the back of the van until on hand brushed against the side of her rib cage that was bruised. She cried out in pain and slumped sideways.

"No wonder she's bruised. She's got a lot of spirit. Maybe we should bite her, boys. She'd be an interesting addition to the pack. Besides, I'm sure you'd like to try her out."

"Um, you said we couldn't..." The second voice sounded confused.

So the older voice had to be Max, she thought. True to Sam's characterization, he was sadistic. He was playing with his goons. Better to keep them confused and stupid than smart enough to think about what he was doing, or what he was roping them into doing.

One hand yanked the blindfold from her eyes and she looked at them. The three men who'd come into the house were there, and they weren't any smaller than she'd remembered them. There were three other men she didn't recognize standing in front of her. The oldest was the man who'd removed the blindfold.

Someone came up behind her and retied her hands, tighter than they'd been before. "Boys, let's tenderize this little morsel. Maybe she'll quit fighting if we give her something else to think about." The older man held her by the shoulder and drove a fist right into her side, right where she already thought she'd have a bruise. The air came rushing out of her in a hurry and she grunted with the impact, feeling the crack of her ribs under his fist. She couldn't help herself; she cried out.

He stepped back and the next man came forward, holding her head still for him to plow a fist into her eye. Another man came up and kicked her in the knee. A fourth punched her in the stomach, and the last two hit her in the mouth. She felt her eye swelling shut and tasted blood.

The oldest one leaned over to her and whispered in her ear. "Listen, you, we have no problem with hurting a woman, as you've just learned. Quit fighting and trying to escape, or we'll come up with new and interesting ways of making you hurt. I've got men here who like hurting women. I know they'd love to knock out of a few of those perfect white teeth, if we haven't already. Keep quiet and cooperative and we won't hurt you any further. Push me, and I'll give you to them for a toy."

Nadia's eyes opened wide, even the one starting to puff closed. She didn't have a choice. She'd have to go along with whatever he asked and hope that Sam realized where she was. She'd wait for the cavalry. She just hoped Sam didn't get hurt as a result, or all her suffering would be meaningless. She was willing to do whatever this man said to stay in one piece for now. If it turned into a longer stay, she'd have to see about trying to escape again, but she'd wait and see where they took her in order to decide what her options were. She'd have to wait until she could walk on her own to act. Her knee wouldn't support her weight, so they loaded her back into the van (minus the bolt cutters, of course) and took off again.

CHAPTER FIFTY FIVE

"No, Sam, don't! It's not worth it! You're here for Nadia, not for revenge!" Justin's voice was the only thing that penetrated the red haze that clouded my vision. I realized I was holding Stephen Tipton by the throat up against the wall, growling in his face, and pointing my pistol at the side of his head.

He whimpered slightly as I pressed the barrel of the gun into his skin, but otherwise he didn't respond. I took great satisfaction at leaving a red mark on the side of his head with the business end of my gun. "Why did you do it? What did I ever do to deserve this? You bastard," I hissed at him, baring my teeth. "Why?"

"I didn't have a choice." He sounded defeated.

"Bullshit. Everyone has a choice. They may not like their choices, but they always have a choice. Why did you choose to do this to me? You've put me in danger, you've put my friends in danger, and you've put my family in danger. I should blow your brains all over this wall."

Tipton calmly met my eyes. "I don't have a problem with you killing me. I'd like to explain, though, if you'll let me down. I probably don't deserve the chance, but you deserve the explanation."

Logan pulled at my vest, and Justin took my gun away. George grabbed me around the waist, and plunked me down in a chair.

"Let's hear the explanation first, Sam. It might help us to get Nadia back." George sounded oh-so-reasonable, but I didn't want to be reasonable. I tried again and again to get up, until he pushed me hard enough into the chair to bruise my butt. When I tried one more time, he growled. I hadn't seen George growl yet, and was surprised enough to let go of my anger for a minute. He was right. I could listen for Nadia. I crossed my arms in front of me, waiting.

He cleared his throat. "You've met my wife and kid."

"Yeah, and you should be horsewhipped for what you did to them."

"I don't disagree. I think I've finally got my addiction under control, but if I can't go around them, I can't protect them from Max."

"Has he made threats against them?" Logan asked.

"Oh, yes, he has. Since the beginning. I can't seem to talk to him without him promising some kind of dire harm to them."

"Why didn't you report it anywhere?" I asked.

"What am I gonna say, that my werewolf pack alpha is threatening my family?"

I shrugged. He had a point. No cop would take him seriously. He'd end up in a mental ward for sure, and wouldn't be released for three days. That wouldn't protect his family.

He kept going. "I was drunk and high the night I saw you at the convenience store. Max had bailed me out of jail again, and made his customary threats. I convinced him to let me go home, or at least to the apartment where I'd been staying since the divorce, and I drank a fifth of whiskey and took a couple of pills to chase it. I went over to make sure my family was okay, and saw you guys outside, so I watched to see where the cruiser went."

"Not making a case for leniency here, buddy." I glared at him.

"I'd watched you deal with my ex-wife politely. I'd listened to you lecture me over and over. I knew from how you'd talked that you would protect them."

"That's my job. That's what I get paid for. I don't need to be infected with this curse, with being a werewolf, to do that."

"No. You get paid to protect them from me. How could I explain to you that I wasn't the real threat? They didn't understand that. How could I explain it to you if I couldn't convince them? The most I could do was to keep their house on the police radar screen. I was hoping it would be a house that you guys would keep an eye out for if you got called out enough, and that part worked, but then I realized you were looking for me, not for Max."

I kept my trap shut. He was right. We did drive by their house on a regular basis even if there hadn't been a call, just because we'd been there so many times. But we'd never been looking for Max. I saw Justin nod. I looked back to Stephen as he kept talking.

"The night I attacked you, Max threatened to kill my ex-wife. He threatened to bite my little girl. I was ready to do anything to protect them, and there you were, like an answer to a prayer. I couldn't just tell you. I had to show you. I had to bite you so you'd see the danger, and you'd believe me. I had myself convinced, in my alcohol induced state of mind, that you were God's answer to all my prayers asking for a miracle to protect my family."

I stared at him, jaw slack in disbelief. I noticed Justin had a similar reaction. For all that Tipton was a fuckup, he was right. I wouldn't have believed it if I hadn't seen it myself.

He continued. "It was incredibly stupid. Words can't express how sorry I am. Things that sound like a good idea when you're ripped generally aren't. The only thing I can say is that I'm sorry, and I will do whatever I can to make it right."

I stood up from my chair. "Okay, you've had your say, now I'm going to have mine. I appreciate your situation. I do understand the reasoning, even if, as you say, it was incredibly stupid. I can even understand why you felt the need to apologize. But you knew what this could do to a person, and yet you inflicted it on someone else. That I can't forgive. So, we'll get through this night, and then you and I will deal with each other."

He stood up from the corner, where Logan had kept him seated through the discussion. "I guess that's fair. I can't ask you to forgive me. I cannot forgive myself."

I grunted at him, and turned away. Just then I heard a metallic whine over head and drew my weapon, aiming it at the ceiling. Justin followed suit just as Judith joined us in the conference room. George saw us with guns drawn, and brought out his own as well.

The pneumatic lift into the basement from the above ground barn was bringing a vehicle down to meet us. I looked up and saw Max standing on the platform beside the van, two of his thugs by his side, and I suddenly felt nauseous.

The lift hit the ground with a soft thump and the driver eased the van off of the lift. They sent the platform back up to ground level and thug number one (the one on the right with the crew cut) opened the back of the van. Inside, wrapped in a blanket, was Nadia.

She wore a blindfold, but I could still tell one eye was blacked, and swelling bad. Her lower lip was puffy and split, and nearly double in size. She leaned sideways, favoring one side. Her ribs, I thought, recognizing the lean. She leaned a lot like I did right out of the hospital. She also couldn't stand on her own. They had her arms tied behind her, and her left leg kept buckling. That couldn't be good, but at least she'd given them a fight.

Okay, they'd hurt me. They'd hurt my best friend. They'd threatened my family. They'd threatened Justin. They'd bruised my cat. It was time to make them pay. I'd swallowed a lot of anger against Tipton, and I was paying the price now. I felt the wolf inside me starting to perk up, as if it was time to let it out again. I'd just shifted earlier. I hoped it didn't become a daily thing. I'd really hate that. I stuffed it back down, channeling my rage and anger into a blank mask to deal with Max. I pointed my gun at his face. It felt good to threaten him.

He stepped forward. "All right, Samantha. Now it's your turn to show some loyalty to the pack. You need to walk away from this court case that's been filed against Stephen Tipton. You need to declare your allegiance to the pack."

I kept the gun leveled at his head. "And if I don't?"

He laughed. The little fucker laughed at me while I had a gun on him. What had I missed? I heard a sudden intake of breath behind me. One of Max's thugs had gotten behind us, and was holding a gun to one side of Justin's throat with one hand while the other shifted slowly into claws below his chin. I gulped.

It didn't seem to faze Justin much. Other than his gun being taken away, and his hands going back down to his sides, nothing changed in his expression. My heart beat double time, but he had no reaction whatsoever. If he could stand there calmly, I could go through with this.

George kept his gun aimed at the man that held Nadia, and I kept mine trained on Max.

"Seems we're at a stalemate, Max," I said. "If you hurt Nadia or Justin, I'll shoot you. That won't get you the loyalty you want."

He laughed, a derisive, mocking sound that made me cringe. "But if you shoot me, they'll kill you."

"If you hurt these people, do you think I care? All I care is that you'll die first. Don't call my bluff, Max. It isn't one." I kept my gun trained at his nose.

He stepped forward. "Oh, I believe you, Samantha. I've heard all about you and your little gun. I've heard about your scores on the shooting range. I've heard you have a reputation for being one of the best young pistol shots on the police department. I know you'll hit what you aim at, but have you ever killed someone in cold blood?"

"You know the answer to that, Max, if you've read my file. I haven't killed. But I'm starting to consider it right now." My arm was starting to hurt. I'd held that gun steady just a little bit too long. I hoped he'd get to the point soon, and let me put the gun down.

"Maybe you're right. Maybe we are at a stalemate. I've got a proposition for you, Samantha. You can put down your weapon and swear your loyalty to me, and to the pack as a whole, and your friends will go free, unharmed."

Bullshit. I wasn't putting my gun down like that, no matter how sore my arms were getting. "I don't trust you enough to put up my gun. In fact, I think having this gun is the only reason you haven't ordered us all killed. Try again, Max."

"All right. You meet me in an official challenge circle fight, and we'll call it even on the outcome. You and me, hand to hand in a circle. George here can hold a gun on my men and we'll hold your little boyfriend and friend hostage to make sure everyone follows the rules. I win, you swear loyalty to me, and your friends go free. You win, and your friends go free without anyone owing me anything."

I considered. He had me by a good seventy pounds, and a full six inches of longer reach, but I was younger, and, hopefully, quicker. And it sounded like even getting the crap kicked out of myself still protected everyone I cared about, if he was to be believed. What other choice did I have? "What are the rules, Max?"

Justin spoke up despite the claws to his throat. "It's not worth it, Sam. He won't fight fair. Don't worry about us."

"What are the rules, Max?" I asked again. I'd see what he meant before I agreed.

"As the challenger, I can lay the stakes, you choose the form. No one interferes as long as the fight is fair. A challenge circle is the traditional way of solving disputes in the pack."

"Nothing fair about the two of you fighting," Logan said, in clipped tones.

"You've lost the right to have a say in any of this, boy, with your activities over the last few days. You've given up that right by allying yourself with a stranger to the pack instead of your pack mates. You can shut up right now," Max spit at him. "And to think, I'd have offered you the leadership of this pack, and your choice of mate to stay loyal."

Logan sniffed. "Loyal to you. That's not leadership. That's being your puppet."

"Name your terms, then Max, and your stakes." I called. I could see this turning ugly quickly, as Max's men poured out of the van and out of the hallway. We were outnumbered three to one. I didn't like the odds of getting everyone out of here alive. If I took his challenge, win or lose, the others could still walk away.

"Well, since you're new, I won't ask for your life. First blood drawn calls the fight."

"Then I choose human form."

The other wolves seemed shocked at this. They shouldn't have been. Max might've been a vicious fighter, but I'd had some training through the police department in hand to hand combat, grappling with opponents larger than me, and in general self defense. I'd never been taught to fight as a wolf. I stood a much better chance as a human woman.

I am woman. Hear me roar. Or is it howl?

Chapter Fifty Six

Nothing any of the others said convinced me that there was another way to handle this. I wasn't sure we could take them all, even with Adam's secret weapon. Even if we went hand to hand with all of them, I risked them all. I couldn't handle that. And even though we had plenty of guns, there just wasn't enough room to maneuver and take cover to protect the injured and captive. We might as well have walked in here with spitballs.

Max nodded at me when I accepted his challenge. Logan assured me he was stuck with the rules of the engagement, which meant that he couldn't touch me outside the challenge. I had a minute or two to divest myself of my weapons, stretch out, and decide what I'd be wearing into the circle. Max was already stripping to the waist. Yuck.

336 • ADDIE J. KING

I really didn't need to see a man thirty years my senior stripped to the waist, and I wasn't going that far, myself.

George tried to talk me back into the Kevlar, but I reminded him that it hadn't protected me from getting hurt the first time around. There were no guns allowed in the challenge, and Kevlar won't stop a knife. The only thing it would stop is my free movement.

The others all wanted me to carry a knife or some other small weapon. I declined them all. I didn't want Max to have any excuse to welsh on his agreement. I didn't trust him not to cheat, but if I cheated and he found out, I'd lose. I had more to lose than he did, so I didn't risk it. I just couldn't see where it would be worth it.

I stretched my arms above my head and leaned over to stretch out my legs. Since I hadn't had much in the way of strenuous exercise since the attack, I didn't want to risk a muscle spasm at an inopportune moment. I felt like an idiot, leaning and bouncing like a boxer about to step into the ring, but it seemed fitting for the situation.

Max stepped forward. Justin stood off to one side, arms down to his waist, and I could see one hand inching closer and closer to where I knew he had concealed one of Adam's syringes in the belt loops of his jeans. The claws at his throat might not make him a werewolf, but I didn't know how long the man holding him hostage would be able to hold off the rest of the change, and the man's mouth was too close to Justin's neck and shoulders for comfort.

Judith looked pissed. George still held his weapon, but he'd lowered it when Max's goons lowered theirs. I knew he'd be ready to fire if need be. Logan, well, there was no reading his expression. Horror, shock, and awe passed across his face. It was a neat trick to display all of that at once. Of course, I could have read him wrong, but if I had, then I'd have to say he looked like a constipated owl. I'd never seen a look like that on anyone's face.

And then there was Nadia. The man who'd been supporting her gently set her down, and Stephen Tipton, of all people, was holding an ice pack to her eye, and helping to dab away some of the blood on her face. It helped. I still didn't forgive him, but under the circumstances, who could? It made me feel a little better about him as a person, though, to watch him help my friend. I shook my head. It was too dangerous to dwell on that now. I couldn't let myself get distracted.

Max was getting impatient, so I stepped forward to meet him.

He didn't give me much warning, but threw himself at me, fists flying. I ducked the first blow, and his fist passed over my head with barely an inch to spare. I kept my hands up, in a defensive stance, and jerked sideways to miss the opposite fist coming at my ribs. He kept coming, and I kept ducking, and I could tell that my strategy, if one could call it that, was working. I caught a couple of glancing blows, and they hurt, but he wasn't doing me any permanent damage. On the other hand, he was getting pissed off, and getting tired. He didn't have the stamina that I had. Even with the time off for my injuries, I was in good physical shape. That worked to my advantage, and I was glad for the hours I spent on my hated treadmill.

It wasn't really a fight. It was a dance. He tripped me once and tried to kick me, but I rolled out of the way before he could connect.

"Come back here, you slippery little bitch," he panted. Apparently Max wasn't much into aerobic exercise. He was winded, and fighting to catch his breath.

I glided back over to him, and ducked another blow. I realized then why I was winning.

He was relying on brute strength, and it was very clear that he wasn't used to fighting someone that didn't try to stand toe-to-toe with him and exchange blows. I really wanted my ASP baton, the collapsible baton I normally carried on my waist when I was on duty. It would have solved the problem of his longer reach, but then he'd have been allowed a weapon, and I was afraid he'd actually have known how to use one.

As it was, he had no weapon and no access to his wolf advantages. If he cheated, he could lose. I realized he meant to cheat from the very beginning. I'd just have to watch for it.

I was holding my own. The fight couldn't last much longer, though. He was tired, and I was slowing down as well. His punches came slower, which was a good thing. I was slower to duck them. He landed another blow to my side, and I saw Justin wince out of the corner of my eye. He'd jumped every time I got hit. Those claws were too close to his throat for that to continue.

I needed to stop getting distracted. I also needed to actually throw a punch. This whole debacle wouldn't end until someone bled, and it was only a matter of time before he hit me in the face instead of in the body. I ducked and rolled, carrying myself further away from him across the room to give myself a second to plan my attack.

He didn't give me time. The minute I was back on my feet, he launched himself at me, hurtling toward me with the power of a small freight train. I didn't think; I just rolled with him, dropping to the ground and using his momentum against him. I used my falling weight and grabbed the waist of his pants to propel him past me as I landed on my back.

He looked down at me as he flew over my head, and didn't give himself enough time to catch himself with his hands. Instead, the concrete wall caught him by the face, and he collapsed backward.

Blood spurted and flowed from his obviously broken nose. His voice was thick and slurred as he yelled at me. "You fucking bitch, you have no idea what you have just done!"

"I don't care, Max. Under the terms of our agreement, we called the winner at first blood. I drew it, so you lose. Let us leave in peace." I stood silently, my chest heaving with effort and extra adrenaline. "Let us go, and we'll not bother you ever again."

He fumed quietly, so I ignored him as I went over to help Nadia up. I slung her arm over my shoulder and hauled her up out of her chair. "You okay?"

She whispered, "Yes, I'll be fine. Just get me out of here, please."

"That's fine by me. Let's go." I started to walk her away, trying to ignore Max as he glared at me.

Justin stepped aside from the man holding him, as the man began to lose the battle against the change. He took advantage of the distraction to jab the man in the thigh with the syringe. The thug collapsed to the ground snoring heavily, his change reversing like magic as we watched.

Distracted by the instant reaction to Adam's secret weapon, I wasn't paying attention to anyone else in the room until I heard a voice call out my name.

"Sam, behind you!" I spun, dropping Nadia to the ground behind me so I could protect her. I saw two things coming toward me, flying through the air.

One was Max, fully shifted into wolf form, blood still dripping from his face, and saliva hanging in strings from his jaws.

The other was the pistol Justin had dropped earlier. Stephen Tipton's hand was still extended in the air. He'd been the one to call my name, and obviously, the one to toss me the gun. I grabbed it and fired point blank as Max hurtled toward me in the air.

His body jerked, and fell to the ground backward with the force of the bullet. He slowly shifted back into human form, the fur melting off his body as he groaned. I stepped up and put one foot on his chest as I aimed the pistol at his head with both hands.

"Max, I wasn't kidding. You lost. I won. I'm taking my friend and we're leaving. You can do this the hard way, you can do this the easy way, but that's the way it is. I won't let you hurt anyone else. And I'm taking Tipton with me. I may not like him. He and I may have a score to settle later, but you cannot hurt me, or him, or Nadia, or anyone else in this area any longer."

He snarled at me, the wolf still present in his voice. "It doesn't matter what you think, or where you go. I will find you, and I will finish what I started. You're dead."

I leaned forward with the gun, and waved it in his face. "I don't think you understand me, Max. I'm not giving you a choice. I'm telling you that this is the way it is. You want your precious secret protected, these are my terms. It ends now, and no one who wants to walk away from you will be harmed."

His hand reached for his pocket, and I saw the bulge of a knife there. I didn't take any chances. I was in arms' reach of him if he was going to use it. Instead, I fired again, into his shoulder. He screamed, and started to spew threats against everyone again. That was it. I was done. I couldn't worry about looking over my shoulder. I couldn't look out for everyone. All I could do was to find a permanent solution.

Calmly, I leaned in, pointed the gun, and emptied the clip into his forehead. Gray brain matter oozed against the concrete, and I kept firing until the gun clicked empty.

I dropped the gun beside him and drew another weapon from my own equipment in the corner, pointing at the two thugs that were left. "Max's rule is over. Members of the Dayton pack, or their friends, or their families are not to be touched. Leave now, and don't ever come back. Any questions?"

They dropped their weapons on the ground and retrieved their sleeping comrade. The snoring continued as they slunk back to one of the vehicles. I kept my gun trained on them as they drove back onto the lift and drove away.

And then I moved four feet away from him and threw up in a corner.

CHAPTER FIFTY SEVEN

I don't remember much of the ride back to Dayton. We drove slowly, with Adam checking on Nadia in the back of Logan's car. Judith rode with them, and I have no idea what the conversation was about. Justin drove his truck, with one arm around me, and George rode with us. Justin periodically kissed my forehead, but otherwise didn't say much of anything else. He didn't need to. I knew he understood, and he hadn't abandoned me even with the oversight of not telling him the truth about my furry nature.

I was in shock, still shaky from throwing up, still feeling the adrenaline from the fight with Max and its sudden ending. Justin had had to drag me to the car, his arms around my waist, whispering that everything was going to be okay. I couldn't seem to walk on my own without someone telling me to put one foot in front of the other. He finally had to pick me up and carry me the last few steps, hugging me close and saying comforting things into my ear.

I'd never shot anyone before. I'd never fired a gun in the line of duty. And now I'd killed someone. Sure, if I was charged with murder, I might get off with a claim of self-defense, since he had been reaching for a potential weapon. It would be hard to get around the fact that I'd shot him in the brain ten times while I was the one standing above him with a gun after I'd disabled the arm reaching for his knife, but it was possible. Still, it was murder. It was a crime.

Nadia was safe. My family was safe. Justin and John were safe. Tipton's reason for attacking me was to protect his family, and now they were protected. There wasn't much else I could do. According to Adam, Nadia needed to be checked out at the hospital and she'd probably stay for a while, but otherwise, she would recover completely. I stared out the window as I tried to come to grips with what I'd done.

Justin's arm hugged my shoulders as he drove, and I leaned into him. He dropped another brief kiss on my forehead as he stopped at a stoplight, and I let out a breath I hadn't even known I was holding. Just feeling him reach out to me was enough. We'd sort through the heavy duty stuff later. I'd screwed up, and I knew it. He'd taken me in his arms despite my secrets. He'd stood by me and he was comforting me now. I rested my head against his shoulder, listening to his heartbeat, comforted in the knowledge that he was still there for me.

Stephen Tipton had set quite a few things in motion when he'd attacked me. There was no way he'd have been able to see what would happen. He'd been wrong, but he'd done it for the right reason, to my line of thinking. He'd done what he could to set things right, and in the end, he'd saved my life, and the lives of all of us in the barn tonight.

It put what I'd done in an entirely new light. Yeah, I was a criminal. I was a murderer.

And I was okay with that.

THE END

ABOUT THE AUTHOR

Addie J. King is an attorney by day and author by nights, evenings, weekends, and whenever else she can find a spare moment. Her short story "Poltergeist on Aisle Fourteen" was published in MYSTERY TIMES TEN 2011 by Buddhapuss Ink, and an essay entitled, "Building Believable Legal Systems in Science Fiction and Fantasy" was published in EIGHTH DAY GENESIS; A WORLDBUILDING CODEX FOR WRITERS AND CREATIVES by Alliteration Ink. Her novels, THE GRIMM LEGACY, THE ANDERSEN ANCESTRY, THE WONDERLAND WOES and THE BUNYAN BARTER are available now from Loconeal Publishing. This book, SHADES OF GRAY, is the first book in a new series, The Hochenwalt Files. Her website is http://www.addiejking.com

Made in the USA
Middletown, DE
08 September 2022

73490233R00195